SNOWFIRE

Books by Phyllis A. Whitney:

PHYLLIS A. WHITNEY

Snowfire

DOUBLEDAY & COMPANY, INC.
GARDEN CITY, NEW YORK

My thanks to Pam Conklin of Camelback for introducing me to "the mountain" in all its aspects—lifts, and trails and sweeping views, and for placing the friendly hospitality of the base lodge as well as her knowledge of skiing at my disposal.

Thanks also to Joan and David Toms of the Swiftwater lodge, The Antlers. Here I first sampled those memorable evenings of ski talk, firelight singing and fondue, which help to further the mystique of skiing.

SNOWFIRE

Far ahead along the road I could see a sign, and I slowed my car in snowy tracks. A picture of a tall evergreen, with the name JUNIPER LODGE printed beside it, told me this was the place. There was no turning back. Whatever my folly, I was committed.

My ungloved hands were damp on the wheel and that sense of time ticking away which had begun to haunt me so frighteningly was there again. There seemed so little time, and I had no conviction that I was clever enough or bold enough to carry this off and help Stuart.

He had been against my coming, warning me that it might even be dangerous, and he had hated the idea of a masquerade. "They'll find you out," he prophesied, "and then everything will be worse than ever."

I dared not listen. There was no other way. I had to come. The ad in the newspaper was fortuitous—a gift from the gods—and I've never believed in ignoring celestial invitations, even when they frighten me. "Headlong," Stuart used to call me when we were younger and I opposed him impulsively. At the moment I felt that being headlong was all I had. If I didn't hurl myself, nothing useful would happen anyway.

The road had wound out of the village through wooded Pocono hills—hills that had once been sea bottom. There were few houses in this area, and beyond the sign the old farmhouse that now served as a ski and vacation lodge was easily recognizable. It was painted white, two stories high, with a rambling addition built onto the original structure.

The other house—Graystones—was my real and secret goal, but I knew it was lost among thick woods of pine and hemlock that skirted the foot of the mountain, and could not be seen from the road. My stepbrother, Stuart Parrish, had told me about both houses. Graystones stood empty now because Julian McCabe and his sister and small daughter had gone to Maine after the tragedy and had stayed there for the last six months. I wondered if they would come home, now that Stuart had been arrested.

I followed the driveway to one side of the white house, and saw the small, neat cottages spotted here and there under the trees, with snow paths trodden toward several doors. It was early afternoon and the entire place lay silent. Everyone would be out on the ski slopes enjoying the December snows. But Mr. Davidson, to whom I'd talked on the phone, had said to come right away.

Ours had been a strange conversation. The ad I'd seen in a Philadelphia paper had told me that Juniper Lodge in the Poconos was looking for an après-ski hostess to help with guests during the evening hours. The lodge was owned by Julian McCabe, whose onetime championship skiing was still remembered for its precision and graceful daring. To be able to ski was necessary, the ad said. I was able to ski, thanks to Stuart, though I was no devotee and he hardly approved of my skill.

I had stared at that ad for one whole evening. Then I'd cut it out of the paper, packed my bags, and driven to the county seat where Stuart had been imprisoned. Bail had not yet been set, because of the seriousness of the charge. I had already been to see him, and I had found him a good local lawyer.

That was easy to do through the law firm for which I worked. David Boyce, my boss, had been thoroughly concerned for both Stuart and me, and he had driven me out to see him when I'd gone in the first time. He'd have come with me again, but I knew I must now act alone. I would show the ad only to Stuart, confide only in him. I had no intention of telling his lawyer or David what I meant to do. Both were practical men, and my imaginative scheme would alarm them and bring objections.

Only this morning I'd sat on a stool in the small, narrow room with medicine-green painted walls, facing Stuart through a grill of steel mesh that almost hid his face. I'd asked a guard for light in that gloomy place, and only then could I see Stuart through fine mesh that permitted no passing of small objects. These weren't visiting hours, but because I came from Philadelphia, two hours away, it was arranged for me to see him.

Incarceration had not changed him in the least, and for a moment I could hardly speak for looking at him. The tie between us was close. Between us we had shared tragedy. In a sense, Stuart owed me his life—and the death of our mother and his father. We both carried inner scars. After the fire which had left us parentless, it had been I who had built a life for Stuart, and he'd grown dependent upon me. He was a gay, lively, confident boy, yet underneath lay an obscure fear of believing in anything.

Now he was indignant over his arrest, but amused too, and seemingly sure of an early release. He was the least likely candidate possible for a murder charge, and he still did not believe in what was happening to him. We'd been over the whole thing again and again, trying to find an answer.

"Margot was sitting on the balcony outside her room on the first floor of the house," Stuart had told me. "Her wheelchair was near the start of that dreadful ramp that led down into the yard and was supposed to make the grounds available to her whenever she wished. I had always told Julian it was too steep, but there were brakes on the chair and he thought it safe enough. Usually someone wheeled her up and down anyway—mainly because she was indolent. And, after all, what could a slanting ramp mean to a skier like Julian McCabe!"

I sat at the high counter before the row of steel mesh windows, listening unhappily to my brother's optimism. I never thought of him as a stepbrother. After my father's death, my mother had married again when I was five, and Stuart one. He was her new husband's only child, as I was hers, and he had been my charge until the tragedy when I was fourteen and Stuart ten. An aunt had taken us then, and there was money for our schooling and care. But Stuart remained my dear and chosen charge, and he was still that. I knew better than he of what flimsy stuff his bright confidence was made. Through dimming green mesh I could see his young face, still untouched by fear, his look of being accustomed to freedom—and I wanted to keep him that way.

Though counter and screen separated us, he lighted the drab room with his presence, as he could light any room. He had that golden shine about him that gave evidence of superb health and youth and well-being. His hair was a pale honey color and he wore it thick at the back, though not too long. He couldn't be bothered with long hair on the slopes. His eyes were a golden brown and they carried the same characteristic shine. I could remember the times when I'd seen them alight with eagerness when he'd talked to me about Julian McCabe and skiing, and I could remember how I'd hated to see that response in him. I would give anything to see it now.

Stuart was tall and slim and muscular, as a skier should be, and his reflexes were like lightning, his control extraordinary. He was Julian's protégé and was being groomed for the Olympics. That was what he minded most now—that there'd be no skiing for him this year, that precious time was being lost and he was letting Julian down. He couldn't believe that the man he admired most in the world would join those who were saying Stuart Parrish had murdered Julian's wife.

"It will be all right as soon as Julian gets back," he assured me. "He'll pull me out of this."

I wasn't at all sure. I had been prejudiced against Julian for a long time, and he was no hero to me.

"It could have been an accident," I said across the width of that discouraging counter. "If her chair was so close to the top of that ramp it could have gone down out of control. Tell me about it again. I want it all to be clear in my mind when I go to Graystones."

He snorted in a sound that was half laugh, half an effort to discourage me. "You'll never get away with it. Someone will recognize your name, even though it's different from mine. There was your picture in the paper as my stepsister, Linda Earle, right after what happened six months ago."

There had been an attempt to blame Stuart then, but it had come to nothing and I had been briefly noted as his anxious stepsister at the time.

"An awfully poor likeness," I reminded him. "And who's to remember a name mentioned once six months ago? I have to use my own name because they'll ask me for identification when I apply for a job."

I lived in the city, and from the beginning I had not been happy with Stuart's skill at skiing. I had not been happy when Julian McCabe discovered him and perhaps saw in him the fulfillment of his own aborted career as a champion. I'd never wanted to meet Julian or any of those who lived at Graystones. And because I was difficult about it, Stuart had said little about having a sister. So my anonymity was fairly safe.

"Tell me again," I insisted. "Adria was with her mother just before it happened. Isn't that true?"

He smiled wryly. "Adria was having a bang-up fight with her mother and yelling with all the enthusiasm of an eight-year-old. Clay and I were talking in the next room—the library. I never went near Margot at all. I left Clay in the library and went toward the front door. Julian's sister, Shan, was just coming downstairs and she wanted to know what was wrong with Adria, who had just run past her up the stairs. I stopped to talk to Shan for a moment, and then went out the front door. In the meantime Margot's wheelchair went down the ramp full tilt, struck the guardrail above the ravine so that it broke and she was flung upon the rocks in the stream below. You know the rest."

I knew the rest. Her neck had been broken and she had died at once.

6

"Was the guardrail all that flimsy?" I asked.

"No—that's the strange thing. It had always seemed to be strong enough. I'd like to follow up on that. I don't know what the police have done."

"I'll follow up on it," I said. "But what about right afterwards? There was that man in the garden—the caretaker?"

"Emory Ault. An oddball character. Rough and ready. A top skier. But often with his nose in a book. Devoted to Julian, though he never seemed to like anybody else. He's been with the family since Julian was a small boy. In fact, he taught him to ski, and even had a hand in my training, though he doesn't like me. I think he resents the fact that now I can ski better than Julian. Emory was working in the garden and he's the one who claims that I pushed Margot's chair. Though he admits that he didn't see it pushed, or who was with her just before. Why he's lying, I don't know."

"Another thing for me to find out."

Stuart grimaced. "Afterwards he told everyone that the chair came down the ramp so fast that it must have been pushed. The hand brakes weren't on when the chair was found. Emory was the first to reach her in the ravine, and then he ran around the house to meet me walking away from the front door. So he nabbed me and started making wild accusations."

"But they didn't stick. The inquest never charged you. No one proved that you went anywhere near Margot, and both Shan and Clay know you went out the front door. Anyone else could have gotten to her. Any one of them. Unless it really was an accident. So what can possibly have come up now?"

Stuart shook his head, not really worried, holding off the darkness in his own gallant way. "The county sheriff has bulldog blood. He believed Emory and now there's supposed

7

to be new evidence. Enough for the Grand Jury to indict me. Look, Linda, forget about this crazy idea. Nothing is going to be proved against me because there isn't anything to prove. I never had anything against Margot, and everyone knows it. I didn't like her, but I didn't kill her."

"What if someone has presented trumped-up evidence to make sure the person who really pushed that chair isn't discovered?"

"You've been reading mystery stories! But if that's the case, I don't want you to go anywhere near Graystones. Just going there could be dangerous if someone discovers who you are. So go home, Linda, and don't be a darling idiot."

But I had to do what was necessary. This was too good an opportunity to find out something useful and I didn't mean to pass it up. I told him I'd be back to see him soon, and I went out of that dreary place and looked for a phone booth.

There was one in the nearby courthouse, and I shut myself into it and called Juniper Lodge. Clay Davidson ran the lodge and when he answered my ring I said my name was Linda Earle—because I wanted to get over the hurdle of stating it right away—and that I was calling about his ad. He talked to me for a few minutes, asking questions. I told him I was twenty-seven, that I'd worked for a Philadelphia law firm, that I was looking for a job away from the city. Yes, I skied a little, and I seemed to get along well with people.

"Can you start tonight?" he asked abruptly. "I need help —and fast."

This was unexpected, but I didn't need time to think. David Boyce knew I might need a leave of absence in order to be near Stuart, and I'd brought along a suitcase and tote bag because I meant to stay at a motel in the vicinity, whether I got the job or not. I had packed ski clothes and my skis were in the carrier on top of my car—just in case. It was still morning, and presumably I was phoning the lodge from Philadelphia. I told him I could be there that afternoon— and he said to come along.

Whether Stuart liked it or not, I was going to be on the grounds at Juniper Lodge. I was going to have a look at the main house—Graystones—and if Julian McCabe brought his family home, I was somehow going to get acquainted with all of them. And with Emory Ault, the caretaker. Even if Julian came to Stuart's aid—and there were reasons why I doubted that he would—I, as a stranger, might be able to learn more than he could. If someone had pushed Margot McCabe to her death, I was going to find out who it was. I couldn't share Stuart's optimistic view that everything would automatically turn out all right. Innocent men had been sent to prison before this.

When I hung up the receiver I discovered that I was shaking. I stayed in the booth for a few moments longer, fighting my nerves and my feelings. I would have to hold onto my emotions if I took this job. The painful picture of Stuart shut into a jail might spur me on, but I must not let it crack my control.

Before I left the booth I called David, told him of my visit with Stuart and that I'd be staying here for a while. His voice was warm and comforting, and I could imagine how he looked at the other end of the line—calm and unruffled as always, his gray eyes steady, comforting. That was the way he looked to troubled clients who had been cheated through fraud and needed his reassuring manner. It was based on all that was solid, and I had found satisfaction working for him. I wished I could feel something more. Six months ago he had asked me to marry him, but I had shied away with very real alarm. "When are you going to start living for yourself?" he'd asked me. But he didn't understand. I was fond of him, but only that, and at the moment Stuart needed me more than he had in years.

Somehow I managed to kill the intervening hours before I would be expected, and now I sat in my car beside the tall juniper tree that gave the lodge its name, and gathered my forces to breach the first outer rampart. If outer it was. Clay Davidson had been as close to Margot that day as Stuart had. I was eager to meet him—and just a little fearful. I wasn't very good at masquerading, and I wished that Stuart had not put all those uneasy warnings into my mind.

In any case, I'd sat out here long enough. If Mr. Davidson had seen me, he'd be wondering why I didn't come in. I ran a comb through brown hair that curled upward just above my shoulders, and took a quick look at myself in my compact mirror. Brown eyes that were not unlike Stuart's—heavily lashed. A nose a shade too pert, a mouth that was generous in its width and often tensed more than I wanted it to. I wasn't sure exactly what an après-ski hostess was supposed to be like. I could pass as pretty, but not flashy. And it was true I got along with people—ordinarily. But ordinarily I was not as nervous as I felt now. So much depended on whether Mr. Davidson accepted me, liked me—was unsuspicious. The fact that he had not reacted to my name on the telephone was at least in my favor.

I tried to relax as I got out of the car into brisk December air that was not yet terribly cold, and followed foot tracks toward the front porch of the farmhouse. The door to the office was unlatched and I walked into the small pine-walled room. A counter separated the office section from the rest, and there were a few chairs set around, a rag rug on the floor and skiing pictures on the walls. A bell on the counter invited my ring and I tapped it lightly and went to study a framed picture on the wall. It was of a man skiing between the flagged gates in a slalom race, a mountain towering above him and the powder flying from his skis as he twisted his body.

"That's Julian McCabe when he won at Aspen," said a voice behind me.

I turned slowly, swallowing hard.

"You're Miss Earle?" he said, and there was still nothing in his tone to indicate that my name meant anything to him. "I'm Clay Davidson. I'm glad you've come. This is our big midweek night, and our temporary hostess has left without warning. If you'd like to try it out this week, we can talk further about permanency next week."

He was not a particularly good-looking man, but there was something wryly engaging about him. I had the feeling at once that he did not take anything very seriously. In appearance he was only a little taller than my own moderate height, and he seemed to be in his late thirties. His wide cheekbones had a Slavic cast that did not match his name, and his chin was hidden by a neat square beard. He was dressed informally in slacks and a red-checked shirt and seemed rather lazy of movement—not driven by energy like a skier. I found him difficult to categorize. Why, I wondered, would anyone but a former skier choose to work at such a job?

"Suppose I show you to your room," he said, "and then we can have a talk about your duties. You've brought your luggage?"

"In my car," I said. "Where would you like me to park?"

He held out his hand for my key. "I'll leave your car around in back where you won't be blocked when everyone comes in this evening. And I'll bring in your bags."

He left me, and I began to take deep breaths, the way Stuart had taught me to do before I started down a run that frightened me. This was a frightening run, if ever I'd seen one.

The picture of Julian McCabe attracted me, and I returned to study it. It was impossible to see his face because of the racing goggles, but the strong chin I'd seen in other pictures was discernible and all the co-ordinated thrust of his body was visible as he christied between difficult gates. So much of Stuart's safety rested on this man. If Julian came home and took up Stuart's cause, everything would be simplified. But in the very beginning, when Stuart was suspected because of Emory Ault's wild accusations, he had not stepped to his defense. Only a lack of evidence had let Stuart go free, and afterward Julian had gone off to Maine with no word for my brother.

I heard Mr. Davidson stamping his feet on the porch and I moved away from the picture. He came in with my bags and led the way through a swing door into the main lounge. I had a quick glimpse of a long room that stretched toward a wide stone chimney and fireplace at the far end, with sofas and chairs set all about. This would be a warm, comfortable room when the fire was lit.

My employer took the stairs on the right. "Come along, Linda. I may call you that? I'm Clay, of course. We stand on no formality here. In the evening we're all on a first-name basis. Camaraderie and all that. Our guests like it that way. And of course many of them have come here since Julian opened the place, and they know each other."

The stairs were part of the old house, narrow and creaking under our feet. On the second floor a long hall, bare of any rug, led into the newer addition, which in itself was not very new.

"The older part of the house has a couple of hundred years behind it," Clay said. "In this section we're hardly more than eighty. Here's your room. You'll be at the rear, away from the guest rooms. Some people prefer the atmosphere and convenience of the lodge, while others like the modern cottages outdoors. Of course all the rooms have baths. Julian saw to that when he renovated."

I stepped into an attractive low-ceilinged room, with braided oval rugs and old-fashioned furniture that wore its age with grace and distinction. The window was small and cross-paned between blue gingham curtains. I went at once to look outside. Unbroken snow stretched away between the trees of an evergreen forest.

"Is the main house out that way?" I asked.

"Graystones?" He turned from setting down my bags and his gray eyes studied me. "So you know something about us?"

"Of course," I said lightly. "Doesn't everyone?"

He answered my first question. "The house is off in that direction, yes. There's a private driveway that leads to it. But it's out of bounds for Juniper Lodge. The curious among our guests are not invited to wander off that way."

I had been gently chided for any idle curiosity I might harbor, but he was still watching me in his lazy, somewhat appraising way. He seemed to wait for a reply, and I decided to be frank, as far as I was able.

"Of course I know what happened here," I said. "The papers were full of it. But I'd read about Julian McCabe long before. Naturally I'm interested. These are people out of a dramatic story and they lived in a remarkable place."

He seemed to make up his mind to cautious approval. "At least you're honest. We've had a lot of sensation seekers around since Mrs. McCabe died. Not so much among our guests, but in passing motorists with a morbid turn of mind."

I considered that, equally cautious. "I don't know whether I'm morbid or not, but long before this happened, Graystones has fascinated me. One wonders if houses encourage tragedy. It has a rather dark history, doesn't it?"

He moved toward the door. "Would you like to unpack, and then come downstairs so we can talk?"

"I'll come down now," I said. "Unpacking can wait."

I threw my coat across the bed and did not stop to remove my boots before I followed him downstairs. He took me on a tour of the lower house, all except his own rooms which were at the rear. I saw the dining room, the kitchen area, the downstairs rest rooms, and then we settled on the couch before the cold fireplace.

"I light the fire around four-thirty," he said. "People begin to wander back around five and they gather here for drinks and fondue. All that is your province. You'll need to get acquainted with individual guests so that you can introduce strangers to each other, see that no one is left alone unless he wants to be. Greet the newcomers. Circulate and keep everyone happy without being intrusive or a nuisance.

"The big lodges have social directors and all that sort of thing. Our guests don't want to be directed, so keep that in mind. It's not difficult—they'll be full of their skiing feats and mishaps and complaints. They'll want to talk about how much better, or how much worse other resort areas are. Dinner's around seven. Afterwards, we gather here again, usually with a larger group because not everyone comes in earlier. Though we're limited in our accommodations, so we don't have large crowds. Neither do we advertise nor take in passersby. Our clientele has grown pretty selective, since our regulars keep returning and sometimes bring their friends."

"Do you go in for entertainment in the evening?"

"Nothing very grand. Informality is the keynote. Sometimes we have a guitar player or two, some community singing. It's all pretty rustic. Nothing super sophisticated. The people who come here are well-to-do, but not jet set, and they don't need to be impressed with chi-chi. I think you'll like them. I do. Though I suppose I've learned to turn off the ski talk and not concentrate on it night after night."

"You don't look like a skier," I said, venturing.

"You can't tell. These days skiers come in all shapes and sizes. However, I'm not much of a skier, though I can ski. Are you?"

"Not really."

"But like me you've found your way to a ski lodge."

It was not a question, but the words hung between us. "I— I wanted to try something different. I'm tired of cities."

"And so was I," he said. "Tonight you can dress informally. Most of the women will wear pants. After-ski clothes are fine. If you'd like to come down around four-thirty, you can start the fondue. I'll give you a tried and true recipe. Then you can be here with a cheery welcome when anyone shows up."

"I'll be ready," I told him. "In the meantime, do you mind if I walk about outdoors after I've unpacked?"

"Go ahead," he said.

I moved toward the stairs, and he came with me to the foot.

"Linda?" he said as I started up. I looked down at the broad Slavic face turned up to me with its square beard and gray, quizzical eyes. "Julian McCabe and his family are due back any time now. He phoned me yesterday. When they arrive, you'll have to stay strictly away from Graystones. So if you want to have a look at the house and walk around it outside, you'd better do it right away."

"I'd like that," I said. "Thank you." I didn't understand his change of heart, but I wasn't going to argue.

I smiled at him, but he did not return my smile. He was still faintly questioning. He might not know who I was, but he still wondered why I was here.

"Watch out for Emory Ault," he went on. "He's the caretaker and he may not approve of your walking around close to the house. If he objects, tell him you're working for me, and I gave you my permission."

I thanked him again and ran upstairs. While I was hanging up my things, I thought about him. A curious sort of man. While Stuart had told me quite a bit about the residents of Graystones, he had not known Clay Davidson well or taken any particular interest in him. Stuart, when he visited, had stayed at the house, not the lodge. At least Clay seemed favorably inclined toward me, and he had volunteered to let me satisfy my curiosity about Graystones. I would go out and have a look at the house as quickly as possible. Perhaps I'd even have a look at the unfriendly Emory Ault. It was good news that Julian was really coming home. Now I would meet them all. Even though Graystones grounds were forbidden me, I would find a way.

II

As soon as I had unpacked, I put on my coat and went outside. The driveway that led to the house cut away from the lodge complex, winding through an evergreen forest. The snow was thin and recently fallen, bare of all tracks—motor or human—and I felt self-conscious about setting down so conspicuous a trail behind me. I hoped it would snow again before the McCabes came home and discovered they'd had a visitor. The neat, small boot tracks marching through the woods were clearly feminine.

Nevertheless, as I walked, I began to relax and savor the quiet and peace around me. I'd always loved any country trips I'd taken, and I felt at home with trees all around me. I enjoyed the green contrast with the snow, and the sense of permanence in the boughs that extended above me. Some of these trees would live longer than I. How fortunate the McCabes were to be a part of all this.

The forest grew too close for any real view of the mountain, but I was aware of its bulk as I glimpsed its steep rise now and then between tall trunks. The utter stillness made me uneasy after a while, because I wasn't used to it. There was no wind blowing, and thick green branches hung motionless as I walked beneath them. The drive ahead was not entirely trackless, however, and my interest was caught by the marks of small animals which had crossed my path. Rabbits, perhaps, or squirrels.

The drive took a circuitous approach to the house, seeming to wander idly beneath the trees. No one shouted at me to go back, and only small gray and white chickadees seemed to inhabit the woods. I came upon Graystones suddenly around a curve, and I stood very still and stared at it. Stuart had told me its history.

It had been one of those whims rich men sometimes indulged in the last century. Julian's great-grandfather had been much traveled and when he decided to settle down in an untamed part of his home state where only Indians had roamed, he'd determined to build a Norman house such as those he had admired abroad. He had chosen the right setting for it and nothing had ever happened to destroy that setting. The house belonged to wild scenery, with the rugged mountain rising behind and the trees opening up, so that its crest could be seen above the house. The ski slopes were on the far side—there was nothing man made here except the house. On this side the mountain was rock encrusted, with evergreens growing wherever they could take root. Snow blanketed the top where the growth grew stubby and served as startling contrast to black roof.

The gray stone house, with its slate roof, was like such an

outcropping itself. It had been built of fieldstone, with arched, leaded windows and an arched doorway. It was not a large house—only two stories high—but it was starkly impressive. To the right of the front door and set a little back from it, a round Norman tower with a peaked roof and high weather-vane rose above the chimneys. The tower had a gallery at the top, lighted by more arched windows which would offer a fine view. As Stuart had told me, that tower had been built to contain a winding staircase. The house was not what might be called "rational" architecture. By today's standards its irregular lines were impractical and would have been expensive to build. The tower staircase was cold and drafty, Stuart had said, but the house had stood its ground for more than a hundred years. It knew itself and it belonged here, as I did not.

Its cold, inimical presence made me uneasy. There was something about the house . . . something I did not like.

I shrugged off such fantasy and walked toward it across unbroken snow. I knew very well why it set up fearful currents in me. It was because I knew too much about it. A mad woman had lived here once in the days when the rich kept madness secret and hidden in the family. Her husband had eventually killed himself. His body had been found on these very flagstones beneath the high windows of the tower gallery. There had been other tragic, if less spectacular, deaths. And then, generations later, after the car accident in the Dolomites, Margot McCabe had come home a broken woman to this place that she hated and where she too was to die.

The accident had left her a cripple and ended Julian's skiing career. He had been driving the car, and Stuart said she had never forgiven him, never ceased to blame him. Especially since he had come out of the smashup in better condition than she. A badly broken leg had healed well enough to permit him to get around without difficulty and even to ski again—though his championship speed and timing were gone. But he was better off than his wife. In the years that followed she was consigned to her wheelchair.

Now Margot herself had lost her life at Graystones and my brother had been charged with her murder.

No wonder I shivered as I neared the house. No wonder I was filled with imaginings. Dusky trees crowding around seemed to hold cold gray stone in a secret circle of dark enchantment. This was surely morbidity, but I could not help myself. I wondered if it was possible for a house, a setting, to take on a contamination that would haunt it through the years. I had heard that where dreadful things had happened something was left in the very atmosphere to vibrate endlessly and touch the living with a sense of horror. That was how I felt about Graystones.

Margot had not wanted to live here, but it was her husband's home. He had grown up in this very house, and in his own way he loved it. He had learned to ski on the great mountain that rose behind the house, and whose huge humped shape could be seen for miles around. It was here he came home to face the shattering of his ambition and to care for his crippled wife. The old life of traveling the ski circuit from race to race was over.

He was not without money, but the bulk of the McCabe wealth had been left to Julian's older sister, Shan. Shan for Shannon, because of their Irish mother. Their father had known that Julian could look out for himself, but that Shan lacked the ability to live in a materialistic world and would need the protection of the family fortune. I gathered that there had been little love lost between Julian's wife and his sister for this very reason. Margot had thoroughly resented wealth being placed in such unworldly hands, when she could have used it better herself.

To implement his income, Julian had gone into tree farming and made himself something of a specialist in the preserving of forests. He had also opened the farmhouse on the property as a skiing lodge. He had withdrawn completely from all that electric life of resorts and tension and excitement that attended the life of a racer. This had happened when he was twenty-four—five years ago. It was Stuart Parrish who had brought him back to life and given him a vicarious purpose.

In Stuart's telling of all this, I had never found myself able to see Julian through his eyes, or to pity him. It was Margot who seemed to deserve the pity. She had ended with nothing.

Julian had met my young brother when Stuart had gone skiing on the far side of this very mountain. He had seen something in him that he had wanted to develop. From the first I had hated what began to happen. Skiing for pleasure was one thing. Becoming a champion downhill racer was another. In the beginning I'd gone to a race or two, staying in the background, refusing to meet Julian or any of Stuart's skiing friends. Being headlong and stubborn, as usual. As if by not meeting them I could make them go away! After that I had not gone at all. The danger was too appalling. I could not bear to watch. I lived in anticipation of bad news every winter, while Julian whipped Stuart into what he believed he could be. There had been no reluctance on Stuart's part. He discovered quickly that this was what he wanted more than anything in life. He had no fear. Dangerous risks meant nothing to him. He was supremely confident of his own skill and he trusted Julian.

Until these last few years, Stuart had belonged to me. He

had listened to me, depended upon me, perhaps even been protected by me. Julian had destroyed all that. And now perhaps Julian would destroy Stuart himself. It was natural for my resentment of this man to deepen to something stronger than mere dislike.

Slowly I began to walk around the house, gazing at the chevron moldings decorating windows and door, staring up at that high peaked tower with its circling windows and the mountain rising behind. Suddenly I realized that smoke was lifting from one of the chimneys. Someone must have lighted the furnace, or perhaps a hearth fire against the probable return of the McCabes. The sight did not stop me and I walked on, breaking through the thin crust of snow with my boots.

An irregular extension that seemed to be the kitchen reached beyond the tower, and I rounded it to find I could view the rear garden. Flower beds sprawled brown and dead and heaped with snow. And here there were footprints—broad of sole and square of heel.

The back door at the end of the house was rather grand and it was also arched, with heavy iron hinges. Tracks in the snow led in and out of it and had trampled the area nearby. They were a man's tracks—Emory Ault's, no doubt. I half expected him to peer out a window at me—the surly caretaker who would order me away.

But the only thing that appeared was an enormous yellow cat which came around the far corner of the house and stopped to stare at me haughtily. Clearly it was he who owned the place and I who was the intruder. I had always liked cats and I spoke to him tentatively. I didn't pay him the insult of calling him "Kitty." I called him "Cat," which would have to do until I knew him better.

He stood his ground, staring at me with golden eyes slitted

with amber, but when I took a step toward him, he spat at me in contempt and sprang away, to vanish among the bushes.

I walked even more slowly now—perhaps as though I challenged something to happen—and once more there was virgin snow. I knew I was approaching the corner where, after her auto accident, a porch had been enclosed to turn it into a downstairs bedroom for Margot. I could feel the tightening of my muscles, the rising of tension. I was afraid of this place. I did not want to see where she had died—yet I must. Seeing it was to attain more knowledge of what had happened, and that was what I was after—full knowledge, the truth.

On my right hand, deep in a winding ravine, ran a small stream, still unfrozen in the center, and on the higher bank across it stood a dozen or more beech trees which had been struck by some blight. All were dead, and their bare, twisted limbs reached starkly toward the sky. Water flowed past them between deep snowy banks toward a rustic bridge that lay ahead. Beyond the bridge, near the foot of the ramp from Margot's room, the yard narrowed, and here a rustic guard-rail had been set. It had been intended to prevent the very sort of "accident" that had happened here.

I went closer, where I could examine the rail carefully. It was made from a peeled log and there was a new, unweathered section of wood repairing the place which had broken through. As I stood there, shivering, I could picture that day. I could see the chair catapulting down the ramp into the rail—and Margot flung from the chair to her death in the rock-strewn stream below. All was still around me and horror was very close. Because my brother was involved, I was involved. I could feel what had happened through my own senses.

But my mind was still working. I put out a tentative hand and pushed at the rail. It was sturdy and strong. It must have taken a tremendous blow to break through it when the wheelchair had struck. There was something wrong, something I did not understand.

For another moment or two as I stood there trying to fathom what troubled me, the silence remained serene around me. And then without warning tumult broke out.

I heard a car on the far side of the house and the sounding of a horn, heard the car come to a halt on the driveway. As I listened, startled, car doors slammed and a child's voice cried out a greeting, followed by a man's deeper tones. The front door of the house must have been opened by the caretaker, for there were more greetings, and echoing sounds from inside. The child's voice came again—that would be Adria, of course. And that high, somehow eerie laughter would belong to Shan, Julian's sister. She was eerie enough, I'd gathered from Stuart.

The McCabes were home.

I considered my position. Certainly I didn't want to be found here. Yet I knew footprints marked my course up the drive, and the new arrivals would be aware that someone had come this way. Someone who had no business here. While I was wondering about a possible retreat, even flight, the back door opened and slammed shut. Someone ran down the steps and came around the house toward me. I turned to face Julian McCabe.

Stuart had already made him seem larger than life to me, and he was just as Stuart had described him. I saw for the first time that finely chiseled head with its thick black hair, prematurely gray-streaked. Even on the ski slopes he went bareheaded, except when he raced, Stuart had told me. I saw the deep-set eyes, intensely, startlingly blue, with squint lines at the corners which came from sun and snow glare. He had a skier's tan, so there must have been skiing in Maine. His nose was straight, his chin emphatic, his mouth pressed into a tight line that boded no good as he came toward me. All my resentment of Julian McCabe, my feeling that I could never forgive him for taking over Stuart's life with such disastrous results, rose to close my throat and freeze me in my tracks.

"You're from the lodge?" he said, his manner bluntly questioning.

With an effort I managed to answer him. "I'm Linda Earle. Mr. Davidson is trying me out this week as a hostess at the lodge."

I half expected him to pounce upon my name, but he did not. It meant nothing to him. Stuart's caution in never talking about me, since I detested his skiing and might interfere, had paid off.

"I see." His disapproval of my trespassing was apparent, and I wondered if he would order Clay to fire me before I'd started work. But he seemed to swallow his distaste for a blundering visitor and strove for a semblance of courtesy. "I am Julian McCabe. We saw your footprints leading toward the house, so I came to investigate."

He was very tall beside me, and exceedingly forbidding.

"I hope you don't mind," I said, trying to sound lightly ingenuous. "I've heard about Graystones all my life. I wanted to see what it was like."

"And now that you've seen it?" The question was dry.

I stopped trying to be ingenuous—it didn't suit me. "It looks—haunted. I think it frightens me." My own words frightened me. They were the worst I could have spoken.

He moved past me. "Then perhaps you'd better return to the lodge, where you'll be safe. I'll show you the short cut. Clay should have warned you that we're off bounds for the lodge. We've found it necessary to be—inhospitable."

I couldn't let him blame Clay. "He warned me, but I—"

"You were curious, of course," the dry voice went on. "If you'll come this way."

He walked me toward that fatal corner where the wheelchair had gone down the ramp. I could see the windows of Margot's room, with the door to the small balcony, and the ramp, snow-covered now, leading rather steeply to the ground. I swallowed hard and tried not to stare. I was being summarily rushed off the property, and certainly I wouldn't be invited back. Yet I could think of nothing I could say or do to change his course.

The man beside me gave a sudden exclamation, staring at the balcony above us. When I looked in the same direction, I saw that the door to Margot's room stood open, and a little girl with long flowing hair as black as her father's was coming through the door. She still wore her red coat and snow pants, and ahead of her she pushed a wheelchair. My breath caught in my throat.

Her father seemed to freeze into shocked stillness as the child wheeled the light metal chair to the head of the ramp. Then she came around it and seated herself carefully on the green cushion. She was absorbed in her own actions and she didn't notice us watching near the foot of the ramp. Her thin hands reached toward the wheels of the chair and she began to propel herself slowly and deliberately toward the beginning of the slant.

Julian came to life and shouted at her. "Adria, stop! Stay where you are! Don't move!"

The child's hands froze on the wheels, and her blue eyes, so like her father's, stared at us unseeingly. Her face was a mask of terrible fright. She was like a child made of ice. I had seen a small boy in just such a state only last year when I had worked for a time as a volunteer in a hospital ward for disturbed children.

Julian started toward the ramp and I knew he was going to frighten her more. I didn't hesitate to put my hand on his arm.

"Please," I said. "Let me."

Before he could object, I went past him up the ramp. The child did not see me because her fixed stare allowed her to see nothing of her real surroundings. All her attention was focused on some inner terror that was more real to her than anything else. I went down on my knees in the snow and put myself directly into the line of her blank gaze. Softly I began to talk to her. Below the ramp Julian did not move.

"Adria, listen to me. I want to tell you something. I was fourteen years old when my mother died, Adria. I can remember it very well. I can remember how much it hurt me and how lonely I was. I missed her terribly and I cried a lot. You're feeling that too now. That's because you've just come home to this house where it happened. Other people feel the same thing, you know. It's all right to cry, if you want to. My mother died when I was a few years older than you are. You won't believe it, but everything gets better after a while. It really does. It hardly hurts at all now, but I remember how I felt then."

My words came out in a sort of crooning. What I said didn't matter so long as the same idea was repeated over and over. Perhaps I could reach her, and perhaps I couldn't—but I had to try.

I had been careful not to startle her too soon with my touch, but touching was important, and now I rested my fingers lightly on the back of her hand. When she did not draw it away, I lifted her hand and pressed her fingers around my own. All the while I murmured to her, summoning her back to what was real and hurtful—the things she must face eventually—not escaping them, not pretending there was nothing to cry about so that all this misery dammed itself up inside.

When I saw the tears well up in her eyes and felt the pressure of her fingers, I sighed with relief. I didn't know her well enough to put my arms about her yet. I did not dare trespass on her personal privacy, but I went on talking to her.

"That's fine, Adria. Sometimes it feels better when we cry. It lets all that frozen lump inside melt away."

She was looking at me now with those great, swimming eyes, seeing me—and still she did not reject me.

"Everybody says I—I mustn't cry," she faltered.

"But of course you must. Go ahead. You can cry and hold onto my hand at the same time. Do you have a handkerchief?"

She shook her head and sniffed loudly. The tears were streaming and it was all I could do to keep from pulling her into my arms and cradling her in her desperation of grief. I could never bear to see a hurt child. But I must move carefully, even though she accepted me for the moment. It was her father who should have come to take her in his arms, but he did not move to touch her, though he had come up the ramp a little way. I held out my hand to him and whispered, "Handkerchief, please."

He gave me a large white square and I handed it to Adria. She blew her small nose, wiped her eyes, and sobbed with abandon. In a moment or two I think she would have stopped because it is surprisingly hard to keep up a continuous weeping. But there was a sudden rush of color and sound from inside Margot's room.

A woman came through the door. Fortunately, Stuart had prepared me for Julian's unearthly sister. She was dressed in blue velvet pants and something like a violet chiffon poncho that overhung them in points. The chiffon made her seem to float, and she drifted like a cloud down upon Adria, her long fair hair, straight and shimmering, floating like the rest of her. She had gray-green eyes that seemed to drift here and there with their gaze, without any particular focus.

"Darling, darling!" she cried to Adria in her soft, rich voice, and went down on blue velvet knees to envelop Adria in possessive arms. "You mustn't cry like that, darling. You mustn't think about terrible things. You'll make yourself ill. Come away from that horrid chair. Come away inside, Adria —come with Shan."

Adria let this vision in blue and violet lift her from the chair and carry her away from my touch. I doubt that Shan even saw Julian and me. She was all hovering mother as she took the child inside, and we could hear her pleading with her not to cry, until the door closed behind them.

I got up to dust snow from my knees, and found that I was shaking as I turned my attention to Adria's father. My trembling was not because of him, but because I'd suffered with the child and been wrenched by Shan's interference.

"That sort of thing will have her right back where she was!" I said angrily.

Then I realized that he looked quite dreadful. His mouth was drawn with pain, and he looked shaken, destroyed. For the first time I considered what the sight of Adria in that chair of Margot's might have done to him. I didn't like him, but I had to recognize suffering.

"Are you all right?" I asked uneasily.

By an effort he seemed to gain a grip on himself and he regarded me with cold animosity. "Are you going to minister to me now?"

"I'm sorry," I said. "I know you've had a shock. But I

think you can take care of yourself better than your daughter can."

He turned on me with suppressed fury. "Do you think *you* were doing her any good—reminding her of everything she ought to forget, encouraging her to weakness and weeping?"

"She's only a child!" I cried, equally furious. "But she has as much right to her pain as anyone else. I can't think of anything more insulting than to tell someone who is suffering that he's not in pain and he must cheer up and forget all about it. Let her feel it. Let her weep it out, instead of hiding it away to fester!"

We stared at each other angrily, and after a moment he spoke out his scorn.

"You seem to take a lot upon yourself." There was a cruel cut to his words—perhaps, I thought with a flash of insight, because he could not bear to have anyone see him with his guard down. "You seem to be a sensation seeker, a ministering angel and a child psychologist. Anything else?"

Feeling suddenly limp, I realized there was no use in being angry with him. No matter how I felt, he was as hurt as the child.

"Perhaps I'm just another human," I said quietly. "Perhaps I *am* curious, like other humans. And perhaps I can remember what it's like to be very young and have something hurting me. I can still remember how painful it is to be a child." It could be painful to be an adult too, but I didn't remind him of that.

He took a deep breath, as if he too were starting down a slope. "I suppose I should be grateful to you for getting my daughter past a bad moment. But you don't really understand. You see, Adria thinks she is the one who caused her mother's death. She thinks she is the one who pushed her chair down this ramp."

I stared at him, shocked, while confused possibilities stirred through my mind. If this was true, it might mean—why, it might mean exoneration for my brother. It could also mean the destruction of that desperate child.

"It can't be true," I said.

"Of course it's not true!" he told me roughly. "The difficulty is to get Adria to believe that it isn't true."

For the first time there was something wrong about his tone, something false, and I realized with some sixth sense that Julian McCabe did not believe his own words of denial. He spoke aloud to convince himself of something he feared quite dreadfully was true.

My eyes fixed themselves speculatively upon the wheel-chair—that innocent mass of metal and cloth that had no concern with death because it was only an inanimate instrument. Apparently it had not even been damaged in the rush down the ramp which had killed Margot.

"Why don't you get rid of that thing?" I said.

He looked as if I had slapped him, and I realized again that his pain was not only for the child. He had suffered loss as well as she.

I started past him down the ramp. "I'm terribly sorry for saying the wrong things. I know I shouldn't be here. I only wanted to—to look at the house. I'll go back to the lodge now. You needn't bother—I can find my way."

"Wait," he said, and came after me. "Since you wanted to see the house—why not see it?"

"I have. I walked around it before you came. I've looked at the tower and—"

"Come along and I'll show you what it's like inside. I don't really mind showing it off to someone who's interested." His manner had softened toward me, though his eyes were still bleak.

I understood a little. Or thought I did. He was trying to make it up to me for the contemptuous words he had spoken. At another place, in another time, I might have walked away from him because I had never liked anything I'd heard about Julian McCabe, and I liked nothing I had seen about him so far. But I was not here for myself. I was here for Stuart. And I had to know the truth about that wheelchair.

"Thank you," I said. "I'd like very much to see Graystones from inside."

III

He took me in by way of the front door. We stepped across an enclosed porch into a large square hall, sparsely furnished and dark, since it boasted no windows. It was a utilitarian entryway, with a tiled floor where ski boots would do no harm. There was a clothes rack hung with outdoor things, and skis and poles and boots were set all about. The elegance of the house did not begin here.

A door on the right led to the enclosed tower stairs, while on the left there was an entry to the library. Ahead lay the great drawing room that Stuart had told me about, and Julian McCabe gestured toward it.

The first impact of the room was something Stuart had not prepared me for. This was not because of anything it contained, but because of the view offered by bulging bay windows down the length of the room. The tall windows, from which dark garnet draperies were drawn back, made a dramatic framing of the dead beech trees I had seen outside. Thus framed, they were far more striking than when I'd seen them with the ravine at their feet and the forest around. Beyond the glass they twisted fearsome limbs to the sky, while the little stream seethed past gray roots. Behind rose the bleak winter mountain, banked with snow.

Suddenly I knew what had killed those trees. It was fire —and I stood stricken. Before my eyes flames seemed to leap aloft, enveloping gray limbs with a dreadful, searing heat. I knew what fire was like. How could I ever forget? How could I not be mesmerized?

I sensed Julian watching me as I walked away from him down the room and stood looking out at those gray, angular limbs, somehow primitive in their agony, as if the memory of fire remained in their writhing. The wildness touched me with terror. There was terror in the agony of the trees, and yet it was different from the gray terror of the house because of my memory of fire. I responded to a force that I did not altogether understand.

Julian had followed me down the room and stood beside me. I had to speak.

"It shocks the senses," I said.

For the first time he gave me the grave smile that lighted his thin, rather ascetic face, and touched the blue intensity of his eyes.

"The trees burned when I was no more than eight. Afterwards, Father kept them there. He was rather a fierce person —my father—and he liked the picture they made. My mother hated it. She said the trees frightened her and when she was in this room she insisted that the draperies be closed."

I could sympathize with his mother. It took me a moment

to trust my voice. "It's a view that might be hard to live with. Who wants to face grim reality all the time? Though I suppose there's a testing in it. Is that why I feel it so strongly? As if I'd been challenged in some way?"

"A testing?" He repeated the word doubtfully. "How can it test you when it's static? It disturbs, yes—perhaps because it's a reminder of destruction. But it takes life to do any testing."

Yet the sight of those trees tested me in some curious way that I could not explain. It said to me, "Do you dare to do what you've come for, when this is the inevitable end?" I shivered and turned my back on the view. Julian's testing would have been on the ski slopes. I knew about that. This was different.

He led me about the room. "My mother furnished our drawing room, and we've kept it more or less as she liked it. She couldn't stand all the Victorian gewgaws the generation before favored, and she got rid of them. She felt it should be a simple room. There's a heaviness to the Norman style that's best balanced by simplicity."

It was a dark room, I thought, with mountain and trees shielding the one wide window. Oak wainscoting rose halfway up the walls, and a dark wine wallpaper covered the remainder. The ceiling was white and gave the room its one touch of light. The furniture was good and not too heavy, with touches of scarlet and yellow among deep brown and green. Paintings of mountain and forest looked down from the walls and there was a huge stone fireplace between two doors on the left-hand side. One door to the library stood open, the other was closed. It was a glass door with a curtain behind it, and I knew that it led to Margot's room and had once been a door to the outside porch that had been converted for her use. I would have liked to see the room where Margot had spent the last years of her life, but I didn't expect him to show it to me. Instead, he led me into the library, which was only a little smaller than the drawing room.

I knew what I would find here. Those stark trees had apparently left Stuart indifferent, but he had told me about the library. In it were not only the books which had been collected by the generations of Julian's family. This was the trophy room as well, and the room he used for his office.

Deliberately, I went to stand before a tall glass cabinet which held medals and statuettes. These were the rewards, the accolades for skill in facing danger.

He was clearly waiting for some respectful remark from me. There had been a day when Julian McCabe was lionized— known, recognized and admired wherever he went. He was undoubtedly accustomed to tributes, to glory. I could not give him that kind of recognition.

"What was it all about?" I mused. "What made you do it?"

He showed no surprise, but that intensely blue gaze studied me, continued to weigh me. "You're asking the mountain climber why he climbs the mountain?"

"Yes," I said. "I might ask that too."

"Do you ski?"

"Only a little. I do it for fun. I'm afraid I don't care much about form or whether my skis are expertly parallel. I've never been able to wedel, for instance."

He laughed with a certain tolerance. "Oh, that. There are fads in skiing, as there are in anything else. Form isn't something to worship. Control is what matters. Clumsiness and a lack of skill give you no control. When you're good enough, you can forget school rules and find your own style."

I'd heard all this from Stuart and it was something that made me rebel.

"For me the good old snowplow is fine. And I never go to the top of the lift, anyway. Halfway up is enough for me. So I can come down the gentlest slopes, and not very far."

"Perhaps you're missing something," he said and moved toward the door to the hall.

"I have my neck intact, and all my legs and arms."

I paused before a wall of framed photographs, some of them informally posed, some action shots taken on the slopes. There was one picture of Julian with a laughing girl on his arm. A girl with a face I had seen in news photos. Julian was noted for his conquests.

"That's Princess Galitzin, isn't it?"

Julian chuckled. "I wouldn't buy that old story about how I taught her to ski."

My attention moved on and I recognized the great French skier Jean Paul Killy, the American Billy Kidd, and Nancy Greene and some of the others. Stuart had seen to my education whether I liked it or not. Among the pictures of experts was a shot of Adria, graceful on skis and as sure as her father.

But once more it was a picture of Julian McCabe that stopped me. His knees were bent, his body sat well back over his skis, his poles thrusting at the snow as he flew down a steep slope.

"Weren't you ever frightened?" I asked.

"I was always frightened before a race. Keyed-up frightened. That's part of the challenge. But you can't let it psych you out."

Stuart was never frightened. Perhaps that was what promised greatness in him—if it didn't cause him to smash to pieces through overconfidence. He took the moment for what it was worth, neither caring nor believing in the future. An acute thrust of pain reminded me where he was, and that he would not be skiing this year.

With only a glance for the book-lined walls, I followed Julian to the hall door. But before I stepped through it I looked back for a moment.

This very library was the room in which Stuart had stood talking to Clay on the day Margot had died. Adria had left her mother on the balcony of her room and rushed upstairs. Stuart had come out the library door and met Shan, coming down the stairs. Clay had been left behind in the library. Stuart had heard Margot scream as he went out the front door.

"What are you thinking about?" Julian asked as we walked into the hall.

I tried to throw off my concentration. "I'm not sure that I'm thinking. Mostly, I'm just reacting. I've never been inside a house like this before."

Apparently he accepted that. He led the way through the door to the tower, where stairs started up within stone walls. Two other doors opened off the circular room at the foot of the tower. One opened into a spacious dining room, done, I saw, in a light apple green that was a relief after the gloomy drawing room. The other gave onto a narrow passage to the kitchen and pantry. But it was the stairs that Julian gestured me toward.

They were not comfortable to climb, the wedged treads winding steeply upward, but they lent a suitable touch of antiquity that was right for the house. A narrow, fortress-like window halfway up threw light into the tower, and at the second floor there was a landing, before the stairs went circling up beneath the peaked roof.

Julian did not pause at the second floor, but took me up to the gallery at the top of the tower. As I'd expected, its many windows opened upon a distant view. I stood looking out over treetops, out toward rolling hills and little valleys. Behind the tower the slate shingles of the roof pitched upward, but I could look between the chimneys to see the tops of those dead beeches and the mountain behind. It was cold up here, with the stone of the tower all around, and I found myself shivering—though perhaps more with the sense of a place that was haunted than because of the chill.

Julian seemed to be waiting for me to comment on the view or perhaps the uniqueness of the tower, but I could find nothing to say. I was thinking of the great-uncle who had flung himself from one of these very windows, to fall to his death on the flagstones below. The memory of old suffering would always haunt Graystones.

"Thank you for showing me all this," I said a little stiffly.

I seemed to puzzle him—perhaps because my reactions did not match any pattern he expected. How could they, with my brother in jail under a false charge of murder? All my thoughts took turns that were strange, even to me.

"I'll take you down now," he said, equally stiff. Clearly we did not like each other, and as we returned to the second floor I wondered how I was to have any further access to Graystones and its residents.

I think he did not mean to show me the bedroom floor, since here the rooms were private and occupied, but as we reached the corridor door it flew open and Shan McCabe stood staring at us in surprise. Adria was no longer with her.

"Miss Earle," Julian said, "this is my sister, Miss McCabe. Shan, Miss Earle is going to work at the lodge, and since she's interested in the house, I'm showing her around."

Shan looked faintly startled, perhaps because her brother seldom showed strangers around Graystones. In this less impassioned moment I was able to study her more carefully. Long pale hair streamed over the shoulders of her violet chiffon poncho, and her face was pale too, as were her light gray-green eyes. She would be the sort of blonde who would not tan. She looked at me with the same unfocused stare I had noted before, as though she gazed a little past, rather than directly at me. I had the curious feeling of someone who hid behind bright colors, peering palely out at a world that was never quite in focus because she did not care to look at it too closely.

When she spoke, I heard again her low, beautiful voice. "I've finally got Adria quiet, Julian. I don't know what possessed her to go and sit in that chair. I think you should lock Margot's room and let no one into it."

Unexpectedly, Julian turned to me. "What do you think, Miss Earle? Should we keep Adria out of that room?"

I had the feeling that he was mocking me, inviting me to commit myself in some ridiculous fashion. It was difficult to be civil to this man—and I had to be.

"I'm hardly an expert," I said mildly. "I don't know anything about it."

The mockery deepened in his smile, his slightly raised eyebrows.

"I thought you acted with a good deal of assurance a little while ago."

I shook my head. "I acted by instinct, and because I know a little about dealing with a child who is frightened."

There seemed to be a flutter of distress going on beneath the drifting movements of Shan's chiffon. Julian put an arm about his sister, as if she too might need quieting.

"It's all right, dear. I know how much you love Adria. Now, if you don't mind, I'll show Miss Earle the second floor."

He had not meant to do this, I was sure, but Shan's appearance had for some reason changed his mind about taking me straight downstairs. The opening from the tower slanted diagonally into a long hallway which ran nearly the width of the house. Shan trailed uncertainly behind us as Julian led the way to the big master bedroom at the front end of the house, just above the library. It was a man's room and I suspected that it had been changed since the time when Margot could climb the stairs and share it with him. The bed was old-fashioned, with handsomely carved posts, but no frilly canopy, and there were small Indian prayer rugs on the polished floor, their colors delicately muted by age. A brassbound chest stood at the foot of the bed, and beyond it was a black marble fireplace. Over the mantel hung a painting of a snow scene, and in one corner of the room a pair of skis leaned against the wall.

Shan brushed past me and drifted across the room to touch the skis with loving fingers. "These were the very skis Julian used when he competed in the Olympics and won a silver medal," she informed me. "One more year and he'd have brought home the gold. Perhaps you could still have won it through Stuart Parrish, Julian. If only—"

"I'm afraid Miss Earle doesn't know what we're talking about," Julian said and showed me abruptly out of the room.

I said nothing, but I found myself watching Shan. I wondered how she felt about Adria's claim that she had pushed her mother's wheelchair the day of Margot's death. And how she felt about Stuart.

The hall, which had ended at the door of Julian's room, opened upon either hand into two good-sized bedrooms. The one at the rear, overlooking the grove of dead trees, belonged to Shan, and I was given no glimpse of it, for she removed herself from our company by opening the door a crack and whisking herself away inside, closing it after her.

Julian made no comment on her sudden vanishing. He turned to the room that was at the front of the house, above the front door. "Adria? May we come in?"

There was momentary silence, then the child came to the door and opened it to peer out at us with those great blue eyes that I had last seen swimming with tears. She had taken off her outdoor things, and she wore faded jeans and a blue sweater. Her long black hair hung below her waist. At least she had stopped crying, though something about her seemed to hold off her father with veiled hostility. Me she regarded with doubt and a certain suspicion. Shan had evidently been at work countering her earlier response to me.

"You're feeling better?" Julian asked. "This is Miss Earle. She is the new hostess at the lodge, and I'm showing her about Graystones. May we see your room?"

Adria was in the process of unpacking the clothes she had taken away with her to Maine, and dresses, jeans, sweaters, shorts were strewn about the bright, cheerful room. White-sprigged wallpaper was cornflower blue, and again there was a four-poster bed, this time considerably smaller, and with a canopy of blue flounces around the top. The patchwork quilt folded across the foot of the bed bore a design of scattered stars, and there were snow pictures on the walls.

As I looked around, a large, tawny cat rose from the welter on Adria's bed and stretched to his impressive length, his tail twitching a little as he turned his yellow-slitted eyes in my direction.

"This is Cinnabar," Adria said, moving to the bedside where she could stroke the cat's huge body.

"We've met," I told her. "Though I'm not sure he approves of me."

"It's not a he—it's a she," Adria said, and darted a look at her father.

42

I saw the curious whiteness about Julian's mouth, as though he held back sudden anger.

"Stop that nonsense!" he told his daughter. "Of course he's a male cat."

Adria pulled the cat to her, and he permitted her hugging with dignified indifference. "Cinnabar belonged to my mother," she informed me.

There was something uneasy in the climate of the room. Something a little frightening. I turned my attention uncomfortably from child and cat, and my gaze fell with a sense of startled recognition upon a small carved figure on a bureau. Still unpacked, in my suitcase back at the lodge, was another figure so similar that I knew at once who had carved this one.

Stuart had given me mine when he was sixteen and was beginning to show a talent for such work. But this carving of Adria's must have been done in his adult years, for it was far more perfect in its execution. Both figures were of a skier, and the stamp of Stuart's work was unmistakable.

I had never seen this carving and I could not take my eyes from it. The skier held his poles out to each side, his knees were close together, slightly bent and turned, his body contraposed to the skis as he came down a slope in a christie turn. Even a portion of the slope had been carved underfoot, so the figure's skis could dip across the fall line.

Adria saw the direction of my gaze and ran across the room to pick up the small polished figure. She did not look at her father as she held it up to me, and again I sensed hostility against him.

"It's beautiful, isn't it?" she demanded of me.

"It is indeed," I said, and took the carving from her, turning it about in my fingers.

Once I had thought Stuart might become an artist, a

sculptor—but that was before he had met Julian McCabe. I glanced at Julian and saw that the whiteness about his mouth had intensified. Adria saw it too, and went on deliberately.

"I know you told me to put this away, Daddy. But I couldn't. I love it too much. And Stuart never did anything wrong. He couldn't have because—because—"

Her words broke off. There was a brief silence in the room, a rising tension between father and daughter.

"Let's have no more of that," Julian said roughly.

The child took the small skier from my hands and carried it solemnly back to the dresser, where it held a place of honor. When she looked at her father again there was a flash of quite terrible entreaty in her eyes, a plea for help, but he had turned away and did not see—perhaps did not want to see. Yet when he spoke again, his voice was more gentle, as though he forced himself to be kind.

"I know Stuart was your friend, Adria, but I don't want you to be hurt when the truth comes out."

If he was trying to reassure her, he did not succeed. She looked at him without hope. She knew her father believed she had pushed that chair, and so did she. Margot's death lay between them. I felt torn with pain for Adria, but there was still my brother, who must come first. I had to speak out.

"Then you really believe Stuart Parrish is guilty?" I asked Julian.

He glanced at me with a surprise that changed quickly to distaste. "I never enter into casual gossip, Miss Earle. I'm sure this is a matter which doesn't concern you."

From his viewpoint, I deserved that, but I had to go on. "I've read the papers," I said heatedly. "I can't help knowing something about what has happened."

His distaste for me increased. "We'll leave you to your unpacking," he said to Adria, and motioned me ahead of him through the door.

In the hallway, he told me briefly that there were two smaller bedrooms, now unoccupied, at the rear of the house, and I knew that one of them had been used by Stuart when he had visited Graystones. But I was shown nothing more. Julian led me down the circling stairs to the lower anteroom, and took me to the door.

"Thank you for showing me the house," I said lamely.

His gaze wandered over the top of my head, and the very curve of his lips dismissed me scornfully. "You're quite welcome, Miss Earle. If you go around this end of the house you'll find a path that follows the stream for a short distance. Stay on it, and it will take you quickly back to the lodge. The drive is the long way around."

As I walked away, I heard the door close behind me. If my rescuing of Adria had at all ingratiated me with Julian McCabe, that advantage had been lost because I'd not been able to stay silent about Stuart. I'd been headlong, as usual, and I could not resent Julian's behavior toward me. He believed that I had been prompted by mere curiosity and that I was indifferent toward the suffering of others. I felt sorry that this should be so, but there was no way to change his thinking.

At the bottom of the ravine the brook flowed placidly between icy banks, and the path wound with it beneath hemlock and spruce and pine. The grove of dead beeches was left behind with the house, and I walked without paying much attention to my surroundings, lost in thought. If Adria had pushed that chair, she might very well champion Stuart, knowing he was innocent. But what had prejudiced Julian against my brother? How was I to follow up these begin-

45

nings of knowledge if the house was to be barred from now on? As was certainly likely.

Around a turn in the path that brought the lodge into view, I came without warning upon a man. He stood with his back to me, half shielded by a tree, and he seemed to be watching the rear of the lodge intently. I noticed his massive head and broad shoulders before I saw other details. He wore a sheepskin jacket, brown corduroy trousers and a green alpine hat with a small red feather tucked in the band. I supposed that he must be a guest from the lodge.

"Good afternoon," I greeted him.

He turned slowly, with no air of being startled. He must have been in his late sixties, but he was still a handsome man, his face lean and weathered, and he carried himself well, with a sense of dignity. For a moment he looked at me in guarded suspicion. Then his shaggy gray brows drew down in a scowl.

"How did you get here?" he asked roughly, and I heard for the first time that harsh, ugly voice that was to haunt my dreams for a long time to come.

I could only gape at him in astonishment. I knew now that this was no guest, but must be Emory Ault, the Graystones caretaker. I managed some sort of recovery.

"You must be Mr. Ault," I said. "I've been at the house. Mr. McCabe has been showing me around. I'm Linda Earle, the new hostess at the lodge."

"Hostess?" he echoed the word in derision.

"Yes. Mr. Davidson gave me permission to walk through the grounds. He said to tell you so if you objected to my presence. And Mr. McCabe has just been showing me through the house."

His annoyance with me seemed extreme and I wondered if I could talk him into relaxing and accepting the presence of an intruder without such indignation.

"I've heard about you," I said, carefully pleasant. "Every-one knows that you taught Julian McCabe to ski. And I believe you had a hand in training Stuart Parrish as well. So you must be a builder of champions."

"Parrish!" he said, and there was a bite to the way he spoke the name. "That was a waste of time from the begin-ning."

I knew by his tone that this man, more than any other, was my brother's enemy, and I must be wary with him. At least I seemed to have distracted him from what he considered my trespassing on Graystones land. When I started past him he turned to walk beside me, and I saw that he moved with a decided limp. A reminder of that injury Stuart said he had suffered long ago on a ski slope.

"I don't know what your game is," he said in that grating voice, "but you'd better be careful. You'd better not try anything. Do you understand?"

Quite suddenly I understood all too well, and in the same instant I realized that this could be a violent man. How it was possible, I didn't know, but Emory Ault knew who I was. This meant that he would undoubtedly report me to Julian and bring a quick end to my foolish game of espio-nage. That is, unless he was not entirely certain, and I could somehow bluff him out of his belief.

"I don't know what you're talking about," I said. "I haven't any game. I'm not trying anything. I hope I can be a good hostess at the lodge because I need the job."

I hadn't known I could sound so convincing, and I think I shook him a little—whatever his belief.

"If you don't mind, I'll go back to the lodge now. I'm sorry if I've upset you for some reason I don't understand."

This time he did not try to stop me and I walked toward the lodge at a moderate pace, subduing my impulse to run wildly out of Emory Ault's malevolent reach. I had never before had a physical sense of fear toward anyone—but I'd experienced it sharply against this man. As a result, all my sensitive antenna were alert. The violence in Emory Ault had some secret source, and I had better find out what it was. And how he had recognized me. That is, if any time was left for me to accomplish these things. For the first time I began to wonder how he had felt about Margot McCabe.

The last few yards to the lodge door I was unable to control my frightened reaction. I flung myself across the yard, and Clay Davidson must have seen me coming for he opened the door to let me in. I almost fell into his arms, and he righted me in some surprise.

"You look as though the wolves were chasing you!"

"Not wolves—a grizzly bear. I've just had a run-in with that awful Emory Ault. He—he really frightened me."

Clay was interested, but unimpressed. He pulled at his beard skeptically. "Oh, come now. He's grouchy, but hardly dangerous. What did he do—order you off the property?"

I was recovering a bit, and I realized that I dared not be entirely frank with Clay.

"He tried to. But he couldn't very well when I told him Mr. McCabe had been showing me through Graystones."

Clay Davidson whistled in surprise. "You work quickly. Or do you carry spells in your pocket like Shan?"

"If you like, I'll tell you what happened," I said. I was feeling a strong desire to talk to someone. And in contrast to the McCabes and their caretaker, Clay seemed like a friend. There was a good deal I could talk about harmlessly, and perhaps relieve my tension and sort out my own thinking at the same time.

"Come along to my office," he said. "I've just made a pot of coffee and you can join me in a cup and tell me about what's happened."

IV

The après-ski crowd had returned from the slopes to gather before Clay's roaring log fire. And I was circulating among them.

I had put on a gold-colored shirt and dark green pants, and brushed my hair until it swung above my shoulders with a springy gloss. I wanted to look well tonight so that I would be kept on at this job—at least for as long as Emory held to silence. For a few hours I had kept expecting a call from the house, or even the appearance of Julian in person to confront me. But so far nothing had happened. Whatever his reason, Emory had not yet spoken out. Even his silence seemed ominous, however.

I was beginning to hate this role of subterfuge which threw me into a web of lies and deception and uncertainty.

How could I know that anything I was doing was right? Always there was the old seesaw of doubting myself that stemmed back to my childhood and the night of the fire. If I had not given all my efforts to getting Stuart out, if I'd taken those few moments earlier, would my mother and his father still be alive?

But I mustn't open that door, and I slammed it hastily in my mind.

I also needed to look well tonight because it gave me a courage that I needed after my talk with Clay. Somehow, perhaps in a reaction to Graystones, I had been too ready to count him as a friend, and I had held back very little in my account of what had happened at the house. Clay had seemed to encourage me to talk, and he had listened with obvious interest. But when I was through, he'd had disconcertingly little to say, and I began to feel that I might have gone over to the enemy camp. After all, he worked for Julian McCabe, and there was no reason to trust him. At least I had been on guard when it came to my identity, and that he still did not know.

At dinner I sat with Clay at a corner table in the big dining room. We had talked little then, because he was constantly jumping up to see about one thing or another. The meal was hearty and flavorful—good country food— with two boys from the nearest village serving at the table. By now I was beginning to get the feeling of the lodge. It was all rather fun, and if so much had not been hanging over my head, I could have enjoyed it.

I had met most of the guests before dinner and found them an intelligent, sophisticated group. Some were married, but there were a few young singles too, arriving in pairs, or pairing off during the evening. A ski lodge was often a place where lasting friendships were made. The slopes could be different. There easy acquaintances were struck up, but everyone eventually skied off alone and perhaps never met again.

Since this was a small, private lodge, it had no license and no official bar, and was therefore more intimate, less of a public place. Clay provided a table of mixers, mineral water, small dishes of olives and onions, with cocktail shakers and ice available, so those who brought their own liquor could serve themselves. The fondue I had made before dinner bubbled in an electric chafing dish and guests speared rounds of bread on long forks, and swirled them in the cheese mixture with expertise. The ski talk went on tirelessly —accounts of falls, difficulty with certain moguls, the good runs and the bad. There were good-natured controversies over teaching methods and styles, comparisons of one resort with another. Our particular mountain could not offer the altitude or the long runs of the West, but it had considerable diversification in its trails and the obvious advantage of nearness to large city populations.

With candles on mantel and coffee table, the lamplight not too bright and firelight throwing wavering shadow patterns on the ceiling, ice tinkling in glasses, and the murmur of voices, it was a comfortable, attractive gathering. And for me, not altogether real. Though perhaps that was the idea—an illusion that offered escape from everyday reality, a release for those who worked hard and needed time off for play.

When a few chords from a guitar sounded, I turned to see that a woman had seated herself on a stool at the opposite end of the room from the fireplace. It was Shan McCabe, her long pale hair flowing over her shoulders as she bent her head above the guitar. She wore a full-length robe of pale green silk, corded with gold at the waist, and there was a long string of amber beads about her neck. Her hands were pale on the strings of her instrument, and when she raised her head and smiled vaguely about the room, I realized for the first time how beautiful she was. By firelight her eyes were more green than gray, and she had not troubled to darken thick golden lashes. Her lipstick was a deep apricot which might have been grotesque on anyone else, but somehow complemented her golden pallor.

The woman in a red sweater whom I'd been talking to uttered an exclamation of pleasure. "Oh, good! Shan hasn't been with us this season. When the whim moves her and she comes down to join us, she's marvelous. Listen."

Shan began to sing, giving her attention to the guitar as though she loved it, paying no heed to those who turned away from the fire and drew their chairs in a circle about her. She might have been alone, singing only to herself, her voice pure as crystal. The song was "The Green Green Grass of Home," and she sang in a slow tempo, touching the words with her own sense of sadness, of sorrowing. It was a singing to break your heart.

I stayed at the fireplace end of the room, behind those who had gathered around the singer. Standing, I could see over their heads to the great, gilt-framed mirror that occupied an alcove wall at the foot of the stairs. I'd already asked Clay about the huge floor-to-ceiling mirror and he'd told me it had once graced the lobby of a movie theater back in the thirties. Margot had picked it up at some auction long ago. Now the glass gave me a double vision of Shan and I could see the delicate purity of her profile when she raised her head and closed her eyes, singing the last bars of the song.

When she finished there was a soft round of applause, and then those who knew her began to call out the names of songs for her to sing. She gave the room her pale, lovely smile that focused on no one and struck the chords for "Where Have All the Flowers Gone?" This time others joined in and the long room swelled with sound.

I looked about for Clay and saw him standing near the dining-room door, his eyes fixed upon Shan with an intensity that caught my attention. I began to watch him instead of the singer. When someone asked for "Shenandoah" she let the organ sounds swell in her voice, and I saw a strange longing on Clay's face that made me wonder what Shan meant to him. All her songs were of longing, of something lost, or about to be lost—something yearned for. And that longing was in Clay's eyes, on his wide mouth above the neat beard.

Again I glanced toward the mirror and saw that a man had come down the stairs and was standing at the foot, watching Shan, only his reflection visible to me. It was Julian—Julian who practically never came to these gatherings, Clay had told me. I could feel myself tensing at the sight of him. Had Emory spoken out? Had Julian come here to talk to me? But he seemed to be making no move in my direction.

He did not join in the singing or attract the attention of any of the guests, but stood quietly near the stairs, watching and listening. I had the feeling that he did not belong to this room or with these people. Boxed in by tight walls, there was a restraint upon him. He belonged on the mountain, carving his turns in the snow, meeting the elements head-on. Where Clay was apt to move lazily, his action more mental than physical, Julian had the tension of a coiled spring about him. He would always need release in conquering the obstacles of a downhill racer. I had the deep instinct that this would apply to his life as a man, as well as a skier.

He would overrun obstacles, sweep them away, accomplish what he wished, whatever the cost. I found it disturbing that I should appraise him so—and for the first time I sensed my own danger more fully than even the encounter with Emory had made me do. What did Julian want, and why had he turned against Stuart? The old question took on a new and more frightening significance.

The crystal of Shan's "Roll, you river . . ." reverberated. In the mirror Julian turned his head and looked at me, straight across the room. His eyes held mine for a long instant, and then I dropped my own and moved out of sight of any reflection. I could not tell what his look had meant, but somehow I was aware of a dangerous response in me that I did not like and would not accept. Julian was our enemy— Stuart's and mine—and I must feel nothing toward him but doubt and suspicion. Yet, deny it as I might, there had been some invisible cord stretched between us at the moment when our eyes had met and held. It had been a physical thing—attraction, repulsion, what? I winced away from it, put it out of my mind, refusing its implication. Attraction between Julian and me there must not be.

When she had played long enough, Shan rose from her stool and went as silently from the room as she had drifted in. No one made any effort to stop her or speak to her. Apparently, one took the gifts she offered and asked for no more. I found my way across the room to stand beside Clay.

"She sings beautifully," I said. "What a strange person she is."

He gave me his usual wry smile. "Dryads are always strange. Undoubtedly she lives in the woods and the stream when she's out of our sight."

"She's more mortal than that," I said a little tartly. "From what I've seen she's smothering Adria with too much protection and affection. I told you what happened today."

"The trouble is that there are no other wood sprites around for her to love. And she isn't very successful at loving adult mortals. A child must suffice."

He surprised me. I had been impressed earlier by his apparently pragmatic outlook, and now he sounded almost visionary.

"You're talking like a poet," I said.

The broad face turned toward me, faintly mocking. "But of course—since that's what I am. A poet manqué. A failed poet. I am a writer, you know."

"No, I didn't know," I said in surprise. This explained him a little. A writer might very well hide away at a job like this, earning a living while he worked at his writing. I wanted to ask what he had published, what sort of things he wrote, but his face had a closed look that held off any questions.

"Did you know Mr. McCabe is here?" I said.

That seemed to startle him. "Where? I haven't seen him."

We were out of sight of the stairs and I drew him toward them. "He was over there watching Shan a moment ago."

But when we neared the stairs there was no one there. A woman spoke to Clay, calling him away, and I went back to my duties as hostess.

The skiing crowd did not keep late hours, and by ten-thirty everyone had gone off to the cottages or upstairs to their rooms. A day on the slopes could leave one ready to turn in early, and early risings were also the rule. The midweek crowd usually stayed for two or three days, and then hurried back to Philadelphia, or New York, or wherever they came from.

When the downstairs room was empty, I helped Clay put

things away, empty ash trays, and set the furniture in order so that guests would not come down to disorder in the morning. He was anything but talkative and I dared not put the questions I wanted to ask about Shan and Julian.

Just before I went upstairs I inquired as to whether I had done as he wished, or if he had any suggestions for me.

"No suggestions," he said. "Keep on as you're doing and you'll be fine."

His words approved me, yet I felt that he was holding something back. As I started up the stairs, he stopped me.

"Don't get too involved with the McCabes, Linda. You can get burned that way."

I hesitated with my hand on the railing. "What do you mean?"

For once there was nothing wry in his answer. It seemed direct, even concerned for me.

"You must have been a breath of healthy fresh air up in that place this afternoon. Stay that way. There's not one of them—not even the child—who isn't twisted miserably askew. Don't let any of them damage you."

Damage *me,* I wondered wryly. Perhaps I hid more damage than any of them. But I wondered what he meant, and if the McCabes had hurt him in some way why did he continue to work for them?

"Thank you, but I'm quite safe," I assured him, raising my false courage again, and went up the stairs.

When I reached the top and looked down, I saw he was still there, staring after me as though something disturbed him that he did not want to express. I said, "Good night, Clay," and went along the upper hall to my room at the far end.

I was feeling thoroughly weary by this time—and more

than a little disturbed. On this first day of my masquerade I had learned nothing at all that might be helpful to Stuart. I had aroused the suspicions of Emory Ault, and I could feel time slipping away. I was not sure how long I could hold this job, yet before Stuart came to trial, I must find the evidence which would free him. I must not fail in my attempt to prove his innocence. This one thing held me to my goal.

My room was dark and as I reached for the switch I sensed movement and a faint sound in the darkness that brought fear to my already tense nerves. For all I knew, the malevolent Emory Ault might be waiting for me. Then light flooded the room and I saw the great orange cat in the middle of my bed. He had sprung to his feet when I opened the door, and he stood staring at me with haughty displeasure, as though I were again the intruder. His presence chilled me as though an evil breath had touched the air of the room. There was something wrong about this cat being here. I had left my door closed, and he could only be inside if someone had opened it and let him in. Deliberately.

"You aren't welcome here, Cinnabar," I told him. "This is my room, and I don't think you're my friend."

His ears twitched and his yellow eyes regarded me with a sharp interest in which there was certainly no liking. I gestured toward the door, clapping my hands.

"Come on—you don't belong here. Out, Cinnabar—out!"

I would never have dared to touch him, and fortunately it wasn't necessary. He leaped to the floor and moved like a jungle cat to the door, slinking into the hall, a swift-moving orange shadow, to vanish down the stairs. I hoped Clay would find him and put him out. His presence in my room was upsetting. Whoever had let him in must have brought him here from the house. Was it Shan? That seemed possible.

I wondered again about that curious exchange between Adria and her father when the child had claimed that the cat was a "she." What had that been all about?

But I was tired and more than anything else I wanted to get to sleep. Before I could make a move in that direction, however, someone tapped on my door and when I went to open it I found Clay standing there.

"I'm sorry to trouble you," he said, sounding unexpectedly cool. "Mr. McCabe is downstairs and he wants to speak to you for a moment, if that's possible."

My heart thumped in my throat as I thought of exposure. Julian knew who I was and I was to be sent packing. Clay watched me with the same chill that had sounded in his voice, and I knew that whatever it was, he disapproved.

"If you don't want to see him tonight—" he began.

I shook my head. "Of course I'll see him. I'll come right down."

Clay started ahead of me along the hall, but before he reached the stairs I stopped him.

"Did you find the cat?"

"Cat?" He looked around.

"Yes—Cinnabar. He was in my room on the bed. Someone must have let him in. I left my door closed when I came downstairs but the cat was there."

Clay's manner softened a little, as though he condoned the cat's presence. "That would be Shan's doing, I'm afraid. She had him with her when she came. I'm sorry, but Shan's whims are hard to reason with. The cat belonged to Margot and he's half wild. I hope you didn't touch him."

"I've met the animal twice before," I said, "and I wouldn't think of touching him, even though I like cats. I simply invited him to leave, and he went out behaving as though I really had no business in that room."

"I'll look for him and put him outside," Clay said and ran down the stairs as though he wanted to avoid any further questioning about the cat.

I descended more slowly, and in the great movie palace mirror I could see the dying fire at the far end of the room, with Julian standing before it. Clay had not turned out the lamps as yet, so the room was still warmly lit. Our positions were reversed from earlier, when I had stood by the fire looking toward the mirror. Now Julian had his back to me and there was a certain dejection about the set of his shoulders that touched me unexpectedly. He was not a man who should ever be beaten, I thought with a flash of insight, and I went toward him with a new gentleness in me that was unasked, unwanted.

When I stood at his elbow, I knew he sensed me there, though he did not speak or turn around.

"You wanted to see me?" I asked.

He continued to study the dying embers of wood as though he sought some answer in them. When he spoke, his words came hesitantly—from a man who, I suspected, was not hesitant.

"Will you come to lunch at Graystones tomorrow, Miss Earle?"

This was the last thing I'd expected and I was slow in responding. When I couldn't find quick words to answer him, he turned to me with an entreaty he must have found hard to make.

"Please come. I know you think we're a strange lot, but we've been through some rather bad times. This afternoon you were kind and understanding with Adria. Nothing else matters. I haven't known which way to turn in dealing with my daughter, and if you're to work here, you might have enough free time to make friends with her. She's a lonely child, and my sister—" He broke off.

In the firelight his eyes seemed almost black and there was pain in them. Once more I knew that here was a man who suffered. Whatever the cord which had stretched briefly between us when he held my gaze in the mirror, it was gone. Here was only someone who was hurt and my heart went out to him. I forgot that he was Julian McCabe. He had lost a beloved wife, and he was truly concerned about his daughter. How could I not try to help him? Yet I moved tentatively.

"I'm not sure how I could be useful," I said. "I think your sister has already turned Adria against me."

"You must forgive her. She loves Adria rather desperately. But I think she isn't always good for her. I've seen examples of this sort of overmothering, protecting and condoning before—with disastrous results. Yet I don't want to hurt Shan."

"Perhaps it's you who's hurting Adria most," I said quietly.

Pain seemed to deepen in his eyes. "I'm trying to do what is right for her. It's not easy. When I look at her—"

He broke off but I knew what he meant. When he looked at Adria he saw Margot—dead. I ached for the child and pitied him. But I must think of Stuart too, and the truth —whatever it was—that must come out, whomever it injured.

"Of course I'll come," I told him.

He smiled gravely and I felt a twinge of guilt because he had no idea of my identity, no idea that he might be letting an enemy into his home. I no longer wanted to be his enemy, yet it couldn't be otherwise. Stuart had to come first. I must never forget that.

"Thank you, Linda," he said, and held out his hand.

I put my own hand into his, trying to remember his identity. Telling myself that this was the man who had been at one time a world idol. This was the man who might destroy—or save—my brother. His charm and attraction must not touch me. I must be immune. But as he held my hand in warm pleading he could not put into words, I wondered if I was.

When he released me, I went toward the stairs. Clay was nowhere about and I did not glance in the mirror as I climbed to the second floor. In my room I went uneasily about getting ready for bed, my uneasiness compounded by many things—not all of which were evident to me then. When I was comfortable in nightgown and robe, I unpacked the rest of the things in my suitcase—among them the small carving of a skier that Stuart had made for me. I set it on the dresser and studied it thoughtfully. This figure had not been carved with the later skill Stuart had brought to the one he had made for Adria. My skier stood upright on his skis on level ground, ski poles thrusting to either side. He wore a peaked stocking cap, and his features were crudely delineated, yet one had a feeling that the carver had known the joy of skiing down a mountainside and had put something of this feeling into the tiny figure he had created.

I was about to leave the carving on the dresser, as Adria's sat on hers. Then I had a second thought and put it back in my suitcase. The carvings were too similar. Someone who had seen Adria's skier might guess that the same person had created both.

Before I got into bed I opened a window and let the cold night air come in. It was blindingly dark out there beneath the hemlocks back of the house. The cottages were not visible from this rear window, and the woods were too thick for the lights of Graystones to shine through. I was not used to such blackness, and I was glad to get beneath warm blankets and close my eyes.

My thoughts were all for Stuart as I lay there, but there was a quivering darkness beneath them that I knew and dreaded. I did not want to think of *that* now. I turned on my side, then on my back again. I tried vainly to bring in other thoughts, to stop the rising tide of memory. But when this fiery thing came upon me, there was never any fighting it. At last I closed my eyes and lay still. I let it come.

I could smell the smoke again. Hear the crackling of fire. It was wintertime and the windows were all closed. Something pulled me from my sleep. I rolled out of bed and ran in cold bare feet into the hall. At the far end flames bloomed in frightful beauty. My mother's room was down there— the room she shared with my stepfather. Stuart's father. I knew I must run down there and pound on their door. They had been out late last night and they were undoubtedly sleeping heavily. I must wake them quickly.

But I was afraid, and I turned toward my brother's room instead. I ran through the door and found him sleeping soundly with moonlight on his face. In a moment I'd shaken him awake, pulled him from the bed and into the hall. He would have run toward his father's room in spite of the flames, but I held him back, and we screamed our warnings together. I don't know whether they heard us or not, but I was pulling Stuart toward the stairs and out the safe front door. We ran through the cold to our neighbor's house and the fire alarm was turned in. After that everything blurred and I could never remember the full details of what happened.

I know there were questions and speculations, but no one could be sure what had really happened. Our parents were found near their bedroom door overcome by smoke. The flames had cut across the hall between them and safety. If I had gone there first I might have saved them, but I never told this to anyone. On all sides I was praised for saving my young brother, and Stuart clung to me, broken-hearted, terrified. All that was safe and sure in his life had been wiped out by the flames. I was all he had left. And now he was mine—son, brother, friend. I had to make it up to him for the fear and doubt in my own mind. Doubt of myself. From then on, any who threatened him had to reckon with me. He had no need to fight his own battles, because I was always there to fight them for him. I had been a naturally gentle girl, but I changed where he was concerned. I was the lioness with her cub, and no one tried to thwart me. Now Stuart was in the gravest danger ever, and only I could help him.

I tossed in my bed. But the waking nightmare had taken its course and at last I slept.

When I wakened suddenly in the middle of the night, I sensed the utter blanketing stillness all around, and I lay for a moment with an unexplainable chill striking through me. I was intensely aware that my bedroom isolated me from the rest of the house. Those guests who were staying overnight at the lodge had been placed in rooms at the front. Mine was at the rear, and the rooms next to mine were unoccupied. But nothing happened and gradually the thudding of my heart lessened. Still, I was very cold, and sleep receded as I lay there shivering. Finally I reached for the bed lamp switch, and when the room brightened I got out of bed and rummaged in the dresser for another blanket. Luckily I found one in a bottom drawer, and carried it back to spread on my bed.

Then I remembered something else. Something I had not

taken out of my suitcase, but had left in a pocket in the lid, locking the case and setting it in the room's closet. Now I brought out the case and opened it to take the magazine from the pocket. I huddled under my blankets with the light on, so I could read.

This issue was dated some months before, and the magazine was a popular one, given to newsworthy articles, and commanding a large circulation. Its cover bore the title "The Griefs of Graystones," and above the words was a color picture of Julian McCabe in his great days as a skier. This was no racing picture, and he was without goggles or helmet —bareheaded as he skied for the pleasure of it. He looked rather like Adria's carved figure, his knees turned and bent, exhilaration on his face, his gaze fixed ahead, watching for danger.

I flicked the pages to the article, knowing exactly where it was. The first pictures were of Graystones, taken from an angle that emphasized the tower. Though it was a summer picture, the house still looked bleak and harsh against the rise of mountain behind. There were more pictures of Julian, and two of Margot—one obviously a studio portrait, the other a candid shot taken at Loveland a year or so before her accident. In the latter she was laughing up at some man whose back was turned to the camera. I did not think it was Julian. I could study her face better in the portrait.

Short fair hair curled softly about her cheeks and she had the rounded forehead and chin of a rather touching child. Her blue eyes looked trustingly out from the page, and while she was no beauty, she seemed utterly feminine and appealing. It was hard to imagine so soft and gentle a creature turning hard and unforgiving because of the accident for which she blamed her husband. I could see why he must have loved her deeply, and suffered over her crippling,

64

why he must suffer now because of her loss, suffer pain when he looked at Adria, who might have caused this loss.

There was a single picture of Adria, also on skis, though not very clear, but no picture at all of Shan. Probably a dryad would be camera shy. There was also, of course, a candid shot of Stuart, taken at the time when Emory had first accused him, and one last picture of Emory Ault angrily waving off a photographer. The lodge was given only scant mention in the article, and Clay Davidson was neither named nor pictured.

Now, however, it was the article which interested me more than the pictures. I had read it several times after its publication, but now I read it again, with a new feeling of awareness because I had met the people portrayed—all except Margot. And I read it with a new suspicion. There was nothing very scandalous or startling in the treatment, though it made interesting reading. The writer had not played up the sensational, though he had not avoided facts. Julian was the hero of the piece, but only because that was the natural circumstance. Some space was given to the value of his tree farming operation, which took place on the far boundaries of the property. His interest in professional skiing was also mentioned.

Stuart was not the villain, however. Not even "allegedly." Shan was presented as a shadowy figure that gave little of her elusive essence, and she came in only briefly. All appeared to be factual and objective, except for one subtle aspect that I had not been aware of until now. Margot McCabe did not come off at all well. Nothing was stated bluntly, yet one sensed a woman who had been spoiled and protected as a young girl, who had craved admiration and attention, and had turned bitter when her severe accident chained her to a wheelchair.

When I finished reading I looked once more at the name of the writer. It meant nothing to me, and now I knew it was not his real name. I had the growing conviction that I knew very well who had written this article about Gray-stones, and that only Clay Davidson could have done it. Somehow, I disliked the fact that this should be so. It seemed less than admirable that, working for Julian as he did, he should use Graystones as the basis for a commercial article and sign a pen name to it.

I wondered at the bitterness that seeped through when it came to Margot, and the way he had kept Shan almost entirely out of the piece. I remembered his eyes upon her earlier this evening, though what all this added up to, I didn't know. I wondered further if Julian had seen the article, and if he knew who must have written it—and how he felt about that.

Clay was now an enigma. I mustn't trust him again with full accounts of what went on at the house. I must find out as quickly as I could where he stood in relationship to the family—and to my brother, Stuart. But I had thought about this enough for tonight. My watch told me it was three-thirty in the morning and I had better get some sleep. But as I reached out my hand toward the bed lamp I heard a faint, light tapping on my door.

For a moment I froze in uncertainty. Surely no one who meant me well would come tapping on my door at this time of night. Still, even though the rooms adjacent to mine were empty, there were sleeping guests farther down the hall who could be awakened and summoned if there was any need. The faint tapping came again.

I got out of bed and into my slippers, drew on my warm robe and went to the door. "Who is it?" I whispered.

"It's Clay," the answer came.

I unlocked the door I had cautiously bolted earlier, and opened it a crack. Clay stood well back across the hall and he was fully dressed.

"Are you all right?" he asked. "I seldom sleep well, and I was out walking about in the snow when I saw your light. I wondered if you might be ill. Or if—" He broke off, as though he did not want to finish that "if."

Suddenly I had to talk to him, and we couldn't keep whispering here in the hall. I opened the door further.

"Come in for a moment," I said. "There's something I'd like to ask you."

His hesitation was slight, but he did hesitate. I picked up the magazine from the bed and held it out to him. At once he came into the room and closed the door behind him.

"Where did you find that?"

"I brought it with me. I told you I've been interested in Graystones for a long time. Tonight you said you were a writer, and this piece seems to have been done by someone who knew the facts intimately. I'm sure none of the McCabes would have told these things to a reporter."

He crossed the room, walking as lightly as Cinnabar, and stepped to the window. "I ought to have a night light put out here at the rear of the house. There's one among the cottages, but we need one here as well."

"You mean you aren't going to tell me?" I asked. "Has Julian seen this? Does he know you wrote it?"

He turned from the window, making up his mind. "Of course he's seen it. He asked me to write it. He knew there was going to be an article and he thought I could put the whole thing in perspective more honestly and with less emphasis on the sensational than the average reporter. I'll admit that I didn't want to write it. It wasn't easy to do."

Somehow I felt enormously relieved to know that Clay had not been guilty of going behind Julian's back.

"I'm glad Julian knows," I told him.

Clay's look was thoughtful. "What did you think of the article?"

"That you were carefully fair. Except perhaps to Margot. I don't think you could have liked Margot very well."

"I detested her," he admitted. "I can't honestly be sorry she's dead. I suppose some of that came through in my writing."

"Didn't that make Julian angry? The way you handled her?"

"I don't know. By the time the piece appeared he was in Maine, and he's never commented on that aspect. At least you must have found that I leaned over backward to be fair to your stepbrother, Stuart Parrish."

I could only gape at him in utter dismay.

He laughed softly and came to ease me into a chair. "There now—sit down. I've shocked you. I didn't mean to bowl you over as soon as this."

"How—how did you know?" I faltered.

The mocking smile was back again above the square beard. "I knew when you phoned me about the ad. I recognized your name. That's why I told you to come right out. I didn't want you to get away. As a writer preparing an article, I read back through all the accounts I could find that dealt with Margot's death. There was a picture of you—though not a good one—and your name was given. I remembered."

"Does Julian know?"

"I'm sure he doesn't. He wouldn't read any of the newspaper accounts and they were kept from Shan and Adria. So I suspect your secret is safe. If Julian had guessed who you are, you'd be gone by now. He'd never tolerate your presence as a—shall we say—spy?"

"I'm only trying to help Stuart," I said. "What are you going to do?"

He spread his hands blandly, still gently mocking. "Nothing. For the moment."

"But if you're working for Julian—" I began.

"That's why it's better if you're here where I can keep an eye on you and know what you're up to. He might not appreciate it immediately, but perhaps that's the greatest service I can pay Julian."

"Isn't he likely to fire you if he finds out who I am, and that you've let me stay? In the end, he'll have to know."

He moved his head in denial. "I don't think he'll let me go. Besides, by that time perhaps he'll understand. And if you should turn up someone else who was to blame he'd have to admit I was right. I say *if*, mind you. For myself, I rather think they've got the right man."

"No!" I cried. "It wasn't Stuart. It couldn't have been."

"Why not?"

"Because I know him. I know my brother. He couldn't hurt anyone. Besides—you were in the library talking to him. The room next to Margot's. When Stuart went out in the hall you could have gone through that connecting door to her room yourself. If you'd wanted to, *you* could have pushed that chair!" I knew I was talking recklessly, but I had to counter the attack on Stuart, even if Clay let me go at once in indignation.

"Do you think the investigators didn't think of that?" he asked, undisturbed.

"Then why—why Stuart, and not you?" I didn't really believe it had been Clay. I was flailing out.

"Because the door, my dear little sleuth, was locked between the library and Margot's room. It would have been possible for anyone to go into the drawing room and get to Margot through the door from there. But the library door was locked, and I didn't have the key. In fact, the key was not even in the door that day, though Margot herself must have locked it. I was in the library when she screamed and I tried to get through to find out what had happened. I couldn't because the door was locked. Whoever got to her went through the other door, from the drawing room, or from outside via the ramp and balcony."

I stared at him blindly. I had known nothing of the locked door, but it made no difference. One explanation had been eliminated—which only meant that I had to find others.

Clay stood up, his look not unkind. "You're more tired than you know. You'd better get back to bed. After all, you've a hard day ahead of you tomorrow, what with luncheon at the house. You'll need your wits about you there."

"Clay," I said before he could open the door, "I'm sorry I spoke so wildly. It *has* been an upsetting day. I'm not used to masquerading like this. Stuart didn't want me to try it. He said it would never work."

"Who knows—perhaps it will. And if that's an apology you're offering for accusing me of Margot's death, I accept." He was smiling at me now, however ruefully.

"I'm glad you know," I said. "It makes everything a little more—comfortable. But, Clay, there's something else I haven't told you. Emory knows—I think. He was almost violently angry with me this afternoon. I don't know how he could know, but he does. Yet he hasn't gone to Julian, and I don't understand why he hasn't."

"So that's it? I wondered why you seemed almost terrified

when you came back this afternoon. And of course he could know. I suppose you've been to the jail to see Stuart a few times. Emory's been there frequently to talk to the county sheriff, and he's been across the street at the courthouse a few times. He might have seen you, had you pointed out to him. From the first, he's been down on Stuart—though it's never been altogether clear why. Unless his evidence really is sound."

I paced about the room a little frantically in my robe and slippers. "I've got to know what he has against Stuart! Clay—will you help me?"

He moved toward the door to put his hand on the knob, and I saw that he had once more turned cool toward me.

"You're on your own," he warned. "I'll say nothing to Julian for now. But I'm first of all on his side. I owe him that."

He opened the door and went out, closing it softly behind him. I turned out the light and got numbly into bed. I felt trapped among enemies, with no way to turn. If only I could have gone to Julian, I thought a little wildly. If only I could talk to him honestly, make him see that Stuart was innocent. He, of all people, could help me. And he, more than anyone else, could not be approached.

V

The next morning I slept late. I had not asked Clay whether he wanted me to help with the guests at breakfast time, and since he didn't call me, I stayed in bed, dozing off and on after the sun was up, then lying awake, trying to marshal my forces for the encounter ahead at lunchtime.

Shan, I suspected, would be my main problem because she would block me when it came to Adria. I had sensed a passionate jealousy in Shan. A possessiveness toward the child. It was the only area in which she seemed to show real feeling. If only I could coax her into accepting me it would be a step ahead. But I did not think it would be easy.

For the last few moments that I lay in bed, I thought about Julian—dark, formidable, haunted by grief, turned from his small daughter by his own belief in her guilt, yet wanting rather desperately to help her, to believe her innocent. Even without his obvious need I would have wanted to help Adria, if I could. She, of them all, was most in danger of being destroyed. But there seemed very little I could do when her care lay in Shan's hands. And not even Clay could be wholly trusted as an ally.

When I had bathed and dressed, I went downstairs to the dining room, where Jimmy, one of the boys who served as a waiter, was clearing off tables and setting things up for dinner that night. I gathered that lunch was not served here, since guests were expected to be out on the slopes and would probably eat at the base lodge. I told Jimmy not to bother about me and went out to the kitchen to make myself toast and coffee.

Clay was nowhere about and I found myself at loose ends. Since nothing seemed required of me, I got into my car and drove to town to see Stuart. We faced each other once more with steel mesh between, our time limited, and he listened a bit restlessly to my hurried account of what had happened since I had made that phone call to Clay Davidson.

"If Julian's back, he'll be coming to see me," he said confidently when I concluded. "All the rest of this espionage bit is foolish and a waste of time. You're going to look silly, Linda, when he finds you out. And Emory's sure to tell him."

Stuart's bright confidence had apparently not been quenched and I could only hope that it never would be. But I had less assurance than he about the way Julian would act.

"If you could depend on Julian, you'd have known it before this," I pointed out. "Stuart—what about that locked door Clay mentioned? Was he telling the truth?"

My brother turned his honey-colored head and looked about

the narrow wedge of room as if he was seeing it for the first time. From the beginning it had been difficult for him to accept the reality of a jail.

"I don't know anything about locked doors," he said impatiently. "But I want to get out of here. I want to get onto the slopes again. Look, Linda—tell Julian who you are and tell him I need to see him. He hasn't come before because he thought I was all right. But now I need his help. Maybe he can put some pressure on to hurry up my bail at least."

"If he'd wanted to give his help he'd have come before this," I repeated.

Stuart's golden-brown eyes rested on me with complete disbelief. He had never for one moment lost his faith in his mythical hero.

"Julian was crazy about Margot. He's been knocked out by what happened. That's why he hasn't come. That's what's wrong with him now. But he'll pull himself together when he knows I need him. You'll see, Linda. Because he needs me as much as I need him. More than anything else in the world, Julian's a skier. Now he's a spent skier and he can only succeed through me. He'll want me back on those slopes and if he thinks things are going badly with me, he'll do everything he can to get me out of here."

A mythical hero in a mythical land! Sooner or later Stuart had to face reality. Since the fire nothing really dreadful had ever happened to him, and he carried no blame for that on his conscience. From then on I'd always promised him that rose garden. Until now. Perhaps the way he was reacting was partly my fault. Perhaps I had spent too much time protecting and humoring him. Now he could scarcely believe in the seriousness of his own predicament—though he was beginning to feel the sense of imprisonment that he had shrugged off at first as temporary. Somehow he had to come to grips with what was happening. He had to help me as he had not done so far.

I put both my hands against the mesh as though I could touch him through it. "Darling, listen to me. You mustn't fool yourself about Julian. He's lost in his own suffering and except when it comes to his daughter he can't see outside the cage of his own hurt. I don't believe he's thinking about you at all."

I'm not sure Stuart heard me with any comprehension. He had never been one to believe what he didn't want to believe.

"At least you can try to help me," I went on. "I've asked you so many times, and you've never given me an answer. Stuart, who do *you* think killed Margot?"

He laid his own hand against the mesh under one of mine. "Linda—I don't know. I don't know anything. As far as I can tell, it had to be an accident."

"When the chair went down the ramp hard enough to break that guardrail?"

He shook his head helplessly. "I know what that rail was like. It was a stout job. I don't see how it could have broken through. Anyway, there's nothing I can tell you."

This was what he had said from the beginning, and from the beginning I had not entirely believed him. I was sensitive to unspoken thoughts when it came to my brother, and I felt there was something he was holding back. Something he was hiding, or else something that was hiding from him. Perhaps something that lurked deep in his own consciousness that he did not know he knew—or could not bear to look at? So that he'd shut it away, refusing to face what might incriminate someone else?

But there was no use now in trying to pluck at the lock

he had closed against me, and I turned to the subject of Clay.

"What do you really know about him, Stuart? I think I like him. But last night I saw him looking at Shan as though he might be in love with her, as though he might be more involved with the McCabes than he pretends. Do you know anything about that?"

"Clay—Shan?" He laughed. "I don't know Clay all that well, and I don't think anybody knows Shan. But it seems unlikely. Margot was mortal enough—but not Shan. If you have to go ferreting down that sort of silly road, try out Clay and Margot. You might get somewhere there."

"He didn't even like Margot," I objected. "It shows in that magazine piece we saw months ago—'The Griefs of Graystones.' I've just learned that Clay wrote it, and Julian asked him to."

Stuart whistled softly, but before he could comment the guard came to tell us our time was up, and I had to leave. I tried once more to impress on Stuart the seriousness of the situation, so he would give some real attention to helping me. He only shrugged, and I went out to my car and drove back to the lodge.

By the time I had parked and gone up to my room to change, it was time to start for Graystones. In boots and coat, with a scarf over my head, I started along the short-cut path. It was another bright day. There had been no more snow and the path had been beaten down with footprints between lodge and house. Today I left no well-marked prints behind me as I had yesterday approaching by way of the drive. I half expected Emory Ault to accost and challenge me again, but he did not appear.

Instead, around a bend in the path I came upon an outcropping of rock on which Adria was perched cross-legged.

She wore blue today, with a peaked ski cap that let her long black hair escape over her shoulders. She was rolling snowballs between mittened hands and a small pile of them had grown beside her, like a heap of white cannonballs.

I stopped and smiled at her. "Ammunition?" I asked.

She nodded solemnly, not returning my smile. "In case someone comes along that I don't like."

"Then I'm glad you haven't thrown any at me."

"I was trying to decide whether to or not. I've been waiting for you to come along."

"That's a pleasant surprise. Would you like to walk to the house with me?"

The little girl stood up on her rocky mound and looked down at me. "Shan says you're snoopy. Are you?"

"Perhaps no more than anyone else. I'm interested in people. And I'm fascinated by the interesting house you live in." Here I went being deceptive again, when I'd have liked to be honest with this child.

Her blue eyes that were so much like her father's studied me, and I sensed something that lay between us—something more than words from Shan. Yesterday I had come to her rescue in that bitter moment when she had lost control of her emotions. At that moment she had clung to me because I was there. But in doing so she had given me more of herself than she might have intended. I had the feeling that now she wanted to get herself back and hold me away, show me that I meant nothing to her. Perhaps she remembered her own wild cry that she had pushed the chair which held her mother, and felt ashamed, so that her own words turned her against me.

I chose a course that led away from dangerous ground.

"Yesterday when your father took me into the library at Graystones, I saw a picture of you on the wall. A picture of you on skis. You must be a very good skier, with your father for a teacher."

"I'm pretty good," she admitted, and jumped down from her rock pile to come with me, leaving the snowballs behind. "Dad's going to take me skiing this afternoon. He doesn't want to, but he will."

I heard the hint of hostility again and the hurt. She seemed to be considering something soberly, and when she went on her words were unexpected. "Would you like to come with us?"

"I'd like to very much," I said, recognizing that she had once more made a turnabout. "But I'm not a very good skier, so perhaps you'd better ask your father first."

"He'll say it's all right. He says yes to anything I ask him." There was a flat note in the statement, as though she knew he did not pamper her out of love.

"Then I hope you ask him sensible things," I said.

She walked beside me, scuffing at the snow with her boots, occasionally darting quick upward looks to see how I was taking her words.

"My father and Shan worry about me a lot." This sounded more complacent.

"You're very lucky," I told her, and made an open play for sympathy. "I haven't anybody just now to worry about me."

Her quick sidelong look studied me. "That's right—you said—you said your mother died when you were fourteen. But don't you have a father—or anybody else?"

"My father died when I was very small. Again, you're lucky. You live with your father, and you have a loving aunt."

I had said the wrong thing. At once there was a withdrawal from me, a guarded closing in. On one hand she seemed to discount Shan's affection. On the other, she knew very well that her father was ambivalent toward her.

"He does love you, you know," I said gently.

She answered with a touching wisdom that went beyond her years. "I suppose he does. But when he looks at me, he thinks of—of what I did to Margot. And then he hates me."

"I don't think so. And I don't believe you did anything to Margot."

Something like hope shone for an instant in her eyes, then vanished. "You don't know anything about it!" she said roughly. "You weren't there. You don't know how angry I was with her."

"That's right—I don't know. Perhaps some day you'll tell me. Do you really remember pushing her chair?"

Adria's blue eyes were enormous as she stared at me. "I—I think so. I heard her screaming, and—" She broke off, turning her head agonizingly from side to side like a small animal caught in a trap. I felt trapped too, and helpless. I couldn't deal with her fear and her self-blame. Any more than I could deal with my own. I knew very well what Adria might be suffering.

A drifting pile of cumulus clouds had hidden the sun, and shadows of hemlock fell across our path. Beside me Adria pulled away, increasing her pace.

"Come along!" she said impatiently. "Don't be so slow. I hate it when it gets dark in the woods. I'm not like Shan."

I hurried my steps, picking up this change of subject. "What is Shan like?"

"Oh—different from me. Different from anyone. She loves the woods. In the wintertime she doesn't stick to paths. She wanders all over. Do you know the story of Undine? Shan read it to me once. I think she's like that. Only she belongs to the woods, not to the water. Clay says she's a dryad. He says mortals can't live with dryads. Sometimes I—I'm afraid of her. I don't want to turn into a tree."

"How did your mother feel about her?"

"My mother didn't think about her at all. Not unless Shan did something she didn't like."

"What a curious thing to say," I ventured. "I mean, to live in the same house with someone and never think about her. I don't believe that's possible."

"It was for Margot." Again Adria's voice had hardened. "When I was little, I guess she thought mainly about my father and going to all those fancy places and wearing beautiful clothes. My father is rich, though not as rich as Shan. But after Margot was hurt in the car accident, she never thought of anyone but herself. Even Shan says that. And, of course, of getting even with my father."

These were sadly mature thoughts for a little girl of eight.

"Do you really believe that's true?" I asked.

She scuffed along beside me, kicking at the snow. After a moment she shook her head. "No. Margot thought about me too. I know she did. But she wasn't angry with me then, the way she is now."

It was my turn to dart a look at the child. She was staring calmly ahead, indifferent to my response, talking almost to herself.

"Now of course she's furious. Because she knows what I did."

"If she knows, Adria—that is, if there's anything to know—she's more forgiving now. I don't think you need to worry."

Her tone grew a little frantic. "Shan says people can come back, you know. Especially those who die violently. Shan has seen that ancestor who threw himself from the tower of Graystones. She's seen him on the tower stairs a few times. And she says Cinnabar—"

She broke off, as though realizing she had said too much, and hurried ahead of me along the path, rejecting me as though I'd suddenly become dangerous to her. I could see why Julian was disturbed over the effect Shan must be having on the child. But I dared not argue against Shan. I must do nothing which would put Adria further away from me.

"Cinnabar came to see me last night," I told her.

She whirled about on the path. "She did? How did she behave?"

Now I recognized the reason for the feminine pronoun, and I could have shaken Shan for putting this idea of reincarnation into Adria's mind.

"The cat was on my bed when I went up to my room last night. It didn't seem pleased to see me. When I suggested leaving, it walked out of my room. I wonder how it got there in the first place?" I found it difficult to keep saying "it," but I had to tread with caution.

Adria pulled doubtfully at a strand of black hair that hung over one shoulder. "That's very queer, isn't it? After she had to be in a wheelchair and the farmhouse was turned into a lodge, Margot never went there. So last night she must have wanted to see you about something. I expect she can walk right through closed doors, if she wants to."

This was going too far and I had to object. "Adria dear, the cat is only Cinnabar. I think perhaps Shan put him on my bed. Though I don't know the answer to that either."

But I had lost her. She flung away from me and ran toward the house, which was coming into view ahead. I followed her slowly, feeling more disturbed than ever. Increasingly, I was drawn to this tragic child, yet I was torn because my first loyalty must be to Stuart, and if Adria had really had anything to do with her mother's death, the truth that would save Stuart had to come out. At what cost to a haunted eight-year-old? It was as if there were walls all around, pressing me in.

As I walked toward the house, the sight of its stark tower and cold stone chilled me all over again. Graystones seemed a place dedicated to death and tragedy, and I felt a reluctance to set foot inside its walls.

Adria was nowhere in sight when I rang the bell beneath the arch of the front door.

This time a maid let me in—a cheerful young girl from the village, who was apparently expecting me, and whose informality might have given earlier residents of the house a turn.

"You're Miss Earle, aren't you? Come on in. Mr. McCabe's in the library over there, waiting for you."

She wasn't going to announce me, but this time I knew the way. I thanked her and went to the open door. Julian sat in an easy chair with a magazine on his knees, his dark head with its wings of gray bent over the pages he studied. Beyond him, the door to Margot's room was no longer locked, but stood open a crack. When Julian saw me and stood up, dropping the magazine to a table, I noted the photograph of a skier on its cover. A devotion to skiing was something I would never understand, but I was well acquainted with it, thanks to Stuart. Today I could even pity Julian a little because of all he had lost. But today he no longer seemed the dark, dynamic presence I had glimpsed in a mirror last night, and I was glad to have that image dispelled.

He smiled at me gravely. "Thanks for coming, Linda. You don't mind if I call you that?"

"Clay tells me it's the ski thing," I said lightly.

He overlooked my false flippancy. "I saw Adria come running in just now. Did you meet her on the way here?"

I nodded. "Yes. She was telling me about Cinnabar. I tried to tell Adria that Cinnabar is only a cat, but she ran away from me."

A tight look pressed whiteness about his mouth again, but he said nothing.

As if he had heard his name, the big orange animal slipped through the crack of open door from Margot's room and strolled leisurely into the library. Julian looked a little sick.

"I've got to lock up that room for good. Shan keeps putting the cat in there." He watched while Cinnabar crossed the library, indifferent to our presence, and leaped onto a window seat, where he began to wash himself.

"I think she put him into my room at the lodge last night," I said. "What is she trying to accomplish?"

"I'm not sure. Shan's motivations are never exactly obvious. But she may be wary of any friendship between you and Adria that might shut her out. My sister has been taking care of Adria from the time when she was very small."

"Your wife permitted that?" I said, venturing.

He got up and closed the door to Margot's room. It was as if he closed the door upon my questions.

"How did it go with you at the lodge last night?" he asked as he turned to me. "Did you have any trouble with your duties?"

He was not, I realized, making idle conversation. He was curious about me, probing lightly.

"Clay seemed to think I was all right," I said. "You have a pleasant group of people coming to the lodge. Perhaps I'll be more at ease tonight."

"I keep wondering why you've sought out this sort of work. Why this instead of a law office?"

"I love the country," I said readily. That was true enough.

"I suppose I can accept that, since the country is my own choice."

"You're lucky to be able to choose," I told him.

I wished I could be more at ease with Julian McCabe. I'd been thrust with strange intimacy into life at Graystones—for reasons he could not guess—and I found it hard to relax and behave naturally with any of them.

"It's too bad Shan has never married and had children of her own," I went on, still venturing. "Then she wouldn't be focusing so exclusively on Adria."

My timing couldn't have been worse. Shan herself came through the door from the hall at that instant, and she had heard my words.

She was floating in chiffon again—this time pale watercress green over brightly flowered pants, and with several strings of beads hanging about her neck. I was reminded of a hippie dressed by a couturier. Her gray-green eyes turned in my direction and there was no liking in them, though her manner was one of amusement when she spoke in her low, beautiful voice.

"But of course I've been married, Miss Earle. I was married several years before Adria was born. Unfortunately, I had to —dissolve the attachment, and I took my own name again afterward. But we don't talk about that. I've forbidden it. As for my focusing on Adria—who else would, if I hadn't? Not her mother, certainly. And her father was away a lot every winter. Not that I have to explain any of this. Adria *is* my child. Possession and all that."

Her tone was gentle, as though she explained something to someone immature and not entirely bright. She relaxed into a chair and regarded me with interest, waiting for my reaction. I couldn't have been in a more awkward and self-defeating spot, and I was grateful to Julian for coming to my rescue.

"Of course we've been discussing you," he told her. "What is happening to Adria can't go on. Miss Earle has had some experience with disturbed children—which Adria is on the way to becoming. But more important than experience is her natural instinct to take the right course with Adria. I think we must make use of this if Miss Earle is willing. In any case, there must be no more of your putting fantasies about her mother into Adria's head, Shan."

His sister remained undisturbed. She noticed the cat on the window sill, still busy with his toilet, and snapped her fingers at him.

"Cinnabar, come here! Come, Cinnabar! You belong in on this fascinating discussion."

Cinnabar stood up and stretched rather haughtily. Then he sprang from the window sill and padded across the room to leap into Shan's lap. She laughed softly, huskily, and he pricked up his ears at the sound.

"You see?" Shan said to her brother. "Cinnabar is listening. What you were saying is important to us, isn't it, Cinnabar?" Her fingers scratched the cat gently between the ears, and he began to purr, the sound deep as a boiling kettle. He was entirely indifferent to the emotions around him, concerned only with his own pleasure. As Margot had been? I wondered wryly.

But Julian had had enough of the cat. He moved to pluck Cinnabar from Shan's lap and put him firmly into the hall. Then he closed the library door with a slam and stood with his back to it, as though the cat might somehow come through again in spite of him.

"You've got to stop this, Shan! I won't have you playing this terrible game with Adria. You're terrifying her. I've turned to Miss Earle because I'm at my wit's end."

There was a tense silence. Shan bent her head like a child

who has been reprimanded. This time he had reached her, and I saw the shine of tears before she closed her eyes.

I put my prodding question gently in the long silence. "Miss McCabe, do you believe Adria actually pushed her mother's chair down that ramp?"

Julian stiffened, and Shan's head came up as she stared at me with a pale resentment that seemed all the more deadly for being contained in a veil of gentleness. "I haven't any doubt of it. Though none of this is any business of yours."

"But then what about this young man who's being held in jail and will be brought to trial? Are you going to sacrifice him to protect Adria?"

"Of course!" Shan cried. "I'm not going to tell anyone else that I think Adria might have pushed that chair. Do you think I want to destroy her? I only want to comfort her, help her."

Her indifference to Stuart's plight made me reckless. "Do you think it comforts her to believe her mother has come back in the form of a cat to torment her?"

Shan's eyes were wide with innocence. "But, Miss Earle—what if it's true?"

Julian started to shout at her, and then stopped himself. I wanted to shout at her myself.

Julian flung up his hands in despair. "We don't need to discuss any of this, Linda. The problem is Adria and her own self-torture. Which you've helped to inflict on her, Shan. There's no getting away from that."

"I've inflicted nothing on her!" Now Shan's outrage was anything but pale. "She came running to me on the stairs that day and she said her mother was screaming because she'd hurt her. What else is there to believe?"

"What I want to believe," Julian said more quietly, "is that Stuart Parrish went into that room and pushed Margot's chair. What I want to believe is that the right man is sitting in that jail."

I almost cried out a denial, barely managing to hold it back.

"I know what you want to believe," Shan said. "And I think that's just fine. Though sometimes I wonder what Stuart thinks of you. After all, you were supposed to be his friend. You brought him into your house. You trained him to the point where he was about to become a champion. Because *you* could no longer be a champion! Yet just because Emory makes wild claims, you drop Stuart and refuse to go near him. He's had too much pride to ask you for help. He's never made a move in your direction since you dropped him, but I wonder what he thinks."

This was an unexpected championing and I was momentarily grateful to Shan. I could have told them both what Stuart thought. I could have told them that he still believed Julian would come to his aid. But once more I could not speak out. I knew now that my first instinct had been right, and that Julian would do nothing to help my brother.

I looked up from the clenched hands in my lap and found his eyes gravely upon me. "We're upsetting Miss Earle, Shan. Linda, I'm sorry. But perhaps it's a good thing for you to see the strain we're under just now. Perhaps you'll forgive us for our impossible behavior and recognize our need where Adria is concerned."

With an effort I kept my voice from quivering. "If I'm to be of any use I need to know more than I do. Why did Adria and her mother quarrel that day?"

Now Julian was impatient with me. "What does it matter? Let's not dredge up old troubles. They often argued. The only thing we need remember is that Adria adored her mother, no matter how rebellious she might be at times."

Shan was watching me and she paid no attention to her brother's words. "I've always wanted to know the answer to that question myself—but Adria has never been willing to talk about it, if she even remembers. Which I doubt."

We were all silent for a few moments. Julian's attitude, and the emotions which drove him were at last coming clear to me. He longed to believe that Adria hadn't pushed Margot's chair, and that Stuart was guilty. He wanted as a father to do everything possible to save his child. Yet when he looked at her, some dreadful gorge rose in him, and he saw her as the instrument of Margot's death—and he still loved Margot. He couldn't believe in Stuart's guilt, as he wanted to, and he felt a little guilty about this. Here was something I might be able to take advantage of when the chance came my way. I hated the person I was becoming—always calculating, always ready to snatch at the easy chance. I didn't want to be like this—and yet it was necessary.

There was no further discussion because at that moment Adria opened the door and came into the library. She had put on a dress of the same watercress green that matched Shan's chiffon, and as she entered the room she glanced from one to another of us knowingly—a child who was all too aware of the adult emotions surging stormily around her.

"Were you having a fight?" she asked sweetly. "Daddy, you do look mad. And Shan's going to cry." She looked at me, her eyes appraising. "Miss Earle looks as though she might go off like a firecracker."

"And you," I said coolly, "are a little girl who hasn't yet grown up enough to understand that other people besides yourself have feelings."

Shan gasped softly, but Julian said nothing. I was aware of the way he watched me. Surprisingly, Adria came to stand beside my chair.

"You don't really like me, do you?" she said, clearly interested, as though I were a novelty she had never experienced.

"Not all the time," I told her, smiling to soften my words. "Though sometimes I do—very much."

She gave me her most winning smile in return and spoke triumphantly to her father, as though she had scored a point. "Daddy, I've invited Miss Earle to come skiing with us this afternoon. That's all right, isn't it?"

"Of course," he said stiffly. "If Miss Earle wishes." But I could not tell by his face whether he wished it or not.

"I'm not very good on skis," I warned him. "I'm not even intermediate. You'll both be impatient with me. But I'll go to the slopes with you, if Adria would like that. Then you can ski off on your own and pick me up when you're ready to go home."

Adria regarded me with a kindly air. "Don't worry—we'll teach you how to ski better. It's fun to be good, you know. And Daddy—is it all right if I call her Linda? She's a friend, isn't she?"

Shan made a sound of displeasure, rejecting such intimacy, but Julian smiled in rather touching relief.

"Yes, Adria, Linda is your friend. And I don't think we have to be Victorian."

At least we had relaxed to some extent and left dangerous topics behind. If Shan was not pleased with this new turn she seemed to recover herself sufficiently to behave more pleasantly toward me, and the climate had changed by the time we went into the dining room for lunch. The change was welcome. My nerves felt raw from irritation, and I could sense Julian's inner torment all too well.

I found this room the pleasantest in the downstairs area. It was light with apple-green wallpaper, and the furniture had the grace of good Duncan Phyfe. The mantel was of veined pink marble with figures of Chelsea porcelain set upon it. Below, a wood fire burned, giving additional light and life to the room. Julian sat at the head of the long table, with me on his right and Shan at the far end. Adria was across from me, and she seemed unexpectedly bent upon charming me, coaxing me to like her. I did not trust her at all, yet something in me yearned over her. Her own bravura attitude gave her away. She was a lost little figure, for all that she was surrounded by Shan's doting and her father's tortured concern. Perhaps my directness was good for her. I mustn't capitulate to the point of foolish indulgence as the others had done. Someone needed to pull her back into the real world. I thought of Stuart and his gay confidence in Julian, his assurance that his predicament was more amusing than frightening, so that he was not trying to fight as he should. A wavering glimpse reached me of some similarity between Adria and Stuart, even though they were so different, but it was no more than a flash and I could not see it clearly or understand its meaning for me. Mainly I felt a growing urge to uncover the real Adria buried beneath the levels of artificial charm and frightening emotion. I had the feeling that she could be an attractive, happy, intelligent child, granted the opportunity. What had to be discovered, no matter how great the cost, was the truth about the pushing of that chair.

I'm afraid I contributed little to the luncheon conversation, and that sometimes I was not even attentive. My fingers touched the heavy English silver, that was an heirloom, the blue and white Staffordshire china that must have been in the family for generations. I ate my food—and nothing registered acutely. Once or twice Shan expressed regret that Julian had no one else in training to put into Stuart Parrish's place. Stuart had been scheduled for the amateur competition at Kitzbühel in Austria, and Garmisch, Germany, both in January. Then the Wild West Classic at Jackson Hole, Wyoming, in February—all just as a start for the season.

In his day Julian had been an amateur turned pro, and now he began to speak of his interest in professional skiing. He felt there had to be more places where the champion skier could go from amateur racing. It was only right that he should be able to earn an income and not be required to depend forever on the donations that were needed to keep his amateur standing.

I knew a little about this, since it was Julian who had sponsored Stuart for the amateur circuit and furnished the support which enabled him to ski instead of working for a living. Sometimes I had worried about Stuart's future in such a life.

"Television's the goal," Julian said. "Once we get advertising money coming in—the money that follows the crowds—professional skiing can be assured of its future."

"At least a good beginning's been made," Shan said. "The television presentation of the last professional racing was terrific, and the audience response was good."

Julian nodded. "Now we have to carry on. It's a bit dreary when our best skiers have to wind up on ski patrol or running a shop or teaching, because there's nothing else they're trained for. Often it's the older skier who has the stamina and muscular endurance, if only he could keep on. To say nothing of the experience that backs one up on the slopes. Yet there's been no place for him if he wants to earn a living using his skills."

Without meaning to, I started to yawn and managed to swallow with difficulty. That was reflex action. My instinctive reaction when it came to talk about skiing was to go to sleep —as I'd sometimes done with Stuart.

"We're boring Miss Earle," Shan said, slyly prodding at me.

Julian apologized. "Skiers go overboard on shop talk, and I imagine you'll get more than enough of that at the lodge. Tell us something about yourself, Linda."

"I'm sorry," I said. "I didn't sleep too well last night. All this country quiet—I'm not used to it. But I'm afraid there isn't anything exciting to tell about me." The last thing I wanted was to talk about Linda Earle, lest giveaway comparisons be made with Stuart's life. "Yesterday I had a curious encounter with your caretaker on the way back to the lodge. He seemed quite disturbed to find me on Graystones grounds."

"I'll speak to him about you," Julian said, and I realized at once that I'd made the wrong comment. I wanted no discussions about me with Emory Ault, who for some reason I didn't understand had held his tongue about me so far.

"Perhaps he senses the same thing in you that I sense," Shan put in, her eyes turning dreamy. "People have auras about them, you know. Yours troubles me. It's wrong for Graystones."

"What color is her aura?" Adria broke in eagerly.

But Julian forestalled any answer. "Never mind, Shan. Let's not go down that road. If Linda has any sort of aura I'd say it's a healthy one."

I'm not sure how I got through the remainder of that luncheon. I found myself moving as if along some dangerous ridge, from which a steep hill sloped away on either side— descents which I lacked the skill and knowledge to traverse. At the foot of each lay a crevasse and complete disaster. It was like experiencing a waking nightmare, and I was glad when we finished dessert and coffee and could rise from the table.

"Let's get ready to go skiing right away," Adria pleaded. "By the time we're dressed and we drive around the mountain to the base lodge, it will be at least an hour from now. So let's hurry. Shan, are you coming with us?"

Shan fluttered her green chiffon. "No thank you, dear. We'll ski another time—you and I alone."

"I'll go back to the lodge and change my clothes," I said to Julian.

He nodded. "Fine. We'll pick you up there."

I could look forward to the afternoon with no pleasure, but at least we would be free of Shan. Surely on the slopes the only dangers to beset me would be physical ones which would include a few tumbles in the snow.

VI

I did not hurry on my way back to the lodge. Let them wait for me, if necessary. I needed time to relax, to let my tensions unwind, and to think about the things I had learned in the last few hours at Graystones.

The first disturbing point was that Julian had definitely turned against Stuart. But still I didn't know why he half believed Emory Ault's wild claims, or why he had deserted his protégé without even a hearing. Opposing this formidable fact was Shan's unexpected championship of Stuart. He had never said much about her, except to indicate that she might be a bit wacky and far out. Certainly he'd never claimed any friendship with her. None of this furthered what I needed to know, but at least it was some small progress.

Superimposed upon my questioning and seeking was the

distress I felt about Adria, and my increasing sense of disquiet when it came to Julian. Last night there had been a strange enchantment upon me when I'd looked into his mirrored eyes across the room. I had found myself disturbingly open to the appeal of a man I did not even like, and this had upset me. It had been a relief to find nothing of this pull in effect today. Yet I'd found myself engaged by pity for him, by a wish to help him if I could when it came to Adria. Strangely, almost by chance, Adria seemed drawn to me, curious about me—perhaps because I fitted no pattern of that indulging affection she'd known too much of in her young life. There had been a time when I had indulged Stuart too readily in just this way. I had protected him as Shan was trying to protect Adria, so that he now found it difficult to come to grips with reality.

This was a flash of uncomfortable self-recognition and I shied away from it. I had never tied Stuart to me. He had cut his bonds easily in growing up, and had begun to slip away from me with his first meeting with Julian. This was as it should be, even though it hurt me. All this I saw quite clearly, but there was, nevertheless, an aching in me for the young brother I had lost. It had been satisfying to be needed.

The sound of something flying sharply through the air past my ear brought me back to my surroundings. A heavy object had crashed through overhead branches, whizzed by my head, and fallen heavily to the path before me. I walked toward the knife-edge stone that lay on the path. There was nowhere it could have come from unless it had been thrown at me. I was more angry than frightened, and I whirled about on the path.

Evergreens closed in behind me around the last turn. Because of low-crowding hemlock branches and thick layers of blue spruce, I could see nothing. There was no wind, no movement among the trees. A deep stillness pressed around me. I turned toward the lodge and began to walk more quickly, hardly believing what had happened, and more troubled by the silence than by the fact that I could see no one in the woods around me.

When the second stone was hurled, it grazed my shoulder and this time I was frightened. I ran toward the lodge, slipping on the icy path, but managing to keep my feet. No third stone followed me, and I burst through the back door, to find one of the maids in the small vestibule watching me in surprise.

"What are you running away from—bears?" she asked.

I didn't want to explain. "Where is Mr. Davidson?"

"He's somewhere around, I guess. I haven't seen him for a while." She shrugged and went on with her mopping.

I hurried into Clay's office and found it empty. My breathing had begun to quiet and I gave up searching and went upstairs. This time no orange cat waited in my room, and it seemed a haven of safety. Who could be trying to frighten me? Because it must be that. Surely the stone thrower would have had sufficient opportunity to hit me, if he'd wanted to. I needed to consult Clay, but that would have to wait.

Now it was necessary to get into my ski clothes and I changed rapidly, pulling on long johns, which fortunately came in two pieces these days. Since it wasn't very cold, I left off the tops. I put on heavy socks and over-the-boots stretch pants. Ski styles changed faster than everyday styles, stretch pants were supposed to be out this season. But it was really up to everyone to do his own thing, so I didn't worry. My clothes were good and too expensive to be put in the rag bag because of styles. While Stuart never cared what he wore on the slopes, he agreed that it was fine for a girl to feel attractive. Especially if she didn't ski very well. So he'd helped me choose my clothes. I liked the dark brown pants with a tiny white pin stripe running down them, and the beige parka that had cost enough and was very well cut. Now the styles were matching parka and pants, but again I wasn't going to worry. I'd bought a yellow turtleneck sweater to wear under it, and Stuart had given me a lovely Ullr medallion on a silver chain to wear against the sweater. Ullr was the Norse god of the skier, and "Ullrs" were often worn or carried by skiers in one form or another for luck.

Mine was particularly beautiful—a round of silver with the small figure of Ullr etched upon one side. This version showed him as a little old man with a long beard, a stocking cap, wind-tossed scarf, carrying a Norwegian crossbow in one hand and a ski pole in the other. He was on skis, of course, his knees bent as he schussed along. On the back, nearly filling the circle, was etched a filled-in diamond—the symbol of that black diamond which warned skiers of the most difficult slope. I'd laughed over that, since I was not likely to be found on even a moderately difficult slope. But Stuart said it was to encourage me. I'd loved his present and I certainly needed anything I could wear for luck.

I put my after-ski boots on last. They were gray reindeer hide, comfortable, a protection against puddles and slush, and good-looking for walking-around purposes. Except when it was very cold, I let the parka hood hang down my back and went bareheaded, my hair held with a brown grosgrain ribbon band that also kept my ears warm. Stuart had said that I made a charming snow bunny—which was a term applied to beginners, usually female, who haunted the slopes, and did not flatter me. It was not, he explained, the feminine counterpart of "ski bum," since the bums were real skiers who had simply become hooked on skiing.

When I was ready, I went down to my parked car and took

out my black ski boots and got my skis from the carrier, shouldered them, and walked toward the driveway to wait for Julian and Adria.

Clay must have seen me there, for he came outdoors, having slipped on a jacket. "Hello, Linda, how did it go at Graystones?"

"All right," I said without enthusiasm. "I'm full of information. For instance, I've learned that Shan has been married before, that Julian doesn't mean to help Stuart, and that Shan is making Adria believe in reincarnation."

"Reincarnation?" Clay echoed, letting the rest go. "What are you talking about?"

"Margot," I said dryly. "She is supposed to be coming back in the shape of that cat—Cinnabar."

Clay looked shocked, when I'd have expected him to be derisive. I hurried on to the main thing I wanted to tell him.

"On the way back from the house someone threw stones at me. Twice. They missed, but they came awfully close. Why would anyone do such a thing? Do you think it's Emory Ault?"

Clay stared at me. "That's going pretty far, even for Emory."

"But there's no one else it could be. Only Shan and Adria. I don't think Shan likes me, but I can't see her throwing rocks. And I don't believe Adria wants to frighten me off."

"You'd better tell Julian," Clay said. "I've warned him before this that the old man is getting out of hand. Julian's too fond of him to listen. I think Emory's a bit crazy—and that may be important in Stuart's defense. If he's really taken to throwing stones it may help you out."

"But why would he? Why should he try to frighten me, even if I am Stuart's sister?"

"Perhaps he doesn't want anyone around attempting to find out the real truth about Margot's death."

I thought about that soberly. There was a big question in my mind about Emory, but for the moment it took me nowhere, and I went down another road.

"I think Shan's a bit crazy too. I don't think she's good for Adria."

Clay startled me by reaching out to grasp my arm, squeezing through the parka sleeve. "Don't ever say that. Not around here. Shan may be close to nature, but she's probably more sane than any of us."

I stared at his hand where it had closed about my arm, and after a moment he loosened the pressure and withdrew it, his face flushed and dark.

"I saw the way you looked at her last night," I said gently.

There was no liking for me in his eyes. "Shan is my wife," he said.

I gasped, staring at him, trying to grasp this revelation. "But—but Stuart never told me—!" I found myself floundering. "And Shan said her marriage had been dissolved, whatever that means."

"In this case it means that there's no legal divorce. It's her term, not mine. She simply doesn't recognize that we're married, and no point of it is ever made, since she took back her maiden name. It all happened years ago. Before Julian's accident. Before your brother came on the scene. I used to live at the house then. But no one talks about it, so Stuart wouldn't know."

"I'm sorry," I said, and I was truly sorry. I liked Clay. He was not looking at me now, but staring off through the trees, his expression remote. What I had seen last night had been a betrayal he had not meant to make, and he probably found it distasteful that I had noticed.

"Here comes Julian," he said curtly and walked away from me, disappearing across the front porch of the lodge.

I was doubly upset—not only because of the stone throwing, but because Clay had been my only ally, and was now offended with me. Julian braked the car and got out, a tall figure in dark forest green, bareheaded as always. I think he sensed something wrong, for he gave me a sharp look. However, he said nothing as he dropped my ski boots into the trunk, and took my poles and skis from me. I got into the front seat beside an Adria who was bright in scarlet from head to toe.

"Nobody is going to lose you on the slopes in that outfit," I said.

She looked off into the woods, not meeting my eyes. "Margot always used to wear red."

Her father made no comment as he got behind the wheel. We followed the narrow road that wound around the foot of the mountain away from Graystones and the lodge. Adria sat silently between us. Now that we were on our way to the ski area, she seemed to have lost all interest in the trip. When she did speak, it was only to sound a warning.

"There hasn't been much snow for a few days. The trails may not be any good."

Her father glanced at her soberly, perhaps sensing her loss of interest in the afternoon she had presumably looked forward to.

"What's wrong, Adria? You wanted to go skiing, didn't you? You know the snow machines were out all night making powder and the grooming crew has been at work."

She offered no response and I was aware of her small, delicate face in profile, blue eyes staring straight ahead, her body all too tense beneath the bright outfit.

"What slopes would you like to try today?" Julian asked.

Adria turned a quick, sly glance upon me. "Let's go down Devil's Drop."

"I doubt that Linda's ready for that," Julian said dryly, "and you're certainly not."

"Oh, I am! I am!" She was suddenly urgent in her entreaty. "I told Cinnabar I was coming down it today."

"Well, you're not." Julian gave me a look over Adria's head, and I saw in it his helplessness and entreaty, his rising anger against forces he could not counter.

"I hope you'll stay with me for a while on the easy slopes," I said. "Remember—you promised to teach me. What slopes do you think are right for me?"

At least she had roused herself from lethargy and was back in our world as she began to consider possible trails.

"Encore's too easy. Maybe you can try Nordic or Hemlock. Do you think so, Daddy?"

"Nothing's too easy for me," I hastened to put in. "I'll be happy to start with Encore."

We drove through more stands of hemlock, pine and spruce as the road began to climb toward the base lodge. We passed cars coming down from the ski area, and there were others behind us climbing toward it.

The base lodge was long and low, with two A-frame redwood sections walled with glass. The sloping roofs wore a frosting of snow, and beyond them rose the mountain with ski trails plainly marked and small figures gliding down them. Julian found a parking space among rows of cars, and we got into our ski boots. I buckled mine as Stuart had taught me, fastening them in the middle notches. Thanks to him, I had boots that were right for me. Leather, because they were more yielding than the stiff plastic boots the experts could use, with enough space to wiggle my toes, but not too much, and with heels that fit snugly below the ankle bone without pinching, yet held my foot rigid. The wrong boots could be agony and they could mean accidents too. I whacked my heel down smartly to get it well into the boot, and show I knew what I was doing. When I'd clipped the buckles shut and stood up, I felt, as usual, rather like a clumping elephant. Both Julian and Adria were ready before I was, and they walked with more grace than I managed as we plodded across broken snow to the lodge, taking care not to hit anyone with our skis or poles. I could almost hear Stuart's voice: "Whether you're carrying your skis or wearing them, you have to keep an eye out for the other fellow. Don't go about behaving as though you were the only skier on the slopes. Maybe you're a snow bunny, but don't be a dumb bunny."

We rounded the end of the building and found ourselves in a wide, level area at the foot of the trails. The sun was high in a cloudless sky and the scene dazzling bright. I took my sunglasses out of a pocket and put them on, cutting down the glare. Directly ahead of us was a chair lift, with T-bar, J-bar and poma lift off to our right. Rather gentle, soothing music was being broadcast through loudspeakers around the base area, calming to ski nerves. Nearby, a class group was floundering down a slight practice slope, trying to follow instructions. At least I could feel superior to them.

Julian went inside to get a lift ticket for me, since he and Adria had season passes. While he was gone we sat down on a low wooden bench and put on our skis. I had step-in toe and heel bindings that would release no matter which way I fell, and of course the regulation safety straps that would keep me from losing a ski if I fell out of it. Aside from the inconvenience, a runaway ski could cause serious accidents on a slope. By the time Julian returned, we were ready and standing up with our ski poles grasped through straps, their basket ends thrust into the snow. Adria looked more at ease and confident now.

The first ordeal would be the ski lift. Thanks to Stuart, I could cope, though in the beginning I'd been thrown by rope tows, tossed off T-bars, and tried to plow another skier under while I was riding a J-bar. At least I had learned not to stay in the path of danger when I fell off so I'd get plowed under myself. In a way, the lifts were worse than the skiing, but at least I knew what to expect.

It developed that we were to go up in the Triple Chair and when Julian started toward it I began to make low moaning sounds of protest. Chair lifts were the easiest for going up, but for some strange reason the easy lifts were usually for expert skiers who could come down the professional runs. As a rule the arm-tugging rope tow which could act like a bucking bronco was for the beginner.

Julian reassured me kindly. "Don't worry. It's true that the chair takes us to Devil's Drop over on the far left, but there are easier ways down and we'll stick to Encore until we see how you do. If you like, we can get off at the halfway station for our first run."

This being a weekday, the lift line was short and we took our places, with Julian in the lead. When it was our turn to get aboard, we placed ourselves three abreast, with Adria in the middle, and Julian, being the heaviest, on the tower side, our ski poles in one hand, and the other hand behind us to catch the chair as it swung up beneath our knees. It was possible to be banged off your feet if you weren't careful. This I could now manage with some dexterity—since the chair halted only briefly, this was necessary. Then we were aboard and away, the chair rocking gently as it left the station. I tilted up the front tips of my skis to avoid piles of snow on the ground, remembering the time my tips had caught and I'd gone headlong out of the chair. Julian pulled the blue safety bar down in front of us, and I held onto it tightly with the inside hand that wasn't gripping my ski poles. Now, for a little while, I could enjoy myself. The lift ran up through a narrow slit cut between trees and as our chair rose high above the ground I experienced an odd sense of release, of freedom. It was as if I were being lifted into a clear and blameless world filled with air and light. Far below the swinging chairs which followed their shadows up the mountain, lay a clean corridor of snow running steeply up the cut, and marked at intervals by the blue posts of the lift. Along one side a trail of footprints marched down, left perhaps by an attendant or by some chair passenger trying to retrieve possessions he'd dropped from the lift.

Beyond the trees on either side of the cut, trails wound down the mountain, and skiers, each encased in his own private world, followed them toward the base. Our chair swung over a ravine, at the bottom of which was a narrow spring-fed lake that furnished water for the snow machines. We moved smoothly now. One tall blue lift tower after another was left behind, and the rise of the mountain steepened. Our shadows, complete with long thin skis, sped up the slope beneath us. In chairs behind and ahead, the bright colors and varieties of ski dress were in evidence. Adria wasn't the only one who wore red.

The halfway point was growing close now as the chair creaked toward it, the machinery rattling like clattering milk bottles. Our shadows rose from the snow to meet us at the station. Once more I lifted my ski tips lest they be caught by the edge of the platform, and in a moment we were sliding out of the chair, Julian gliding ahead down the ramp, with Adria next, and I on the outside, following last. I swallowed my usual impulse to hold back (while my skis ran out from under me!) and pushed with my ski poles to slide down the snowy ramp, snowplowing quickly away from the end, so there would be no pile-up behind me. We had arrived, and the usual moment of truth lay ahead of me.

At least I was temporarily cut free from all the problems and worries that beset me. I couldn't think about Stuart now. Or about diabolically thrown stones that whizzed past my head. I couldn't ponder the problem of Adria or Julian's suffering or the fact that Shan was Clay Davidson's wife. All these things whirled dizzily through my mind and were lost before the immediate problem of getting myself down a ski trail without breaking my neck. Perhaps that was why skiing was good therapy. It freed one for the essential, physical matter in hand. Or perhaps "under ski" would be a better way to put it.

Julian said, "I'll see you down the first run, if you like, Linda," and went skating off toward the top of the Encore trail.

"Come along," Adria said. "This run is pretty boring, but you don't have to go down it twice."

For me it wasn't boring. I persuaded Julian to go over to the next, more professional slope, even though he was entering from the halfway point. Then I got Adria to start ahead of me down Encore—and was left on my own. Even for me, the run was easy enough to give me no trouble. The snow was well packed, but with a rough surface that offered purchase for my skis. I set my edges and started down using stem christies back and forth, traversing the fall line, occasionally slowing myself with a snowplow—trying nothing fancy, my skis clattering over the hard pack. Here the moguls weren't bad, though I hated those disconcerting humps of hard-packed snow carved by many skiers turning at the same point. At night the snow cats would get out and chop the worst ones down for busy skiers to set up again the next day.

Someone behind me shouted, "On your left!" and I got out of the way of a descending skier who was obviously not altogether in control. At least he hadn't shouted "Look out!"— which would have told me nothing. Not all the dangers of skiing had to do with the trails and one's own skill.

This was my first skiing of the winter and I discovered to my surprise that somehow during the long months of lying fallow I had improved. I seemed to have greater confidence, more skill than last winter. I wished Stuart could see me. I was doing something entirely on my own, and I wasn't doing it badly. The experts might scorn my stem turns, but I felt a sudden exhilaration over such improvement. These moments of elation, of growing confidence were what skiing was all about. Speed would never be my thing, but this—this experience of snow underfoot, the mountain slipping past, with a cold wind on my face, a warming sun overhead to make the snow sparkle with diamonds, plus a modest competence achieved—for a few moments all this was wonderfully heady. When I joined Julian and Adria at the foot of the run, my blood was tingling and I knew my eyes were bright.

Julian smiled at me, the harshness of his face softening. "I watched you come down, and you're not bad at all. Someone's been teaching you well."

I could have told him the teaching was his, even though once removed. Strange to realize this was so.

"Let's go up again!" Adria cried. "You're fine, Linda. We'll try Hemlock this time." She seemed a different child on the mountain. There was therapy for her here too.

I was braver now, and while I left Devil's Drop to Julian, I managed Hemlock several times, thanks to an off day when the lift lines were short, and we could go up again quickly.

I even went to the top of the chair—the top of the lift—once I was acquainted with the run, and there we pushed over to where Devil's Drop fell away, and watched Julian go down until he was out of sight beneath an overhanging cornice of the mountain.

He too had come to life and was a different man, now that the slopes called him. It was as if ice had been momentarily thawed by that inner fire with which he met the mountain and the snow. It was marvelous to watch him as he went down with a twisting grace and great speed and control, a lithe figure in his dark green, fitting the scene about him, belonging to it.

Adria watched in rapture. "My father's still the best in the world," she told me when he'd dropped from view. "Stuart Parrish thinks he's good, but he'll never touch my father."

I said nothing, and we went back to the top of Hemlock and I skied down in Adria's wake. Perhaps the sight of Julian's perfection went to my head and I tried to be better than I was, for I caught one ski tip on a mogul and went sprawling and sliding across packed snow. My skis released, dangling from their thongs, and I crawled hastily to the side of the trail where I'd be out of the way of others coming down. Adria heard me fall, and she made an uphill turn and skied to a stop. Then she sidestepped up the edge of the trail and came to help me to my feet. The injury to my newborn pride was greater than any physical hurt. I put on my skis in a state of chagrin and made the rest of the run with less careless aplomb. Adria was surprisingly considerate and made no fun of me. "Everyone falls," she said, offering comfort.

When we reached the bottom she said nothing of my mishap, but pleaded with her father to go over to the big ice palace which had been built for children, where there were tunnels to crawl through, and surprising scenes to be discovered inside. Julian let her go and took me into one of the upstairs A-frame lounges that overlooked the skiing area.

The room was cozy and warm. We sat at a polished wooden table next to a great triangle of glass panes, and Julian ordered glühwein. The carpet on the floor was a warm, deep red, and there were slanting brown timbers overhead. Only two or three other tables were occupied and we sat by ourselves in the quiet room.

Julian had helped me off with my parka and I sat fingering my silver Ullr on its chain. When I let it swing free of my hand, he stared at it with sudden intensity.

"What's that?" he said. "Where did you get it?"

His questioning was so abrupt that I wondered uneasily if he had seen it before—if perhaps Stuart had shown it to him before he gave it to me. I answered carefully.

"It's only an Ullr medallion that was given to me. I suppose they come in all sorts of forms. I wear it for luck—the way other skiers do."

"What's on the other side?" he asked.

I turned it so he could see the shaded diamond, tipped on its point—that symbol to warn the inexpert.

"This is supposed to encourage me to greater efforts than I want to make," I said.

He laughed and seemed to relax, but now and then his eyes strayed to the medallion as though something about it puzzled him. However, he talked on casually enough, telling me about the room we were in—that on Saturdays it was well filled, and there was usually a banjo player to entertain in the afternoon.

I found it pleasantly quiet now. Yet I couldn't relax and enjoy this moment as I'd have liked to. With no effort needed to stay on my feet, everything else came rushing back—all my concerns and fears and oppressive secrets. I'd have given anything to face Julian honestly and talk to him about Stuart. But this I could not do.

Instead, I asked if he missed the competition skiing and traveling about to the best skiing areas here and abroad. He didn't seem to resent my asking. His eyes rested on the mountain slopes beyond the window, the green of trees and brilliant white of snow shining in the sunlight. Faintly from outside, music came to us. The tune was "Moonlight in Vermont." I wondered how these slopes would look by moonlight. There was night skiing here, I knew.

"I suppose I miss it to some extent," he said, finally answering my question. "Though not as much as I did in the beginning. The excitement gets into your blood, the need to meet a challenge, to prove yourself. The exhilaration of winning. I suppose no one knows what it's really like unless he's done it."

I knew something about it from Stuart. Skiing could be a passion, a religion.

"The mystique," I said, sipping hot, spicy, mulled wine.

"Don't put it down if you haven't felt it."

"I'm only trying to understand. For instance, how can people give whole lifetimes to working at this sort of thing?" I waved my hands to include the entire ski area. "It's a playtime world. It's not real. Even running a lodge for skiers isn't—"

His laughter cut into my words. "The work ethic, you mean? But this may be a better way of earning a living than most, my little Puritan. Perhaps in our age it's a man's playtime that enables him to get closer to the natural things he's lost. Perhaps it keeps him from being swallowed whole by what you call the real world—which can be a pretty greedy monster. Out here there's time to look at the sky, at the hills, at the earth. Even into yourself. All this may be closer to reality than you think because here you can get back to being part of the universe. I don't count any of these lives lost. Those who come out from the cities envy us."

"I know there's a bond—a very real one—between people who ski, and I know that must count for a lot."

"Yes, there's that. Strong friendship can develop when you have skiing in common. Even après-ski is more fun because skiing has turned you on."

"But I don't see why the mountain climber must climb still another mountain. Or why a man must cross an ocean in a small boat. Why does one have to be the best and the fastest on a ski slope? To say one climbs because the mountain's there isn't good enough. Where does the drive come from? Why does it exist?"

Unexpectedly, he was as curious about me as I was about him. "How have you remained so untouched, so uninvolved?" he countered. "Hasn't this sort of passion ever touched you?"

"Uninvolved!" I choked over the word. "Honestly! I'm the most involved person I—"

"With other people's lives," he broke in. "What about you? Who are you? What do *you* want?"

I floundered, unable to answer him. He saw with too much perception a question I was afraid to face.

"What frightened you away from life?" he asked softly.

There was a betrayal of tears in my eyes, but I truly did not know why they were there. He saw them and reached out to cover my hand with his. I had a curious wish to turn my hand and grasp his—to be the leaning one, instead of the leaned upon. But I did not move. I sat very still, blinking desperately.

He let me go and sat back and there was a gentleness about him that I'd never seen before.

"I'm sorry," he said. "I had no right to turn that particular screw. Perhaps you'll tell me someday."

How could I tell anyone what I didn't understand myself? I fumbled for a handkerchief and blew my nose crossly. He smiled at me almost tenderly and returned to my original question of where the drive came from that thrust a man to strange heights.

"Perhaps it's not a woman's thing, after all," Julian said. "Or at least not for many women, though there are always a few who rise to a challenge. My wife wasn't one of them. Margot liked the excitement of the resort area for itself. She liked beautiful sports clothes and beautiful people. She thrived on admiration. Even though she skied well and enjoyed it, there was never any passion in her feeling for it."

I wondered if he had minded that, if he had needed a woman who would share the same passion.

"And there is with you?" I asked.

His eyes had a faraway look—a look that saw beyond the slopes outside our window. As if he remembered higher mountains, longer trails. He didn't need to answer my question. It was there in his face, only now there was a sense of loss—loss of the perfection he had once achieved, loss of all that fantastic skill in the face of danger which had once been his. He was like the sculptor who could no longer sculpt, the singer who could not sing. Still, I must probe and try to understand. Because I wanted to understand Stuart as well, I told myself.

"Was it the testing you wanted? Pitting yourself as a man against all those natural obstacles?"

His gaze came back from the distance to study me thoughtfully. "You've come close to it. A man needs to know he can dominate his own fears. It's not the athletic ability that matters most. It's the ability to cope with pressure—and win. That instinct's still embedded in us, but there's little opportunity to use it today. And when a man stops testing himself he's lost, wasted, spent."

I couldn't bear the look in his eyes—that look of loss. "But you aren't any of those things!" I cried.

He smiled at me over his wine glass, and the glimpse of inner privation was gone. "No, I'm not. I have other things to do, and I can still ski. There are many ways for a man to test himself. It's unfortunate if he puts his heart into only one."

Yet he had done that, I thought. As had Stuart. Once more I felt an unwanted stirring in me, a response I had no wish to feel. Julian McCabe was possibly my enemy. Yet how could I see him in that light? For some reason I remembered the stand of dead beech trees outside the drawing-room window at Graystones. I remembered my own unexpected response to that wild scene. As though something in me that had always slept stirred dangerously. Once those dead trees had flamed and burned themselves out. Julian was like that—ice, where there had once been fire, except when I'd seen him on the slopes and some spark had come alive again. It had not entirely died away, and that strange feeling in me that answered wildness reacted to the hint of fire. What would it be like if he ever came fully to burning life again? And how little I knew myself that the very thought brought in me this rising response. This was a frightening thing to realize—that I knew myself so little.

I changed the subject abruptly, bringing it back to the one thing I must never forget.

"What about this young man in jail? Why aren't you taking an interest in his case? I've read that he claims to be innocent of the charge that's been made."

The slight smile vanished, and the deep blue of his eyes darkened as ice closed in again.

"You're still curious, aren't you? I might ask why you're so interested in this case."

"I've read about it." I repeated the old, lame excuse. "Stuart Parrish seems an attractive young man—quite open and honest. It appears that he's going to need help. Yet though you've been his sponsor, you don't mean to help him. Not even if you believe that your daughter pushed that chair."

Julian drank the last of his wine and put the glass down with a jar that set it reverberating. "If you've finished your wine we can go and look for Adria."

He considered me a meddling outsider and I deserved his evident displeasure. There was a swallow left in my glass and I swirled the red liquid thoughtfully, unable to stay silent, no matter how he felt.

"I suppose I hate injustice more than anything else. How can you know what the truth is until you talk with this young man?"

He pushed back his chair, and I set the wine down unfinished and rose to join him. Once more I'd gone too far. But I had no other choice. If he found me out, I'd at least have tried.

There was another bad moment when he helped me into my parka, and the silver medallion swung against my breast. For an instant Julian's hand moved toward it, and I stepped away, fumbling with the parka zipper, covering the shine of silver. His hand dropped, and he said nothing.

We clumped down the stairs in our ski boots and went through halls where muddy footprints had dried, showing the constant passing of ski boots. Outside we walked toward the ice palace and found Adria waiting near one of the tunnel entrances. She came running to meet us.

"Can we go up the slopes again, Daddy? Just one more time?"

Her father shook his head, his face dark and remote, so that he quenched her eagerness. She flung me a half-frightened look and her young face took on that closed and guarded expression that was so like her father's. I wanted to fling words at him. I wanted to cry out the accusation that *he* was bad for his daughter, that *he* took out his own dark haunting upon her. But this was not the time. I walked beside Adria back to the car, coaxing her to tell me about the ice tunnels, though her response lacked her earlier enthusiasm.

Once more we changed our boots and got into the car's front seat. I felt both helpless and discouraged. I'd had my moment alone with Julian, and I had not used it to tell him about those thrown stones. Instead, I'd angered him and turned him against me, with a result that was proving harmful to Adria as well.

When they dropped me off at the lodge, I gathered up my equipment and headed blindly out to store the ski things in my own car. My thanks to Julian had been met coolly, and nothing had been said about our ever skiing together again. With my equipment put away, I went into the lodge. The afternoon was nearly gone, and I would have to hurry in order to be on duty by four-thirty.

Clay was behind the desk when I walked in, and he regarded me almost as coolly as Julian had.

"I've been checking around, Linda," he said. "Is it possible that you made up this stone-throwing bit? Is it possible that you're trying to create a troubled atmosphere in which you think someone will give something away?"

"Nobody'd be likely to admit it, would they?" I cried.

He merely stared at me, and I felt that I'd had enough of both Graystones and the lodge. I'd had enough of Julian and Clay. I told him stiffly that if this was what he chose to think, there wasn't much I could do about it. Then I went upstairs to my room, feeling torn and angry and hurt. But more than anything else, frightened for Stuart—and more than a little frightened for myself. The atmosphere was certainly troubled, and hostility was being created against me.

On the bed Cinnabar lazily washed his face. I unzipped my parka and flung it across a chair. Then I confronted the great orange cat, my exasperation rising.

"If no one else will talk to me, maybe you will!" I cried. "Hello, Margot! Perhaps it was you who threw stones at me?"

Cinnabar yawned widely, rose and stretched. Then, liking me as little as ever, he leaped from the bed and went to the door. I opened it for him and he sped down the hall without another glance in my direction.

More disturbed than ever, I changed into my after-ski clothes, brushed my hair, put on lipstick. I left the silver medallion in a pocket of my tote bag when I went downstairs to start the fondue.

VII

It was morning, and once more I had not slept well, though there had been no further incidents since I'd come home yesterday and found the cat on my bed. The after-ski hours had gone well enough, and I'd given myself conscientiously to my duties. A few new people had arrived, others had gone, but the routine was the same. I'd made the fondue with no help from Clay, and for the most part he'd left me to my own devices. When I went into the dining room for dinner I found he had eaten earlier, so I sat alone.

Julian did not appear during the evening, and neither did Shan, but a young nun who had come along with her skiing family borrowed a guitar from Clay and played her own songs for group singing. She was a cheerful, lively young woman, with red cheeks and a happy air that was contagious. Her songs were modern—a few things of the Beatles, some Simon and Garfunkel tunes, some Rod McKuen. She was very *with it,* and I liked her. It was this sort of unexpected "happening" that gave the evenings a varied and interesting flavor. Next weekend a Connecticut editor who had made up his own small combo was bringing two members of it for skiing and to entertain in the evening. But I hardly expected to be here by then. Too much was closing in on me, hostile, inimical. There would be an explosion of one sort or another before long. It couldn't be avoided. I'd begun to feel almost fatalistic about whatever was to come. Perhaps I must even take some action to bring the hostility that surrounded me into the open. To expose it might be to point an accusing finger.

Now it was morning, and I had breakfasted alone, with the feeling that Clay was avoiding me. I had not even been able to tell him about Cinnabar appearing in my room again. During the waking hours of the night I'd made plans, however, and shortly after breakfast I'd put them into operation.

I could not feel easy about walking through the woods to reach Graystones, but it had to be done. The morning had turned gray, as though there might be snow, and it was decidedly colder. Clouds lay on top of the mountain, but there was still no wind, and the trees stood utterly motionless, with not a whisper running through their branches. Somehow I'd have felt better if they'd thrashed their limbs and shown a little life. At least no stones came hurtling at me from some enemy hidden behind an evergreen. There was no slightest sound anywhere. That was why it was all the more alarming when I rounded a turn in the path and found the man waiting for me. I'd heard no step on the path, no brushing of shrubbery, yet he was there, as though he'd been aware of my coming and had waited silently.

Again he wore the sheepskin jacket and corduroy trousers, the neat green alpine hat with its red feather. Again I sensed that he was a man of confidence and dignity. He might have been master of an estate, instead of its caretaker. His weathered face bore me no liking, and I thrust my hands into the pockets of my coat to hide their trembling as I came to a halt on the path. I knew I must plunge in before I lost my courage entirely.

"Was it you who threw those stones at me yesterday?" I demanded.

Shaggy gray brows drew down in a scowl and I heard again the hard, rough sound of his voice. "You'd better go away as quickly as you can, Miss Earle. No one wants you at Graystones. If you mean any harm it will be the worse for you. I know who you are—I saw you one time over at the jail. But I don't know why you've come here."

"I only want to help my brother," I said. "I think you know that."

"He's beyond help and he'll get what's coming to him. I'll see to that."

"How can you—when he's innocent? Perhaps you're using him as a scapegoat—to protect the person who really pushed that chair?" I wanted to say, "To protect yourself?"—but I did not dare.

He took a step toward me and I saw violence in his eyes. He was a dangerous man, as Clay had pointed out.

"I don't know who pushed Margot's wheelchair," I told him. "But I think you do. And I think you know it was never my brother."

He took his hands out of his pockets, and they were bare, gloveless—the gnarled hands of a man who had worked hard physically all his life. This time I stepped back from him, sensing danger, yet needing to prod him to some betrayal,

118

some explosion. I could see Graystones' tower and roof beyond him, and if he tried anything rough, and I called out, surely someone would hear and come to my rescue.

"Throwing stones won't frighten me away," I warned him. "And if you come any closer I'll scream for help. Mr. McCabe won't be pleased if he knows you've threatened me."

He stopped a few feet away, and let his hands fall to his sides.

"Why are you so set against my brother?" I persisted. "Why are you trying to send him to prison?"

He answered me then. "You know as well as I do. He's got it coming. I heard what he said when he ran out the front door after Mrs. McCabe went down that ramp. I was the one who caught him. He said, 'I didn't mean to do it—I didn't mean to do it!'"

I believed not a word of this, but I couldn't tell why he was lying. "You didn't tell the police that in the beginning."

"I told Mr. McCabe. He said to keep still. So I held my tongue at first, even though I turned Parrish over to the police. But I've been thinking about it all this time, and I couldn't keep still forever. While Julian was away, I went to the sheriff again and told him some things I'd held back. Showed him something I had."

I felt a little sick, and my face must have shown it. Emory Ault stood in silence, watching me, the threat of violence slowly fading from his eyes.

"Look here, Miss Earle," he said, "I haven't anything against you, and if you'll just go away from Graystones and the lodge, nothing will happen to you."

"Is that a threat?" I asked. "What do you suppose Mr. McCabe will think when I tell him what you've done?"

"He'll thank me for turning you away."

"Then why haven't you gone to him? Why haven't you told him who I am?"

"I'll tell him when the right time comes. Don't worry about that."

"And when is the right time?"

He shook his gray head. "I'll decide that. When I make up my mind. It's better if you go away of your own accord. Safer." Again there seemed a not so subtle threat in his words.

"What else have you told the police?" I persisted. "What other lies?"

Again he shook his massive head, rather like a bull who feels the prick of the dart. He had the dignity and the massive quality of a bull, I recognized, and when he decided to attack it would be better not to be in his way.

"How did you feel about Mrs. McCabe?" I asked, pricking him again. "Did you like her or despise her?"

This time I thought he would charge. He snorted angrily, his breath rising in a mist on the chill air. "Go back to the lodge! Stay away from the house, if you know what's good for you!"

His very size was some reassurance, and the fact that he was lame. I was young and quick and I could surely move faster than he could. Leaving him to paw the ground, I took off into snowy woods and lost myself among spruce and hemlock. As I wound my way toward the house at a run, I doubt that he tried to follow me. When I came into the open on the Graystones' drive, I couldn't see him behind or ahead. I ran up the steps and touched the bell.

Adria let me in, and she looked not at all like the lively child I'd seen on the slopes yesterday. Her face was pale, her eyes had a lost look, with dark shadows under them, and her shoulders drooped. She greeted me without pleasure, without interest.

"Hello, Adria," I said. "Is your father home?"

She stepped back from the doorway. "He's in the library," she said indifferently, and walked away, leaving me to announce myself. I couldn't let her go like that, and I stopped her before she reached the door to the stairs.

"There's something wrong, isn't there?"

She turned deliberately and gave me a long, somber look that reminded me of her father. "You didn't come last night. I wanted you and you didn't come." With an air of haughty dismissal that might have been amusing if it hadn't been tragic, she went through the door and up the stairs, leaving me astonished.

Feeling more disturbed than I liked, I went to the library and looked into the room. Julian sat at a desk with his back to me, working on some papers.

"Good morning," I said hesitantly.

He swung about and stared at me. Then his face lighted and he rose to come toward me across the room and take both my hands in his in a warm greeting that astonished me further and left me wordless.

"Come in, Linda. Let me take your coat. I've just been writing you a note. Partly of apology, partly of entreaty. But I'd much rather talk to you, if you're still speaking to me."

I let him help me out of my coat, more at a loss than if he had greeted me coldly. "Why wouldn't I be speaking to you?"

He carried my coat into the hall and hung it up, then returned and pulled a chair close to the front windows and waved me into it. I had the feeling that for some reason he was marking time before he answered me. As though I'd taken him by surprise and he must marshal his forces. I didn't in the least understand this sudden change in him, and I wasn't sure what it augured for me.

"The apology first," he said. "I was rude to you yesterday because you touched on sensitive matters you couldn't possibly understand. You couldn't even know how sensitive they are. But I've been thinking about all this since then, and I know I must allow you your interest in what the papers call the Graystones affair. Obviously, you're generous and sympathetic, and you're imagining a young man who is perhaps being persecuted. Whether you're right or not, I want to avoid talking about this case." He broke off, moving about the room restlessly, as though something drove him today—some emotion he found it hard to suppress. If there was anger here, I sensed that it was not directed at me.

But while I understood nothing of this change to a gentler attitude on the part of Julian McCabe, I wasn't sure I liked it. Something lay behind the words. Whether angry or kind, he'd never seemed a devious man, yet now I had the feeling that he was being devious. I even wondered if he had discovered who I was. But that wasn't likely, because if he knew I was Stuart's sister, that *I* was the devious one, he would explode in furious indignation against me. This must be something else. Something out of character for him, and I didn't like it.

"There's no reason for apology," I said stiffly. "It's true that there's a lot I don't understand."

He came toward me across the room. "Then we can agree that certain matters are taboo?"

"Why do we need to agree to anything? I belong to the lodge. I'm not likely to have much to do with the McCabes."

He smiled faintly. "We spent the afternoon together yesterday. You're here now. I think you're likely to have quite a lot to do with the McCabes. Because of Adria. You've shown an interest in my daughter, Linda. You've seemed fond of her, anxious to help her. Isn't that true?"

"Of course. This morning she looks almost ill." I didn't know where this was going, but I could at least express my sympathy for a tragedy-haunted child.

"Adria had one of her nightmares last night," Julian said. "She woke up screaming and trembling and it was a long time before Shan and I could quiet her. She dreams herself back to the day Margot died and she sees herself pushing that chair. The whole thing is there deep in her consciousness, and I don't know what to do."

I felt wrenched with pity for Adria—and even for Adria's father. I too had dreams of self-blame—though mine had to do with fire.

"There must be doctors—" I began.

"As a last resort," he said roughly. "I don't want to send her away to some hospital or sanatorium for treatment. She needs love around her. Yet there's not one near here who can help her. Shan's love is unhealthy, and mine—" He broke off, unable to finish.

I remained silent, as helpless as he.

"She called for you last night. She called your name repeatedly. I almost came down to the lodge to wake you up and bring you here."

So that was what Adria had meant.

"I'd have come, of course. But I don't know whether it would have done any good."

"You've made a deep impression on her, Linda. I don't think she understands it, or that I understand it, since your meetings with her have been so few. But you seem to have reached her as no one else has."

Perhaps Adria was only trying to flee to neutral ground

from two people she loved who tore her apart. But I couldn't say this to Julian. I simply waited.

He stood before me like a supplicant, and there was a strangeness about him. Perhaps because he was a man who did not know how to plead. He was an autocrat in his way, accustomed to ruling, to doing as he wished, to commanding those who followed him. Now he was beseeching me, and this was a role he did not wear gracefully. I tried to help him.

"What can I do?"

His smile was almost wistful. "I'm not really sure. Perhaps I'm trying to feel my way. What if you came up here for a few nights? We have plenty of room. If you were here, and she wanted you—oh, I'm putting it badly, too abruptly."

This was alarming. I had no knowledge in depth of a child in Adria's condition, any more than Shan or Julian had. I could only offer sympathy growing out of my own experience. Sympathy and perhaps an instinctive way with children. I seemed to have won Adria's respect and at times her liking.

"What can we lose by trying this?" he pressed me. "I can always turn to doctors or psychiatrists later. A little loving common sense might be the best recipe. Something Shan and I seem to lack. We love her well enough, but eventually we do the wrong things, and she responds to us in the wrong way. A lot of the time she pushes away our love and—" again he broke off, though by his expression he might have added, "—and my anguish."

"What about your sister?" I said. "Won't she resent my coming here?"

"I've told her I was going to talk to you about this. She'll do as I wish."

Though not willingly, I was ready to wager. But I wouldn't think about Shan. The memory of Adria on the slopes yesterday returned to me—of Adria as she could be, contrasting with the drooping, nightmare-haunted child I had seen just now at the door. If only I could help her—

"Give me a moment to think," I said.

He moved away from me, and I could almost feel the intensity of the pressure he had put upon me lift. The vision of Adria faded a little, and suddenly I remembered all too vividly who I was and why I was here. I remembered Stuart held in a jail, and the road I must take to release him—not on bail, but entirely free, cleared. There was no question as to whether or not I would accept this request of Julian's. I might not like living in this house under a pretense that could be exposed at any time. I hated the pretenses increasingly for themselves. It was more natural for me to be honest and direct, yet from day to day I was being drawn into a deepening well of subterfuge. I didn't like what I was becoming.

It was fortunate that my interest in Adria, my growing fondness for her at least gave me an honest reason for being here. As far as the child was concerned, I would do whatever it was within my power to do. There was no deceit there, and probably no harm would come of it, unless Julian put me furiously out of the house in spite of Adria's need.

He stood beside the bookcases, watching me, and he seemed to think I needed more urging.

"If you need an excuse for coming, you can probably tutor her. We've had to keep her out of school this term because of her disturbed state. Though if you can help her, perhaps she'll be able to join her class after the first of the year. You needn't keep on at the lodge unless you want to. Clay can find someone else."

There was a long silence between us. I knew I must say yes, yet I hesitated.

"You came to me this morning for something else, didn't you?" he said at last. "Would you like to tell me what it is?"

I stared out the window, and against the far background of the woods something stirred. Emory Ault stood watching the house, as though he waited for me. His gaze was directed straight at me, and I knew he could see me sitting there near the window. Yes, I had come here for a purpose. I had come to talk to Julian about that stone-throwing incident yesterday. And now I could say nothing. Because if he went angrily to Emory, the old man would tell him everything. I didn't understand why he had kept silent so far, any more than I understood why Clay kept silent. But if Emory was pushed, he would tell Julian, and I would be stopped, regardless of Adria. I snatched at the first thing that came into my mind as a substitution.

"It's only a small thing," I said. "But it's begun to worry me. Twice when I've gone back to my room at the lodge, your cat, Cinnabar, has been shut into my room. Clay doesn't know how he gets there—and it makes me uneasy."

Julian seemed to relax. "That's the sort of trick Shan likes to play. I don't know why she should—unless she's simply jealous of you because Adria appears to like you. That's quite possible, you know. I'll speak to her about it. When can you come, Linda? I'm sure a room can be made ready for you at once."

I hadn't said I was coming, but he seemed to need no answer. He knew I'd made my decision.

"There's one thing," I said.

"Yes? Anything you like."

"You mentioned a bargain. You've said I must never mention Stuart Parrish. I don't like that."

He stared at me. "Why, Linda? Why should you care about Stuart Parrish?"

"He's part of the very atmosphere of this house," I said. "What is he like? What do you make of him?"

He came to stand close to me again. "Have you known him at some time? Is he a friend of yours?"

The danger was very close. "He's not a friend," I said. "You've found me sympathetic toward Adria. I suppose I have feelings about other people too. Sometimes people I don't even know. If I'm to understand what troubles Adria, I must understand what really happened here. Isn't it your wife's death that's behind everything? What if Stuart Parrish never pushed that chair, and neither did Adria? What if the person who did push it is still around? Couldn't that be part of what's affecting Adria? Something in the very atmosphere!"

He paced the room again—a man confined by the walls of a house, liberated only on the mountain. At his desk he paused and picked up the note he had been writing me, tore it across several times and dropped the pieces in a wastebasket. Then he sat down in the desk chair and stared at me across the room.

"You want to know about Stuart Parrish. All right—I'll tell you. I've often thought that if Lucifer could ski, that would be Stuart. I don't mean Satan, and all that fallen angel bit. I mean Lucifer the morning star. He used to be called the bringer of light, I believe. I've always seen Stuart that way."

Yes, I thought. Yes, that was Stuart. Lighting up his world with his own magnificence—radiantly alive.

"He was made for the slopes," Julian went on. "I knew it the first time I saw him. He was better at the very start than I ever was. He had a lot to learn, but he learned quickly and easily. I told him I could teach him, and he was eager for the chance to learn. I turned him over to Emory Ault part of the time, because Emory's a great teacher. Emory could have been a champion if he hadn't smashed himself up. He turned me into a skier and it broke his heart when I had to stop. I think he felt it more than he did his own accident. He seemed to feel there was no sense in what happened to me, as there would have been if I'd been hurt skiing. An unexpected icy patch on a road, a sign that children had defaced—there was no excuse he could accept for my being hurt in a car accident. So when Stuart Parrish came along, he gave Emory a third chance to hit the top. The only trouble was that he never liked Stuart."

Julian stopped for so long that I thought he might not go on. I sat very still and waited. His tone softened when he finally continued, as though he remembered someone he had loved and lost.

"Stuart was like the young brother I never had. There was a real affection between us. But I wanted to turn him into the best for his own sake—not just because I wanted to recapture vicariously my own successes, as Shan thinks. I'd outgrown that. I wanted it because Stuart was so good, so beautiful on skis—so made to be a champion. And he had something few athletes have. He was absolutely without fear. Nothing ever psyched him out before a race. He was up there at the starting gate with no knots in his stomach and ready to go. In the beginning I worried about that. Because if you're not a bit scared the adrenalin may not flow when you need it. But his worked all right. He wanted to win and everything keyed him up to that point. I don't think there's much doubt but what he would have won the Nationals in a year, and be in the Olympics in two."

I thought of Stuart sitting in that miserable jail, all his

hopes broken, tossed aside. I might not like championship skiing, but I'd wanted Stuart to have what he'd longed for, worked toward.

"Then why aren't you helping him now?" I said. "Why aren't you getting him out of that jail for good?"

He seemed not to hear me. When he spoke again there was a depth of anger in his voice that startled and frightened me.

"You wanted to know what Stuart Parrish was like. I'm telling you. He was all the things it takes to make a champion. And that means he was single-minded and ruthless and selfish."

I made no sound, but I turned in my chair, struggling to stifle the wild indignation that rose in me.

Julian went on. "I never met any of his family. He kept me away from them and he never talked about them much. I gather that his father and stepmother spoiled him when they were alive. I believe there was a sister too, and I suspect that his ruining lies partly at her door. He was beautiful and young and supremely confident. He thought he could have anything he wanted because his family had always given him everything from the time he was a baby."

It was all I could do to check my own anger, hold back my denials.

"Oh, I didn't mind about his girls," Julian said. "He had his pick of snow bunnies and I suspect he gave them a bad time. But they were young—they had to learn. It was when it came to Margot that I couldn't take any more. She told me he was making a play for her."

"In a wheelchair!"

He winced painfully. "You didn't know her." There was hurt in the simple words. "She was as fascinating and attractive as ever, even though I'd destroyed her. And she wasn't completely paralyzed, in spite of her injured back. She chose the wheelchair rather than to live in braces. She was still alive, she could feel. She was my wife."

"She—she told you this? About Stuart, I mean?"

"Emory told me first. He knew what was going on, when I didn't. When I questioned Margot she admitted it, though she didn't want to. She knew how I felt about Stuart and what I could do for him. But she had to tell me what he was up to, once Emory had spoken out. So it's possible he killed her by way of punishment. He knew I was ready to throw him out, and he had to get even with her. Did you know that the guardrail the chair went through had been tampered with ahead of time?"

I stared at him.

"No, of course you wouldn't know. It had been sawed through and then nailed loosely together. Someone planned to send that chair down the ramp, Linda!"

Hope and reassurance swept back. Stuart might be capable of acting on angry impulse, but a plan for murder was not in his character.

"Why didn't you tell all this to the police when Emory accused Stuart in the beginning?" I asked.

"How could I? How could I be sure, no matter what Emory said that it had really been Stuart? Margot may not have been entirely blameless. She never forgave me for the accident that crippled her, and—" He hesitated. "On the other hand, there is Adria, who may have pushed that chair herself."

It was hard to control my impatience. "Couldn't you have found out the truth from Stuart?"

"He'd have lied, if it suited him. With such pressure on, I couldn't believe anything he might have told me. All I could do was try to stay neutral and give him a chance to defend himself. When they let him go for lack of evidence, there was no need to speak out. I gave him the benefit of the doubt. If it weren't for Adria, I'd be glad to believe him innocent. When I learned that Emory had chosen to tell the police something more, I came home. What it is, I don't know as yet. So far Emory won't talk to me about it. Now the thing must take its course. If Stuart's innocent, it will come out. I don't want Margot's name brought in, as it would be if I had to go on the stand as a witness. And I don't want Adria harassed."

"Isn't a man's life more important than—than anyone's name?"

"Perhaps not this man's," Julian said. "If he's guilty, perhaps others need to be protected."

"I think you're unfeeling, dreadful!" I gasped out the words.

He left the desk and went to stand before Margot's picture on the wall. It was one of those taken on some ski slope—a gay, triumphant figure against snowy mountains.

"Well—I've told you," he said, and his voice had turned hard. "With the result that you think I'm unfeeling. Not that what you think of me is important. But I'm not sure what good all this will do you with Adria. For whatever it's worth, however, there's my picture of Stuart Parrish."

I knew how worthless such a picture was, and I was no longer sure that I could come to this house to try to help Adria. How could I bear to be under the same roof with Julian McCabe when he felt as he did about my brother? For a few moments I sat unmoving, and he let me be.

The shrillness of a woman's scream reached us from the direction of the stairs. For an instant we froze where we were. Then Julian ran through the door and across the hall, and I followed him. At the foot of the steeply turning tower stairs Shan lay in a crumpled heap. Clinging to the railing a few steps above her was Adria, her blue eyes wide with horror.

Julian knelt beside his sister. "What happened? How did you fall?"

"I—I don't know. She pushed me—and I fell."

Adria cried out above her. "I didn't push her. I didn't— I didn't!"

Shan made an effort to sit up and her gaze turned toward the circling stairs. "Not you, darling. Margot. It was Margot who pushed me."

My eyes were drawn eerily upward to where the stairs spiraled out of sight. The hairs on the back of my neck lifted and my skin went prickling cold. Padding with dignity from one step to the next as he came down, Cinnabar moved toward us around the bend, his tail aloft and twitching, his fur ruffled as though something in the atmosphere had touched him, readying him to fight.

Adria cried out and pressed herself against the rail, hiding her face in the crook of her arm. I left Julian to minister to his sister and went up to her. This time I didn't hesitate to put my arms around her and she turned to hide her face against my shoulder, sobbing wildly.

Her slight body was light as feathers in my arms—yet not like feathers because there was life to it. I could feel the throbbing of her heart against my own heart, the fever of her skin against my own skin. Black strands of her hair touched my forehead, and they were wet with the sweat of fear. The suffering and fright of a child was like no other suffering. It had an intensity that thrust cruelly deep, and could leave a mark that would damage for all the years to come.

I knew now that I had no choice. I would come to Graystones, and not only because of my brother. I held the child close in my arms and tried to comfort her.

VIII

Shan had fallen only a few steps. She was not badly hurt, but she was shaken by her own imaginings, and she would listen to no reassurance from Julian. He finally picked her up in his arms and carried her upstairs. The big orange cat stood in his path and Julian went precariously around the animal, leaving it to bar my path and Adria's.

I turned from the child and touched the cat with my toe to prod it out of the way. It lashed at my ankle with claws that stung and then sprang down the remaining steps and disappeared into the hall. Adria's face was hidden against my shoulder, so she didn't see.

"Come," I said to her gently. "Your aunt's all right, I think, but let's go and find out. Sometimes she imagines things, you know. There's no need to be frightened."

Her small pale face looked haunted when she raised it from my shoulder and looked around. "She—she's gone?" she quavered, and I knew she didn't mean Shan.

"*He* is gone," I said firmly. "That cat is beginning to be a nuisance. Come along, Adria. Let's go see about Shan."

She clung to my hand with a trust that left me shaken— for how could I fullfill it?—and came with me to the second floor. We went at once to Shan's room, where Julian had laid her on the bed.

It was the room of a wood sprite, I thought, remembering that Clay had called her a dryad. Forest trees climbed their own hill on the wallpaper, and thin green curtains let a verdant light into the room. Through the gauze veil at the windows I looked out upon dead beeches, the curtains tinging them with green. Even the spread Shan lay upon was the color of moss, and the carpet the dun brown of dead leaves. Here there were no snow pictures on the walls, but only one lovely water color of a deer standing among autumn trees, his white tail a flag as he turned to flee.

Shan lay on the bed moaning softly, while Julian stood helplessly beside her.

"Winter's here now," she murmured. "Ice and snow and death. And the wind! How I hate the wind when it blows around the mountain! There'll never be another spring. I'll be the next one to go. I know that now. She'll see to it."

Julian sat on the bed beside her and took her hands in his to still their fluttering. "Listen to me, Shan. You've got to get over these wild ideas about a cat. I won't have him in the house if he's going to disturb you like this. No one pushed you. You caught one of your slippery sandals on a stair rung and fell. Cinnabar was up on the second-floor level when you slipped."

Shan raised long pale lashes and looked at him piteously.

"You mustn't send Cinnabar away. It would all be worse then."

Julian looked at Adria and me in the doorway and beckoned to his daughter. "Come and tell Shan what happened. You must have seen her fall."

The child drew me with her into the room, never for a moment letting go of my hand. "She—she just slipped and fell."

"And Cinnabar was upstairs, wasn't he?" her father persisted.

Adria nodded vaguely, but there was a veiled look in her eyes.

Shan paid no attention. As Adria clung to me, Shan clung to her brother for comfort and reassurance, even while she thrust away all comforting words.

"Julian—you know I have these queer moments of seeing ahead sometimes. One of them came there on the stairs just before I fell. There's going to be another death. I know it— I know it!"

"But not yours," Julian told her, his voice roughening. "Come out of it, Shan! People die every day. This precognition of yours doesn't always turn out as promised. You only remember the times when it does. If you'll lie here quietly now, I'll send Adria to get someone to make you a cup of tea. And I'll go telephone Dr. Reed. I want him to have a look at you. Linda, will you stay with her while I phone? I'll only be a moment."

"I'll stay," I said, and sat reluctantly down in a small armchair covered with sunflower print.

When the other two had gone, Shan lay on the bed with her eyes closed, paying no attention to me. I began to speak to her quietly. There was something she had better know before Julian told her too bluntly.

"Your brother has asked me to come and stay at the house for a little while, Miss McCabe. And I've agreed. He thinks I may be able to help with Adria. He says you've both been having a difficult time with her, and perhaps a new face, a new voice may be useful."

At least I had succeeded in distracting her from her thoughts of death. She looked at me across the room with unexpected composure. Quite suddenly I wondered how much of her fall had been real.

"You're attracted to my brother, aren't you?"

"I'm not thinking of your brother at all. I'm thinking of Adria," I said with asperity.

A smile flitted across her face and was gone. "You can't help it, I suppose. Most women are attracted by him. He's used to it, you know. He won't pay you the slightest attention. He's never stopped thinking of Margot. And he never will. Perhaps there were times when he hated her, but he loved her too. Isn't that always what love is like—made up of love and hate?"

Something twisted in me that I didn't want to feel. "Was it like that with you and Clay Davidson?"

She turned her head away from me. "I never hated Clay. But Julian loved Margot foolishly, blindly."

"She must have been very lovely," I said carefully. "I've seen her pictures as she was before the accident."

Shan made a small, derisive sound. "She was an absolute devil, Miss Earle. Destructive was the word for her. Spoiled and destructive. Julian gave her anything she wanted. He adored her, and he was useful to her as long as she could live the sort of life she wanted. So she was discreet. After the car accident—which could have happened to anyone—she hated him, hated everyone. Everyone but Clay."

I'd been listening uncomfortably, wanting to know because

136

I must know all I could, yet hating to listen to this distraught woman. But when she mentioned Clay, I stiffened in my chair, fully alert.

"I suppose you've learned that Clay was my husband, Miss Earle?"

I nodded, noting the past tense. Clay had used the present.

"We were living here happily before Julian married. We were here when Julian brought Margot home as a bride. Clay was writing—working on a book he never finished. It was good. I read the early chapters. He would have had a success with it, I think—if it hadn't been for Margot."

Shan propped herself on one elbow and stared at me, her gray-green eyes suddenly a little wild, unfocused.

"Please," I said, "you mustn't upset yourself."

"Margot took him away from me. She wasn't beautiful— hardly pretty, really. But she had something earthy about her that appealed to men. All her satisfactions came from exerting her own particular fascination over them. And she always needed someone new. In a way, I don't blame Clay. It was her fault. But of course I had to dissolve our marriage. It couldn't go on. So Clay went away for a while. He never finished his book, but he started to write for magazines to keep himself alive. I'd have given him an allowance gladly, but he wouldn't take it. I don't need all the money I have. Of course he'll get some of it through my will, if I die first. As I'm very likely to do. That cat on the stairs today! She would like to see me dead."

"You're making all this up," I said. "You rather like playing the unearthly dryad, don't you? Perhaps it attracts Clay, but it upsets Julian."

"And of course you don't want to upset Julian."

I hated this sort of female dueling, even though Shan asked for it, and I glanced uneasily toward the door, wondering where Julian was. It shouldn't have taken this long to call the doctor. Shan worried me more than a little. She seemed on the verge of some emotional outburst that I wouldn't be able to handle.

She paid no attention to my uneasiness, however. It was as though she felt driven to get all these words out before anyone stopped her.

"Clay didn't come back until after the accident. When Julian gave up skiing and opened the lodge. He needed someone to run it, and I persuaded him to give the job to Clay. I knew his writing wasn't going well, and he needed some way to bring in an income that would still give him time to write. There was no longer any danger when it came to Margot. Or that's what I thought. So he took the job and he's done well with it. He's even writing again, and I'm glad of that. But Margot wouldn't leave him alone. She thought she was still madly attractive and that he would come back to her if she flicked her fingers. She didn't have the sense to know that Clay had turned thoroughly against her. When she began to realize that, she hated him and started threatening him. She said she would tell Julian the truth—the truth that he'd never known, because even I had never told him about Margot and Clay. Oh, it's a lucky thing that she died when she did. I've never felt any regret over that. But I'm afraid of her now as I wasn't before. She's come back to Graystones, Miss Earle. Oh, you can laugh at that, if you like, but she still means trouble."

Shan lay back on the bed, spent by her own outburst.

I spoke to her softly. "Who do you think pushed Margot's chair?"

She lay with her eyes closed. "Not that poor young man who's been put into jail. I always rather liked him, you know, though we never had much in common. He felt about

138

mountains and snow what I feel about woods and rain. How I hate snow, snow, snow!"

"Then who—?" I persisted.

"Why, Adria, of course. She was angry. She flung out at her mother as a child will. She mustn't be blamed. She never will be blamed. Julian will see to that."

I speculated aloud. "If Julian becomes convinced that Adria did this, then perhaps someone else goes free," I said. "Is that what you'd like? I don't mean Stuart Parrish. I mean the person who really pushed that chair."

Her eyes flew open—more green than gray in the swimming green of her room.

"Graystones isn't a safe place for you, Miss Earle. You've come here to make trouble. I've sensed that from the first. I sense a great deal, you know. Often I know things that are hidden from other people. I should hate to see anything unfortunate happen to you here."

"Are you threatening me?" I asked.

A flush came over her pale skin. "Go away, Linda Earle. Just go away and leave us all alone. If you won't go now, I'll try to see that you don't stay for long. And I'm not going to let you take Adria away from me."

While I hesitated, wondering how to meet her antagonism, Julian came back to the room.

"I've been talking to Adria about your coming here, Linda, and she seems to like the idea. Have you told my sister?"

It was Shan who answered. "She's told me and I think you're being foolish, Julian. There's an aura about this girl that means trouble. She means difficulty—and danger."

Julian was unimpressed. "I'm afraid you color these auras you see to suit yourself," he told his sister.

A maid came into the room bearing a tray, with a teapot and cup. Julian left her to minister to Shan and beckoned me into the hall. There he drew me toward the stairs, out of Shan's hearing.

"Don't mind the things my sister says. I'll persuade her that your coming here is for Adria's good. Shan's been a mother to my daughter since Margot died, and perhaps before. She's jealous of her prerogatives."

A picture of what Margot had been like was beginning to form in my mind, making me feel a little sorry for Julian, who had apparently been a loving husband. Though I didn't want to feel sympathetic toward him when he had behaved so badly toward Stuart. Always there was this twisting in me toward him, away from him. I'd have little rest in this house.

"You will come, won't you, Linda?" He pressed me.

I had no choice. This was what I must do.

"I'll go back to the lodge and pack my things," I told him. "But I won't let Clay down when it comes to my chores this evening. In fact, it will probably be better if I'm away from Adria some of the time. She mustn't take me for granted."

Julian came with me to the front door and when he opened it, Emory Ault was waiting near the steps.

I turned to Julian quickly. "Will you tell Mr. Ault that I'm coming to stay in the house?" I said. "He doesn't approve of my trespassing in your woods."

"It's all right, Emory," Julian told the old man. "Miss Earle is to look after Adria for a while. She'll be staying here."

I braced myself for the inevitable. Sooner or later Emory was going to speak out about my identity. But still he did not. He only nodded to Julian, gave me a dark look and disappeared, limping around the end of the house. At least I could set off through the woods knowing that for once I wouldn't be followed.

Back at the lodge I sought out Clay. Shan had told me a great deal. I could understand a little better now Clay's distaste for Margot McCabe. I wondered how strong that distaste had been, how much he had come to dislike and perhaps even fear her. Enough to have taken some action after Stuart left him in the library next to Margot's room? How true was his story of a locked door? I liked Clay and I didn't want to distrust him, but for Stuart's sake I must trust no one.

Clay was in the kitchen conferring with the cook over tonight's menu. When I asked if I could speak to him, he finished up and came into the lounge with me. We sat on a couch before last night's burned-out embers. The room was dark with shadows in the daytime, and a little cold—not warmed by fire and candlelight as it had been the night before. To dispel the gloom, Clay lit two stubby candles on the coffee table and shadows danced.

I told him about Julian's plans for me, and Clay listened soberly, now and then stroking his neat, square beard as he did when thinking seriously about something.

"So you're really getting close to home in your efforts, Linda."

"Adria likes me. Perhaps she needs me. And I've become fond of her. If I can help her in any way I want to try."

Clay picked up the poker and thrust it into burned-out logs. They fell with a crash and gray ashes spilled through the grate onto the hearth.

"I believe you're sincere when it comes to Adria," he said. "But what will happen when Julian learns the truth about who you are, as he must eventually? He won't put up with you then. And won't that be harder than ever for Adria?"

"I have to try," I said doggedly.

"Then perhaps I'd better tell him first. Perhaps I'd better stop this before it goes too far."

I put my hand on his arm, entreating. "Don't, Clay—please don't. Give me this chance. For Stuart's sake."

His smile was slow and a little wry, but he covered my hand lightly with his own. "You're an appealing child. It's too bad that you've been caught up in Graystones' intrigues, through no fault of your own. However, I don't suppose you can do much harm at this late date."

"I suppose you mean that whatever evidence might have existed in the beginning has been obscured by this time?"

"Perhaps," he said lightly. "But what interests me is what I'm to do for a hostess tonight."

"Julian doesn't mind if I keep on with my work here. I'll be with Adria most of the day. I'll do a bit of tutoring, perhaps. In the evening her father can take over."

"Poor Shan," he said softly.

"What do you mean?"

"We should have had a child. She needs one of her own desperately. But I never thought she'd make the right sort of mother. An ability to smother another human being with love isn't exactly a virtue."

Julian's words about Stuart flashed into my mind. "Clay, do you think Stuart was spoiled?"

"Of course. Didn't you always hand him everything on a platter?" But he was smiling at me not unkindly, taking the sting out of his words.

I moved away from something I didn't want to think about. "Sometimes Julian believes that Stuart pushed Margot's chair. That's what he wants to believe."

"Good. It's safer for him to believe that."

"How can you say such a thing when you don't believe it yourself?"

He seemed to shy away from me. He stood up and dropped the poker back in place. "I don't always know what I believe. But never mind about that. Have you any feeling, Linda, that you may be entering dangerous territory by moving up to the house?"

"The only danger I've felt has come from Emory Ault. And Julian has spoken to him."

"What about the cat in your room? Do you think Emory did that?"

"Hardly. I've told Julian, and he thinks it was Shan, as you do. But I'm not afraid of Shan."

"Then you're braver than I am," he said cryptically, and started toward his office. "Do you need any help in getting yourself moved up to Graystones?"

I shook my head and went upstairs to pack. At least there was no Cinnabar in my room this time, since Shan was in bed and waiting for the doctor. Clay's last words about her haunted me. What could he have to fear from Shan? Even though she no longer wanted to live with him as his wife, she had seemed interested in his welfare, his success as a writer. If there had been anything between Clay and Margot, Shan had seemed to blame Julian's wife, not her husband. But his words left me uneasy, nevertheless.

It was true that I could not face Graystones without trepidation. More and more I'd begun to feel that something menaced me there. Some secret thing that thrived on darkness and conspired against me and wore a mask behind which I couldn't penetrate. When I thought openly of each one in turn—of Shan, of Emory, of Clay—there seemed to be no mask, and I could imagine none of them as the source which frightened me. There was nothing hidden about Emory's menace. But perhaps that was only because the mask was so concealing that I couldn't see past it to that hidden, frightening thing.

My suitcase was packed and closed, and before I zipped

my tote bag I reached into the inner pocket and felt the cool surface of the silver Ullr in my fingers. The touch of it confirmed the next move I must make. I hadn't told Julian when I would come to Graystones, and once there my freedom might be curtailed. Before I closed that door upon myself, I had to see Stuart again. Quickly I took the medallion from the bag and slipped its chain over my head. Then I buttoned my coat over its silver gleam.

When I started for the stairs with my bags, Clay was waiting for me in the room below, and he came to carry them down. I had the feeling at once that he wanted to say something more to me, and when we reached the door I paused questioningly. His words surprised me.

"More than anything else, I admire courage," he said. "Julian has it. I'm not sure I have. I'm not at all sure, Linda, that I'd do the right thing rather than the expedient thing if my own safety was involved. Will you remember that?"

What was he trying to tell me? What was he warning me of? I felt a sudden sense of relief that I would not have to spend any more nights at the lodge.

"I don't know what you're talking about," I said.

"You're not supposed to. But keep it in mind, nevertheless. You do have courage, Linda. Perhaps of a particularly foolish and vulnerable kind. You lead with that small square chin constantly. I think I don't want to see you hurt. If the time comes when you take to hating me, try to remember that."

He surprised me further by bending to kiss my cheek—lightly, affectionately. Then he gave me a little shove out the door and came with me to place my bags in the back of the car and helped me secure my skis on top. When I was behind the wheel I thanked him and told him I was going to drive to town to see Stuart. He said nothing at all, but as I turned into the road, I could see him in the rear-view mirror standing there looking after my car. He was a strange person, Clay Davidson. I did not understand him at all, but I had warmed toward him considerably.

It began to snow as I drove toward the interchange to Route 80, but it was a light fall, and nothing to worry about, the flakes melting as they reached the pavement. I was glad, nevertheless, not to have a long drive ahead. I could see the big hump of mountain most of the way, its long back lost in swirling snow.

When I pushed the bell that would bring admittance to that small brick building that was the jail, I found there were other visitors today, and I had to wait my turn in the hall. When I was called, the other stools in the narrow room were occupied, and when I faced Stuart through that now familiar mesh screen, I had a greater sense of his imprisonment than ever.

I spoke in a low voice, aware of other voices in the room. I had a great deal to tell him, and I hurried. First I had to let him know that Julian was unlikely to come to his aid, but that he was willing to hold to a neutral position and let matters take their course.

Stuart looked at me in disbelief. "That's not like Julian. I don't understand what's come over him."

"Sometimes he thinks you pushed that chair," I said. "But he's not sure."

A little of the shine had gone out of Stuart since I'd seen him yesterday. His honey-colored hair looked dull and the brightness in his eyes had been quenched. What had happened was beginning to get through to him, and Lucifer no longer lighted his surroundings. I had wanted him to face reality, but I hated to see that facing change him like this. At my words he stared at me for a moment longer with that same disbelief, and then he bowed his head beyond the wire mesh.

"I never thought he'd do this to me. I never thought he'd accept Emory's lies."

"After all this long silence, you still believed that Julian would help you?" I scoffed a little to rouse him.

There was a break in his voice when he spoke. "I thought he was trying to find a way out that wouldn't let me be blamed." He turned toward me and I saw the hurt in his eyes. "It's not like Julian. It's not in character for him. Linda—are you telling me everything? Is there something else involved? Some risk to someone Julian wants to protect?"

I wanted to put my hands out to him. The screen barrier was cruel. I wanted to hold him as I'd done when he was a little boy, but if I was to help him now, I had to be blunt and truthful at last.

"I haven't told you nearly everything. Julian says you made a play for Margot."

The utter disbelief was back in his eyes to reassure me. "A woman in a wheelchair?"

There could be no doubting him. That was what I had said in another connection about Clay.

"She seemed to have lost none of her appeal for Julian."

"That's true," Stuart agreed. "He never really looked at her as she was. Everyone else knew what she'd become. Other people have been injured as badly as she was, and they still had the courage to make lives for themselves. But not Margot. She only wanted to destroy. But only Julian and Adria could be fooled by her. Linda, she tried to get at him through me—but I wasn't having any. Julian was my friend, my patron, everything. I tried not to let him see the disgust I felt toward her. But that's all I felt."

"Did you feel disgust strongly enough to push that chair?"

I asked quietly. There were things he had not told me, as I was beginning to realize, and I had to shock him into telling me more. "Did you fix that guardrail so it would break and throw her into the ravine?"

He looked at me and I saw honest shock in his eyes. "Guardrail—what are you talking about?"

"It was deliberately damaged, weakened ahead of time."

"But you know I'd never do a thing like that, Linda."

I knew and I couldn't bear the look in his eyes. I fiddled with my purse on the counter before me.

"No one can turn me against you," I promised him, "but I can't fight with my hands tied behind my back. I have to know more than I do. At Graystones they tell me bits and pieces that I can't put together. Emory knows who I am, and so does Clay. So far neither of them has spoken out to Julian —and I don't know why. Eventually, I need to go to your lawyer with something definite. I've stayed away from him since coming here because I have nothing that will help."

He watched me and I knew that for the first time he was frightened. For the first time he could see the walls closing in forever, and the armor of his own innocence no longer protecting him. I had the feeling that he guessed why Emory and Clay were saying nothing, but that he didn't mean to tell me. A light was breaking through the fog for me.

"Stuart, who are *you* trying to protect?"

He looked away across the small bare room and I knew that if I had touched a sensitive nerve, he did not mean to answer me. I was aware of nearby voices, was for a moment aware of the anguish of others, and then my own swept back. I went on, trying to numb my own feelings because I knew I must hurt him more.

"Emory says that when he came around the house and met you running from it, when he caught you and held on, you cried out that you didn't mean to do it. He said those were your words. He told me so himself."

Stuart shook his head in disbelief, but he had been touched at last by hopelessness. "I never said anything of the kind. I said, 'What's the matter—what do you think I've done?' He couldn't have misunderstood me. For some reason he wanted a scapegoat. I never liked him, even when he was teaching me on the slopes. And he didn't like me. In the beginning it was only his word against mine, and it didn't get him anywhere. Linda, what about Emory? What is he hiding?"

"If he didn't like Margot, maybe he—" I began.

"It could be. Linda, you've got to find out!"

"I'm trying," I told him. "But now Emory has found something more to tell the police."

"More lies," Stuart said. Suddenly he pressed both hands against the mesh. "Linda, you've got to get me out of this. I've got to talk to Julian, convince him. When will I be out on bail? You said that sometimes Julian believes I pushed that chair—what does he think the rest of the time?"

"That Adria pushed it," I said limply.

His hands dropped from the mesh, and he stared at me in astonishment. "Adria! But that's impossible. She was crazy about her mother. Margot could do no wrong as far as Adria was concerned, even though Margot used her at every turn."

"It appears they had some sort of quarrel. No one knows what about. There's a possibility that Adria lost her temper momentarily and behaved wildly, as a child does. Perhaps wanting to hurt, but not being truly aware of the consequences."

Stuart shook his head dazedly. "Not that little girl. Never."

"She seems to like you," I told him. "And so does Shan,

148

for that matter. At least Shan has come to your defense with Julian."

This seemed to surprise him even more. "I never paid much attention to Shan. She's pretty offbeat. I don't go much for flower children."

"I expect snow bunnies are more your type," I said dryly.

He flashed me his old smile, so filled with teasing affection that it was as if we were back on a safe, normal plane and I felt a catch in my throat. "They must be missing me, Linda —those bunnies. When am I to get back to them?"

"Perhaps when you tell me who you think really pushed that chair."

The brief moment of being himself in the old way faded. He sat silent for a little while, and when he spoke his voice was low, toneless.

"Perhaps the person who supposedly found her dead. I doubt that anyone inside that house touched the chair. If Adria gave it a push and it rolled a little way, perhaps someone else saw and helped it along. Someone outside who could easily run up the ramp. Perhaps that's why Margot screamed so wildly—because she saw what was coming." He shook his head as though to shake away the disturbing memory of that scream. "I can still hear her. I heard her as I was going out the front door. I never liked her, but I can remember that scream."

"Are you talking about Emory?" I asked in surprise. "It was Emory who found her. But then why wouldn't you say so before this? There'd be no reason why you'd protect Emory."

"No," he said, his tone still lifeless—like the look in his eyes. A look that twisted at my heart. "No, there'd be no reason why I would protect Emory."

He seemed to have gone off into some country where I couldn't follow. I didn't know what he was talking about.

"If you think it was Emory—" I began, but he cut in on me quickly.

"What possible proof have I that Emory ever touched that chair? There's nothing to hold back from you—there's nothing I know. I was on the other side of the house when it happened. If I tried to speculate, they'd laugh at me. They'd think I wanted to get back at Emory. Wouldn't they? Even though he could have pushed the chair, then come to cut me off."

I could only nod, feeling as helpless as he. There was no way in which to turn, and my visiting time was nearly up. But I had to ask him about one more thing. I hadn't taken off my coat, and I reached inside to pull out the Ullr medallion on its silver chain. I held it up for Stuart to see.

"Where did you get this?" I asked him.

A look came into his eyes that I remembered from his little boy years. He had always looked like that when he was about to lie to me.

"Wait!" I said. "Whatever you're going to tell me—don't. Just tell me the truth, Stuart."

The cocky grin came slowly back, appealing and confident. "I never could fool you, could I? How did you know?"

"I wore it when I went skiing with Julian and Adria. Julian saw it. I think he recognized it, but wasn't sure."

"Did he look at the back of the medallion?"

I turned it over so that the small bearded figure of Ullr was hidden, and only the sign that warned skiers of a difficult slope was visible. "Yes. For some reason it seemed to reassure him."

"Good," Stuart said. "Though I never thought when I gave it to you that you'd ever be around any of the McCabes."

"Did Margot give it to you?"

He nodded, still trying to be cocky. "Julian gave it to her.

But it dated back to her skiing days, and she didn't want to keep it. There was an inscription on the back with Margot's name and Julian's. She had me take it to a jeweler in Philly and have that warning diamond etched over the names and filled in, so they couldn't be seen. When I brought it back to her she gave it to me. For some reason she was trying hard to make a hit with me."

I remembered Shan's words—that Margot had made a play for Stuart.

"So then you gave it to me?" I said bitterly.

"I wore it a couple of times in a race for luck. But it gave me the creeps. I thought it would become you, and you'd never know its history, so it wouldn't bother you. It's a beautiful thing."

There was no reason to feel hurt. I couldn't doubt the pleasure he'd taken in a gift for me that he couldn't have afforded if he'd had it made himself. And if I never knew it had belonged to Margot first, I'd never have been hurt. His logic was simple.

"Linda," he said, coaxing me, "don't look like that. You know I'd give you beautiful gifts if I could. And I will some-day." His face sobered. "If I ever get out of this."

There was no use in chiding him. I stood up, wishing I could kiss him good-by, but barred from doing so. I knew how trapped he felt, and how the desperation which had held off for so long in the face of his natural optimism had now swooped down to possess him.

"Linda," he said, "go after Emory. He's the key—the answer. Get it out of him."

I couldn't have asked for a more disturbing assignment, but I told him I'd do what I could. Then I left the building and walked to where my car was parked. The snow was coming down more heavily now.

Once I was behind the wheel, I took off the silver chain and slipped it into my purse. I knew I would never wear it again. As I drove back toward Graystones, I felt oddly sad. Not sad and frightened for all the real reasons that beset me. But wistfully sad because Julian's wife had given his gift away to another man, and because my brother had in turn given it to me.

As I drove along the interstate highway with the windshield wipers pushing at the snow, I remembered a time when Stuart was seven and he had brought me a turtle which another child had given him. He'd brought it to me because he loved me and wanted me to have something he treasured. And of course we had shared the turtle. This was hardly the same—yet there was something of that loved little boy in the gesture. As I drove along I forgave him. But I did not forgive Margot McCabe. Something of my wistful sorrow was for Julian too.

IX

That afternoon Adria helped me to settle into my room at Graystones. It was small, but pleasant, and located at the farthest end of the house from the big master bedroom. There was an empty room between mine and Shan's, and a bathroom at the end of the hall. One window looked out over slanting kitchen roofs to the side garden, the other faced upon those stark beeches across the ravine with its stream. The room was country-like in its atmosphere, furnished in maple and chintz. I had liked my room at the lodge better, in spite of its being in a public establishment. Perhaps houses had auras, as well as people, and there was an aura to Graystones I did not like. My first sensitive reaction to the place had been borne out.

At least Adria seemed to have recovered from the effects of

Shan's fall, and she did not mention the cat on the stairs again. She welcomed me to the house with an eagerness over this break in the routine, and insisted on showing me my room, and staying with me while I unpacked. I was happy over the change in her and somewhat encouraged. Perhaps I would be good for her, after all.

Shan too had recovered, and while she didn't exactly welcome me to Graystones, she flitted about in her misty way, not really focusing on what went on around her, listening—as it often seemed—to her own voices. Now and then she looked through the open door of my room, where Adria was watching me unpack, and then drifted off again.

Adria was curious, questioning. "Why are you coming to stay here at the house, instead of at the lodge, Linda? None of the hostesses from the lodge have ever moved into our house before."

I had already been thinking of that question, and I'd agreed to Julian's suggestion to use the excuse of tutoring. I explained this to her now, and asked about her schoolbooks. She didn't question my role as a teacher, and ran off to fetch them for me.

We spent some time looking over her books, and she seemed to have no objection to giving two or three hours a day over to schoolwork, apparently liking my interest and attention. I asked if she had any young friends in the neighborhood, and she shook her head.

"There's nobody around here. And I don't want to see the kids from school. I told my father I wouldn't go back there."

"But why not? Haven't you any special friends? Someone you'd like to invite in to play with you?"

Again her dark head moved negatively. "Not any more. I haven't any friends. Except you. Are you my friend?"

"I hope so," I said. "But you need playmates of your own age to run about with outdoors. I'm sure we can arrange something. I can drive over to pick up any friends you'd like to see and bring them here. Perhaps you'd like to have a party some weekend when the other children are out of school?"

I could sense her sudden tensing, her rejection of such a plan. "No—no, I don't want to see any of them! They're all —horrible!"

I couldn't let this pass. "Horrible in what way?"

She ran to look out my window at the dead beeches, not answering.

"Everyone needs friends," I said gently.

"I don't. They—they want to talk about Margot. They— ask me questions."

I tried to reassure her. "All that has probably died down by now. They'll tire of the questions quickly."

"They whisper behind my back. And I can feel them looking at me."

She was too young to be so tested and tormented. Perhaps it would be better for her to stay out of school until all this was resolved. All the more reason why it must be resolved before Stuart ever came to trial.

She came back to peer into my face intently, disconcertingly, and I asked what was the matter.

"Your eyes are such a deep brown, Linda. Not like ours. I mean Julian and me. Does it feel different to have brown eyes?"

I laughed in relief. "I don't think so. Though I don't know how blue eyes feel."

She turned to the window, dismissing the subject of eyes, and her thought moved to a distant time. "I wish I could have seen those trees out there when they were on fire.

Wouldn't it have been exciting, Linda? It was at night, you know. My grandfather thought somebody set the fire on purpose. Maybe somebody who meant to burn up the house. But it only caught the trees. My father was a little boy when it happened, and he says the flames shot so high they hid the mountain."

"A fire isn't pleasant or exciting, Adria. I—I once lived in a house that burned down."

She looked at me round-eyed. "Tell me about it."

"Some other time, perhaps."

Her attention returned to the beeches. "My father said the flames roared like the wind in a blizzard." Her thoughts veered again. "Do you think there's a blizzard coming now, Linda?"

I let the matter of friends and fire go for a moment, and went to stand beside her at the window. The dead gray of the beeches was softened by the curtain of falling snow. Flower beds were turning slowly into irregular mounds of white, and evergreen branches had frosted to their tips with a growing burden of snow that made them droop toward the ground. Black boulders in the stream were crested with white, and the path of the water had narrowed as ice spread out from the banks. Only the bare beeches held no coating as the wind blew the snow from their bony arms. Behind them the mountain was blotted out by lowering snow clouds.

"I haven't heard a weather report," I said. "But this looks as though it might last. I think the wind's rising." Through the glass I could hear the whine of it, and now and then gusts flung snow like sand against the panes.

Adria looked up at me, her eyes suddenly dancing. "Shan hates storms, but I love them. She hates the wind, but I think it's exciting when it howls around the tower. When I go up to the tower room in a storm, it feels as though I were right outside in the middle of it. Do you know what my mother used to say?"

I shook my head uneasily.

"She used to say I was a storm baby. I was born during a terrible snowstorm. My father barely got her to the hospital in time. So Margot said it was natural for me to feel the way I do about storms—I mean sort of excited and—and happy. Sometimes I feel as though I just have to go outside where I can be a part of what's happening. But my father says that's dangerous."

"It very well could be," I agreed. "But would you like to go outside for a little while now—before it gets too bad?"

She was obviously delighted. "Could we really? Of course we'd stay just around here."

"Put your things on," I said, getting into her spirit of adventure. "Then we'll go tell your father and Shan, so they'll know where we are."

"Not Shan. Please! She's awfully afraid of storms. She pulls the draperies in her room and hides herself in bed. Of course it's not bad enough for that now, but she'd say no. Let's just ask Dad. You can persuade him."

We got into ski clothes and boots and tramped downstairs. Julian was at his desk in the library, busy with his work. While the actual management of the tree farm was in other hands, he kept a rein on directing the operation.

"We're going outside to have a taste of the storm," I told him, and he regarded me doubtfully.

"So Adria is converting you to her snowstorm cult?"

"Not converting, exactly. I've never seen a real snowstorm in the country. I'm interested."

He smiled at us. "Run along, then. Stay near the house and come in if it gets too bad. You can find yourself losing direction out in the woods in a real storm."

"Why don't you come with us?" I said. "Then we'll be sure not to get lost."

Adria made a sound of delight, but I knew in the same instant that Julian meant to refuse.

"Please come," I said quickly.

His eyes studied me as though he wondered why I wanted him to come.

"You look tired," he said. "There's darkness under your eyes, and a line around your mouth. The outdoors will do you good, so if you want me, I'll come."

"We want you," I said, and turned away, lest he see too much. I was troubled by the quickening in me. I wanted him to come, regardless of Adria.

He laid aside his papers. "It'll take me a moment to get ready. Wait for me and I'll join you."

When he'd gone, Adria danced about the library with more excitement than I had ever seen her show. "He's really coming, Linda! Oh, I'm glad you're here. Shan said you might make spells, and I should be careful. So you've used one of them, haven't you? To get him to come."

"Spells? Don't be foolish. Why shouldn't he want to give you pleasure?"

She sobered at once. "Because he—he doesn't like to be around me much. And I know why. He looks at me and he thinks about Margot being dead. Sometimes he hates me."

I pulled her small, wool-padded person to me in a hug. "He loves you very much, darling. You mustn't forget that or ever think anything else. Of course he's sad because he's lost your mother—as you're sad too."

"But I—I pushed—"

I cut her off at once. "You didn't!" I cried with a conviction that surprised me. "You didn't push that chair, Adria.

I know you didn't. You must stop thinking such a thing. We'll find a way to prove you didn't. I know we will."

"Prove it—?" A faint hope came into her eyes, lighting their blue depths.

"I've been thinking about that. I have a plan. But I'm not ready to try it, yet. Adria, will you show me your mother's room sometime? Can you take me into it?"

She went at once to the door between Margot's room and the library, and turned the knob. The door resisted her pull.

"They've locked it again. But I know where there's a key. An extra key. The same one Shan used to lock this door after Margot's chair went down that ramp, and—and—"

There was something here I must think about. Who had told me the door was locked between these two rooms that day—*before* Margot died? Clay? Yes—Clay had said that. But I couldn't give it my attention now.

I tightened my arm about Adria. "Never mind. We'll look into that room another time."

"My father won't like it. He's told me never to go in there. Of course I did go, anyway. So now he's locked the door. Probably the other door is locked too—the one from the drawing room. And the one to the balcony locks with a bolt on the inside."

"We'll work it out when the time comes," I promised. "There's your father coming downstairs. Don't let him see you've been upset. Make this a happy time for *him*."

She looked at me strangely, a little puzzled. I doubt if she had ever thought about giving someone else a happy time. The idea must have pleased her, however, because when Julian called to us and we followed him out the front door, she skipped after him happily, with the usually hovering darkness that beset her thrust aside.

The storm had not reached blizzard proportions, but the

snow was falling thickly and wind was whispering around the mountain. High up it would be a gale, and the treetops were bending. We walked about the house, with Julian leading the way across the bridge over the stream that was still alive and running between ribbons of ice. For the first time I walked beneath the scarred beeches and saw their blackened trunks and branches close at hand. Apparently the fire had scorched them on only one side, so that the arms they turned toward the house were mostly gray, while here they were a dull black from that long-ago fire.

Under our feet the snow was deepening, and now and then Adria stumbled into a drift that came to her boot tops. She clung to her father's hand, laughing, and let him pull her out. Julian watched her with guarded amazement and now and then he looked at me thoughtfully—as though her gaiety puzzled him and he did not know quite how to react to it. As a father, I thought, he needed a few lessons himself.

A path between hemlocks opened behind the beeches and began to wind up the mountain. Among the trees the wind could not reach us so easily and the flakes came straight down. In the wind the cold burned, but here in this shelter we had some respite.

"Are we going up the mountain, Daddy?" Adria called to her father over the storm sounds of creaking branches and high, rushing wind. Her cheeks were red, her eyes bright with eagerness.

"Only a little way," he told her. "Just to show Linda the lookout place. Though there won't be much to look at today."

Outdoors Julian himself was as much in his natural element as his daughter, and it was I who plodded, occasionally stumbling into a drift and learning that snow over my boot tops was a chilling sensation. But I wouldn't have spoiled their fun for anything, and in my own way I was enjoying this too. Perhaps mainly because, for the first time since I'd met them, Julian and Adria both seemed untouched by any haunting.

The trail wound steeply, and sometimes I slipped backward a foot for every foot or two I took ahead. My mittens were snow encrusted and a little damp, and my nose was fiercely cold.

Once Adria kindly turned to wait for me. "Daddy and Emory cut this trail down from the top of the mountain," she informed me. "If we want to we can ski all the way home from the top of the lifts. But you have to be careful because there are places where you can drop off a cliff."

She plunged on again through the snow, and a moment later she cried out with pleasure.

"Here's the lookout place, Daddy! I've never been here in a storm before."

She climbed nimbly up what appeared to be a cliff of snowy rock, and her father paused to help me.

"It's not as bad as it looks. There's an easier way up."

I clung to his hand and put my feet where he told me to, climbing a sloping bank until I found we were out on a high ridge, about a third of the way up the mountain. Sheer cliffs dropped away below, but swirling snow now hid the country-side that should be spread out beneath us.

Adria stood on the ridge, a bright red figure, her arms outstretched joyously as though she embraced the elements, her small face lifted to flying snow. In this place the wind struck us furiously and I felt the sting of snow pellets on my face. I had no wish to tilt my head toward the brunt of the snow blast, as Adria was doing.

Julian came to stand with an arm around each of us, steadying us there in the blast of the wind, with the steep drop to the valley falling away invisibly at our feet. Overhead, white snow clouds blotted out the sky, and there was a sense of isolation that shut us in. Perhaps there was a world out there somewhere in the storm, perhaps there was a house called Graystones, but here all was wild and elemental, and the three of us stood alone with the fury of wind and beating snow full upon us. It was frightening and exhilarating. I was aware of the pressure of Julian's arm about me. He looked down at me and I knew he felt the moment as intensely as I.

Slowly a strange feeling of elation began to possess me. I ceased to think of discomfort and cold, because something in me that I didn't recognize was responding to this turbulence and to the pressure of Julian's arm. I wanted to shout into the storm and lift my face to the freezing kiss of the snow. I looked at Julian in something like bewilderment, and he nodded at me.

"You're feeling it, aren't you? It's primitive pain, I suppose. The skier knows it. You can feel triumphant when you stand up to it."

But it was more than that, and I think he knew it too. I sheltered in the crook of his arm, exultantly glad to be there—no longer timid or afraid of the blast. But he did not press this testing for long.

"We'd better go down now," he said. "On a day like this the dark falls early, and this is no trail to travel when the light has gone."

Adria turned reluctantly from her storm worship, batting snow from her eyelashes, wiping it from her face with a wet mitten. Her cheeks were glowing with a health I'd never seen in them before, and she looked radiantly happy, as though she had been fully released from whatever haunted her at Graystones.

"I wish we'd never go back!" she cried.

"I can echo that," I said, and Julian laughed with pleasure and I knew there was release for him as well.

"I don't think I want an ice maiden for a daughter," he said as he started down the steep portion of the trail. "Let's go home and sit before a roaring fire. Give me your hand, Linda."

It was good to have the wind at my back and the vision of a warming fire in my mind as we started down. The going was worse downhill, but I dug in my heels as Julian told me to, and we went down with the snow smoking from our feet, making better time on the downward course. Skis would have been quicker, but this would be a hard trail to ski because it was narrow.

Where the hemlocks opened near the foot of the trail, we could see the beeches, with the roofs of Graystones visible between gaunt branches. The elation I'd felt on the mountain began to seep away. Everything that was troublesome and dangerous still lay ahead, and I knew I had no right to the freedom of the mountain—or to the warmth and comfort of Julian's arm about me. I was anything but free to choose my own actions.

It was fortunate that Adria's happy mood lasted longer than my own. While we went to change our clothes, Julian built the promised fire in the drawing room and ordered hot chocolate for Adria, and hot buttered rum for us. Yet the coziness I'd looked forward to was not there for me, after all. I wanted more than I could have. I knew that Julian's gaze was upon me warmly, and I dared not respond. Too much that was secret and dangerous for me lay between us, and I could not turn to him with honesty and without subterfuge.

Stuart was with me in that quiet room and I could hear the ticking of a clock—the relentless marching of time. What

163

was it Clay had said when he knew I was coming to the house—that I was moving into "dangerous territory"? It was more dangerous than I had known—and somehow I wanted this danger to come closer. I didn't want to turn from it as I must.

Adria was in a chattering mood, behaving more like any little girl than I had ever seen her. Julian seemed to be entertained by her—perhaps still able to carry with him the mountain's spell and hold off the haunting. He too talked in a more natural way, and he made an effort to draw me out. There was a new intensity in him that I had to guard against, to resist, and I was cold before the fire—cold in a way that I had not been out there in the snowstorm.

Once he spoke to me directly, curiously. "What sort of woman are you, Linda—with your nose that tilts in a cocky way, and your mouth that's always in earnest?"

"Never mind my mouth—I know it's too big." I was flushing, squirming inwardly, filled with a ridiculous desire to run away.

"You seem to spend your life looking after others, but what about you? Aren't you responsible for a life of your own?"

I was responsible for Stuart's life, I thought a little wildly, and tried to answer him defensively.

"I have my own life."

"A man, of course."

He was baiting me, his eyes bright with teasing, and I squirmed the more under this pinning down.

"Of course," I said. "There's a man I worked for in the city. I suppose he'd like to marry me."

"But clearly you don't choose to marry him."

"That's not clear at all!" I denied, and welcomed Adria's interruption.

"What *are* you talking about?" she demanded of us both.

"We're talking about Linda's life," her father said. "Here she is looking after skiers at the lodge, looking after you up here. But when does she get to look after herself?"

Looking after Stuart, I thought, and saw a yawning pit at my feet—a darkness I didn't understand and feared terribly. It was *necessary* to look after others—to pay my debt to life.

We were nearly finished with our drinks when Shan came downstairs and drifted into the room, dressed in a long violet robe patterned with yellow flowers and slit to one knee. She seemed surprised, and not altogether pleased to find us sitting so cozily before the fire.

"I couldn't stand being upstairs alone any longer," she said, flinging herself into a great velvet chair that engulfed her, stretching her sandaled feet toward the fire. "The weather report promises a real blizzard, and it's getting worse outside."

"Perhaps I'd better get down to the lodge while I still can," I said. "If it gets too bad, I'll stay there for the night and come back in the morning. Guests will be down from the slopes early today, if they went out at all."

"You don't know skiers!" Shan said lightly.

Adria set her chocolate cup on the coffee table and came to stand before me. "Don't go there tonight, Linda. Please stay here. I need you. It's at night that I need you."

I held her extended hands in mine, both touched and troubled by her appeal.

"If you feel that way I promise to come back," I told her.

"Don't worry," Julian said. "I'll get you to the lodge, Linda, and I'll come after you. Though we'll have to walk, since there's no use trying to plow in this weather and the drive's already impassable."

"That's not necessary," Shan said gently. "Linda can stay at the lodge. Adria dear, you can sleep in my room tonight.

I'll have the cot put up beside my bed, and we'll keep each other company. Then the storm can't hurt us."

Adria whirled to face her aunt. "No—no, I don't want to do that! You're afraid of storms and you frighten me. And I have enough to be frightened about at night."

Julian was a man, beset by feminine vagaries, and he threw up his hands. "Night's no different from day, Adria. You're both behaving hysterically, but settle it between yourselves." He left his chair and went out of the room, impatient and all too nervy himself.

I spoke again to Adria. "I'll go to the lodge, if it's possible. And I'll come back here when Clay lets me off. I'll look in on you before I go to bed. I promise."

Shan drifted out of the room in Julian's wake, clearly offended with me and offended because her own rather Victorian vapors were not being taken seriously by her brother. I had no particular sympathy for her. She wasn't my problem and she was supposedly adult and had lived through blizzards in this house before.

"I'll have to get ready for the lodge," I said to Adria. "Do you want to come with me while I dress?"

We went upstairs together. Stepping into the tower was like entering another world. The wind was howling now and snow obscured all the outdoors, flung against the windows with the force of hail. Drafts whistled around us and I could see why the doors to the stairway were always kept closed in the winter.

Cinnabar wandered uneasily about the upper hallway, and not altogether to my pleasure, Adria picked him up and brought him with her to my room, planting him in the middle of the bed. It was already dark outside, for all that the snow gave the afternoon a ghostly sort of light. I pulled my draperies against those staring beech trees.

Adria laughed at me, stroking Cinnabar, who purred deeply. "There's nothing out there. You don't need to pull draperies at night at Graystones. Unless you're like Shan. She's sure there are faces out there, staring in. I know better. Whatever wants to get in is already in. So there's no use in covering the windows."

Her words had an eerie ring to them, and I answered her as matter-of-factly as I could.

"I'm a city girl. I'm not afraid of anything out there, but it's cozier to be curtained at night, and I'm more used to it when the lights are on."

"After all," Adria went on, "the only spirit that's around here inside is Cinnabar, and you can't shut her out." She bent to nuzzle the cat with a too-elaborate show of affection.

"You don't believe that sort of nonsense, any more than I do," I said impatiently, and paid no further attention as I changed my sweater and combed my hair, pinning it on top of my head, the better to fit under my parka hood. My long johns and ski pants I kept on, since I would need them going and coming.

Adria sensed that her return to tormenting wouldn't work with me and she hopped off the bed and went stirring curiously about among my things. I watched her in the mirror as I put on lipstick and eye liner, but I let her be. There was nothing she could hurt, and I was just as glad to have her busy, instead of watching me with her sometimes disconcerting stare.

"Is it all right if I help you unpack?" she asked.

I nodded. "You can start with my tote bag if you want to."

She began to pull out bedroom slippers and extra pairs of shoes from the bag.

"You like my father, don't you?" she said abruptly to my reflection in the mirror.

"Why wouldn't I like him?" I forced a deliberate casualness into my voice.

"Shan says you'll fall for him, the way girls always do. She says she can already see it happening."

"That too is nonsense," I assured her. "I'm afraid Shan's imagination runs away with her."

I set down my hand mirror, blotted lipstick and turned around on the dressing-table bench. Adria had come to stand directly behind me, and I was startled to find her so near. She held out her hand, almost pushing it into my face.

"Where did you get this?" she cried. "Have you been in my mother's room? Have you been stealing her things?"

The silver Ullr dangled from her fingers on its cabin, and I remembered that I'd taken it from my purse to return to the tote bag pocket. I took it from her gently.

"This doesn't belong to your mother. It's mine. Someone gave it to me a long time ago." I turned it over casually so she could see the diamond marked upon the back, obliterating the lettering that lay beneath.

She looked at it doubtfully. "But—but my mother had one just like it. My father had it made for her especially. There couldn't be two so much alike."

"There are probably many medallions like this. Are you sure it's exactly like the one your mother had?"

"No—there's that diamond thing on the back of this one. My mother's wasn't like that."

"Then I hope you're sorry about making wild accusations," I said.

She looked taken aback and upset, perhaps concerned about having offended me. Her look made me sorry for my deception, but I couldn't let her go rushing off to tell Shan that I had her mother's medallion. Clay and Emory might

168

keep their counsel, even though for reasons I didn't understand. Shan never would.

On the bed Cinnabar announced himself. He stood up and made an unearthly yowling sound. Adria turned around slowly.

"Did you hear that?" she whispered. "She doesn't like what you said. Maybe she knows it's her medallion."

I spoke a bit sharply. "I suppose Cinnabar skis? I suppose he needs an Ullr for luck when he comes down the slopes?"

Adria stared at me for a moment, and then relaxed, laughing softly. "You make it sound silly. Come, Cinnabar, I'll let you out if you want to go. Though I don't think you'll enjoy it outside. Margot never really liked to be out in a storm. She wasn't a storm baby like me." She threw me an impish glance, caught Cinnabar up about his middle and carried him squirming out the door.

I thrust the medallion under a pile of lingerie I'd put in a dresser drawer, and pulled on my boots and my parka. Then I hurried downstairs, glad to meet neither Shan nor Adria, and found Julian once more at his desk in the library. Strangely, I had a sense of shyness at seeing him again. There had been—something—out there on the mountain. Something that reached tentatively between us, and which I must now deny. But Julian smiled at me in welcome, denying nothing.

"I'll take you up on that escort service, if you're still willing," I said a little stiffly.

He nodded. "If you really feel you must go, I'll be with you in a moment."

I waited for him near the front door, peering out at the storm through small colored panes, thrusting back the uneasiness in me. There was nothing moving out there except the wind. No footprints, no Emory Ault lurking behind a tree.

I wondered where the old man lived when he was not working, and I recalled unhappily Stuart's warning that it was he who might hold the key to everything, if only it could be pried out of him. If he intended concealment that might be difficult, and even dangerous. I had already sensed his malevolence.

Julian joined me quickly and took my arm as we went down the steps. "Don't worry," he said. "I've seen worse."

I hadn't. I ducked my head against the wind and the snow sand it flung in my face. The buffeting was furious, and I doubt that I'd have been able to stand without his support. The house vanished immediately, and I'd not have known which way to turn if I'd been alone. Julian apparently knew the path blindfolded, and he found his way without difficulty. It took longer than usual, but the very effort I made warmed me, and I reached the back door of the lodge breathless and laughing a little over my victory.

Julian thrust open the door and we stood for a moment in the vestibule while I stamped snow from my boots, and Julian brushed it from my parka.

"I'm fine," I said, letting the hood fall back from my head. "But I don't want to try it alone getting back."

"You're looking better now," he said, and brushed the hair back from my eyes with a quick, light touch that left me as breathless as I'd been in the storm. I froze in something like alarm at my own response, and he saw and laughed. He knew women all too well—did Julian McCabe.

"Suppose I come for you around ten o'clock," he said. "I suspect everyone will go to bed early tonight. If this lets up there will be fresh powder on all the slopes tomorrow. Comparatively deep powder for around here." Matter-of-fact words that did not hide the warmth in his eyes.

"Which isn't for snow bunnies like me," I said, purposely

light. "But I suppose the machines will pack it down and break up the surface."

He smiled. "You're a better sport than some of the bunnies. And you're doing wonders with Adria."

"You can do more wonders," I told him. "Everything was just right for her when we went up on the mountain this afternoon."

"Thanks to you, Linda." He touched me lightly on the shoulder with one gloved hand and went back into the storm. I shut the door hastily upon a swirling fog of snow, unzipped my parka, and tried to brush more snow from my pants, since I'd brought no others to change to. Clay heard me and came out from the hall.

"Hello, Linda. I didn't expect you to make it tonight."

"Julian brought me, or I wouldn't have. He's coming back for me at ten o'clock."

"You could have stayed here overnight. The radio promises clearing before morning."

"I know. But Adria wants me there. Apparently she has bad dreams at night. Though whether I can help her or not, I don't know."

His look was a little cool. "You're really digging in, aren't you? And Julian hasn't the faintest notion of what he's harboring. I can tell that when he's mentioned you on the phone. You're very clever, Linda. Whatever good it may do you. What do you hope to learn that no one else has?"

He made me angry. "One thing I learned today is something Adria told me. She says it was Shan who locked that door from the library to Margot's room—*after* Margot died. I think you said it was locked while you were in there—when you heard her scream."

He nodded at me almost fondly, though his eyes were still cool. "Shan would do that for me, of course. And of course I would accept her claim that the door was locked—to protect myself. I do not like putting my head in a noose. It's much simpler this way. And makes no difference, since I didn't go through that door. Shall we get your fondue started? Everybody's turning up early this afternoon."

He opened the hall door for me, his manner formal and a little mocking. There was nothing I could say. I went ahead of him into the lounge, where groups of two and three were already gathered, and found myself busy at once.

The fire was a blaze of logs, offering cheer against the storm outdoors, and Clay had lighted a surplus of candles, to give a warmer glow than electricity. I went out to the kitchen to mix the fondue and soon had it bubbling in a big chafing dish in the lounge. The crowd was smaller tonight, but there were a few newcomers who were disappointed because they'd been driven from the slopes before their day was over. There was talk about the various qualities of snow, the preferences and handicaps, the dangers from boiler-plate ice to deep powder. Of course that was one of the things that kept skiing interesting. No slope was ever the same, and weather changes could come within hours. What was an excellent pack could melt and ice over in the same afternoon—and if there was one thing most skiers didn't relish it was ice.

Some of the crowd had gone, but the little nun was still there. I saw her sitting close to a lamp with a book open upon her knees. Her habit was neat and modern, with a trim, light coif, and her skirt was short and unhampering. She saw me nearby and looked up, smiling.

"Agatha Christie," she said, tapping her book. "Good for a stormy evening. But I'll have to stop reading so I can listen to people." She made a small gesture. "They're even more interesting than mystery stories. Take your Clay Davidson, for instance. He was telling me about the novel he's working on.

It's a suspense novel dealing with skiers, and it sounds fascinating. I asked him if he used real people in his writing."

I dropped into the chair next to her. "And does he?"

"He claims not. He says real people would get in his way and not do what he wants. But I suspect he uses bits and pieces—perhaps without ever being conscious where they come from, and putting them together in a new form. I expect you can tell a lot about a writer from his work. His philosophy, his outlook—everything must come through, even when he hides behind his characters."

"A mystery writer must hide behind some pretty nefarious characters. Do you think you can find Agatha Christie there?"

Her smile was gently serene. "Aren't we all mixtures of good and evil? Isn't that why we need something outside ourselves to pull us through?"

"You make me curious about Clay's writing," I said. "I'll get him to loan me something of his to read."

We discussed innocuous matters for a time, and then someone came up to speak to her, and I moved among the other guests until dinner was ready.

The big dining room seemed drafty tonight under the heavy wind, for all that it boasted the wide fireplace of the original farmhouse. A bronze American eagle stood on guard in the center of the mantel, with a porcelain rooster crowing at each end, and there was a spinning wheel near the hearth. It was a homey, comfortable room, with the wide floorboards of another day, and old beams overhead.

Clay and I sat together and talked in a desultory fashion. There was the constant spat of snow against the windowpanes and a great rattling of glass. At times the old house trembled under the impact of the wind. Candles about the room dipped and smoked, dancing erratically.

"I hope the wires don't ice over and go down," Clay said.

"We've had power loss and blackouts before this during storms."

We were both being cautious, avoiding dangerous ground, measuring each other. I told him lightly that Sister Mary Elizabeth had recommended his writing, and wondered if I could read some of his fiction.

He seemed unexpectedly pleased. "If you'd really like to I'll loan you a manuscript after dinner. You can take it along to the house if you want to. If you promise to keep it dry on the way home."

I told him my parka had big flap pockets and I'd take good care of his story and be happy to read it.

"It won't tell you much," he said, and his eyes mocked me wryly.

I ate my salad and did not look at him, and after a moment or two he went on in the same dry tone.

"You're the wrong sort to make a good detective, Linda. I'd never use you in a story. You're so forthright, a child can see through you. I'm sure Adria does."

I thought of Adria and the medallion and wondered.

"I saw Stuart again this morning," I told him. "He says Emory has invented lies about him from the first. He thinks Emory holds a few answers, if only I could get at them."

"Of course." Clay seemed unsurprised. "Emory would lie his head off for Julian. The biggest lie of all, of course, is that Emory Ault was the first to find Margot after her chair came down that ramp."

I stared at him, and my voice rose a little. "Then—who—?"

Clay cast a hasty glance around the dining room, but storm sounds had blotted out my words, and no one was interested in our table near the kitchen door.

"Julian found her," Clay said.

I gasped. "But Julian wouldn't have—"

Clay looked at his plate. "Anyway, Emory jumped to conclusions about what might have happened. He knew that Margot had done everything possible to enrage Julian and goad him into violent action. And if I know Emory, he'd go to any extreme to protect Julian."

Or perhaps to protect himself? I could so easily imagine Emory with his hands on that chair. "Even to blaming someone innocent like Stuart?" I asked.

"Especially Stuart. Emory never wanted him around— because of Margot's wandering eye. This was a way to pay him off, get rid of him and spare Julian at the same time."

"What about your wandering eye?" I spoke deliberately.

The betraying flush darkened his face, and I plunged ahead, pressing on the nerve I'd exposed.

"Shan talks quite readily, you know. I understand Margot broke up your marriage."

He held himself in check very well and even managed to smile a bit grimly.

"Perhaps it's not detective talents you need, after all, Linda. Perhaps just being able to stir up trouble is enough. Unless some of those stirred pots boil over and scald you. Anyway, that's ancient, though perhaps regrettable history, and—"

"Shan says not," I broke in. "She says Margot wanted you back and could never believe she'd lost her fascination."

The slight grimace that crossed his face was betrayal enough of his feeling about Margot. "As I was about to say— it was Julian we were talking about. Not me."

I'd been holding off the thought of Julian, because I couldn't accept what Clay had told me.

"Julian wouldn't let Emory say he'd found her if it wasn't true," I said flatly.

Clay's smile took on a taunting twist. "Julian makes his own laws."

I could hardly swallow the rest of my dinner. Clay watched me covertly, and I knew he was watching. Julian, Adria, my brother Stuart! I could accept none of the three as having pushed that chair. I didn't want to sacrifice any one of them for the other two. And yet I knew that if it came down to a final judgment, it must be Stuart I would try to save. Was it Julian *he* was trying to protect?

"Do you care so much what happens to Julian?" Clay asked softly.

"I care about what happens to anyone who is innocent," I told him. "How do you know that Emory was lying about finding her first?"

"Shan looked out the drawing-room window. She saw Julian down in the ravine. Afterwards she told me. But she'd never say anything to imperil her brother."

Any more than I would imperil mine, I thought.

"Shan was pretty busy, wasn't she?" I said. "Meeting Adria on the stairs when the child was upset and running away from something. Looking out the window. Locking the library door to Margot's room. Which isn't what you told me. Perhaps she even saw who pushed that chair."

Clay's mouth above the neat beard pressed grimly in at the corners, and his eyes had a blaze of anger in them I'd never seen before. All his wry and lazy manner had vanished, making me wonder if it was a sham he liked to wear. Under the shelter of the tablecloth he reached for my wrist, and his fingers hurt to the very bone.

"I'll listen to nothing against Shan. Not ever. I've told you a few unpleasant truths because you needed help with your brother, and I've nothing against Stuart. But there are directions you aren't to take. I hope you understand that."

He frightened me and I tried to twist my hand free from his grasp. The storm came to my aid. There was a tremendous blast of wind that crashed against the old house. For an instant the electric lights flared to brilliance, then died slowly to pinpoints and vanished. The dining room was shadowy with firelight and the light from swaying candle flames. One or two women squealed their alarm, and others laughed nervously.

Clay let go of my hand and stood up, speaking as cheerfully to the room as though he had never been angry with me.

"There's a wire down someplace. I'll go phone the electric company. In the meantime, we've plenty of candles, and we'll keep the fire going. The hot water may run out, but we've got an auxiliary pump for the well, so cold water will hold out. And there's food enough for a siege, if necessary."

He went out of the room and there was laughter and talk again, as the whole thing was turned into an adventure. If anything this proved to be our gayest evening. When we left the dining room everyone grouped about the fire as heat from the furnace gradually dissipated. Sister Mary Elizabeth borrowed Clay's guitar once more and played old songs from the thirties and forties. Plaintive songs that everyone knew, and her voice rose sweetly in the lead. "San Antonio Rose," "Tennesse Waltz," "Star Dust," and "Deep Purple," "Moonlight in the Rockies," and finally, quite wistfully and tenderly, with the snow blowing wildly outside, and all of us shut into a shadowy, firelit world—"White Christmas."

I couldn't sing, though I tried to mouth the words of all the songs to keep up appearances. There was a lump in my throat that kept the words from becoming vocal. A lump of fear and grief, adding up to a foreboding of coming disaster. Somehow the wistful, memory-laden words of sentimental old songs brought tears of longing. I hadn't been born when some of these tunes were written. Behind the longing—for me—there was fear. I had stirred too many pots to near boiling, as Clay had said, and my wrist ached from his grasp.

Fortunately, I had my hostess duties. I kept hot coffee going over an alcohol burner, and sometimes I moved about the downstairs area of the lodge. I looked into the dining room, where the tables had been cleared and only firelight sent shadows climbing the walls. I went into the empty office, and out into the dark back vestibule where I'd left my parka and other things. But I did not dare look into Clay's private quarters. I couldn't face his anger again.

Once I opened the back door cautiously against the wind and found the storm furiously increased. It roared and howled outside, and I pulled the door shut upon an icy blast of snow. Surely I couldn't go out in that. Perhaps I'd better phone the house. The telephone at least was still working. But then I thought of Adria and let my hand fall from the receiver. If the storm was too bad Julian would know and he would call me.

I went back to listen to still another chorus of "White Christmas." Christmas! It was only a little way off and I hadn't thought about it at all. What gift could I bring Stuart except his freedom? Christmas this year at Graystones would be subdued and not very gay, because of Margot's death. But at least I must try to find a gift for Adria. She mustn't be deprived of Christmas.

I'd just poured myself a cup of coffee, when I saw Clay coming toward me across the lounge. He no longer looked angry—indeed, he seemed oddly pleased, and I couldn't imagine why.

"Your escort has come early," he told me curtly. "He's waiting outside because he's covered with snow. You'd better get into your things and go back to the house while you can. *If* you can. The power is gone there too. I'll handle things here."

I had alienated Clay, as I could see. He was pleased that I would have to struggle back to the house through the storm. I nodded to him without speaking and started to move away from him. He held something out to me in a flat envelope.

"You wanted to read one of my stories," he said, and turned away quickly as I took it.

Under the circumstances I was surprised that he had remembered. But when I reached the rear vestibule I tucked the envelope carefully into a flap pocket of my parka so that it would keep dry. I didn't open the door to greet Julian because of the cold that would blast its way in, but I hurried to put on my things, wound my muffler around the lower part of my face, drew on my boots, and shoved at the door. It was pulled from my hand and held steady as I stumbled into the fierceness of the night.

"I'm to take you back to the lodge," Emory Ault said. "Miss McCabe's having one of her spells, and Julian's got his hands full. I told them you should stay here, but then Adria put up a squawk. So come along and stop gawking at me. You'd better take hold of my belt at the back and hold on."

So this was why Clay had looked spitefully pleased. I didn't want to go with Emory, but I had no choice. Wind and snow buffeted me on all sides. I could only put my head down, hang onto Emory's big leather belt with my mittened fingers, and stumble along behind him. Sometimes I was dragged. Sometimes I slid, as my feet went totally out of control in loose snow, my boots unable to step surely in the drifting white masses of powder.

X

We moved very slowly. Lame or not, I was sure Emory could have made better time alone. I was often a dead weight stumbling behind him. At first all my attention was given to trying to stay on my feet, and to gulp air before the wind whipped the breath from my lungs. I didn't attempt to see where we were going. Sometimes a snow-laden branch would slap back as Emory released it. The noise seemed worst of all. The roaring was no longer confined to the treetops, but seemed to rush like an advancing tidal wave along the ground, buffeting us with sound. Often there was a nearby crashing as some ice-laden branch gave way and broke off to fly through the night. The ice must be heavy everywhere, and the slipperiness underfoot was increasing.

We must have struggled through the forest for ten minutes

before I began to take note of our surroundings. There were no longer hemlocks around us. The trees had changed to spruce and pine. The snow itself made a strange light and there was no darkness of an ordinary night to blind me, so that I could see better than I might have expected. As an awareness of the changed forest reached me, fear struck through the physical chill, adding to my misery. This was not the way to Graystones. We were neither on the short-cut path nor the driveway, but seemed to be tramping through an unmarked wilderness. I could no longer tell where the mountain lay—or the lodge, let alone guess the direction of the house. With all my strength I dug in my heels and pulled Emory to a stop.

"Where are we going?" I mouthed at him, filling my throat with snow.

He shook his rugged, wool-covered head. "Can't hear you," he shouted. "Keep going!"

But I had heard him. There was nothing to do but hold on and follow. If I let go of that sturdy leather belt I would be lost in swirling whiteness. I could never find my own way alone.

It was growing harder to keep moving because I was frightened now and weakened by fear. My lungs felt as though they were bursting. My cheeks above the muffler had numbed to the sting of snow, and my fingers were surely frozen to Emory's belt. Then a dark shape loomed before us. It was a small hut, its slanting roof snow-layered, its window ledges piled with white. Emory attacked the door, pulling it open against the wind, and dragged me into a big room where a fire had burned to embers on a wide brick hearth, and candles burned on the mantel. I hadn't the strength to stand and I slumped to my knees. It was almost as though I'd forgotten how to breathe when the buffeting ceased and my every breath wasn't snatched away from me, so that I gasped and shivered.

Emory was taking off his jacket, stamping his boots, dashing snow from his pants.

"What would you do if you had to take a real trek in a blizzard?" he asked me scornfully. "Get on your feet and get out of those wet clothes."

I obeyed him numbly, fearing that if I didn't he'd do it for me. He was muttering violently to himself as he stirred up the fire and added fresh birch logs. I couldn't tell whether his epithets were for me, or for those at the house who had sent him on this fool's errand.

I didn't need to ask where we were. This was Emory's hut. His mark was everywhere. There were skis lined up against one wall, a pair of snowshoes hung on a peg, and boots of every description marched in order on a rack. His bed was a bunk in one corner, and there was a round table in the middle of the floor, with chairs set about it. Against one wall stood an unfinished bookcase, stacked with both hard-cover and paper volumes. Apparently Emory was a reader.

Beside the fireplace there was a wood-burning stove, which added warmth, and on which Emory probably cooked his own meals. A few pans hung from hooks above the stove, with a sink nearby, and running water. The cabin was not primitive and there was electricity—when the wires weren't down —and a door stood open upon a small bathroom. Though the bare wooden floor was rugless and scarred, it was very clean, except for the snow we'd tracked in, as was the entire hut.

All this I saw as I peeled out of my things and went to sit on a low wooden stool, holding out my hands to the wonderful warmth of the replenished fire. Emory moved about lighting more candles, and he brought one to hold before my face, his limp noticeable as he crossed the room.

"Rub your nose and your cheeks gently," he ordered. "There's no frostbite yet, but you need to stir up circulation. I'll phone the house and tell them we've got this far."

I began to relax. He meant me no harm. He had brought me here to break our journey, and he was only obeying orders to return me safely to Graystones.

At the wall telephone he clicked the receiver up and down, and I began to tense again. As long as there was a telephone—

"Phone wires are down too," he grumbled and slammed the receiver on the hook.

"How—how far are we from the house?"

He ran a hand through gray hair and turned his massive head to look at me. "Five minutes fast walking on a good day. Another fifteen or more when I have to drag you through the snow."

"I'm sorry," I said. "If I'd understood how bad it was I'd never have gone to the lodge in the first place."

He shook his head in disgust. "No sense to it. No consideration for anybody else. Just like your brother."

I stiffened on my stool. "I was thinking of Adria. It seemed terribly important to her that I return to the house tonight."

He turned his back on me and went to the small stove, taking off the lid to add wood, setting on a pot of coffee, and opening a can of soup to heat.

My brain was beginning to thaw out, as well as my fingers and nose. I clasped my warming hands about my knees and stared into the fire. Here was my chance to talk to Emory Ault. But how was I to use it? I mustn't be headlong this time. I must step warily. But there was no way to be wary. I had my chance and I must take it.

"Clay told me something interesting tonight at dinner,"

I said. "He told me that you weren't really the first one to find Margot after she was thrown from her chair. Clay says Shan told him that Julian reached her first."

Emory set down the spoon with which he was stirring soup and turned to look at me, his heavy gray brows bristling, his mouth a straight line.

"Davidson's a fiction writer. He makes up fantasies." The harsh voice grated.

"Shan looked out a window," I said. "Shan saw what happened and she told Clay."

The growling sound he made disturbed me, but I held my ground as he came toward me.

"Julian knows I'm with you," I warned him. "You'll have to account to him if anything happens to me."

He came to a halt directly before me and I sensed a black anger raging through him. Perhaps it was always there, though he kept it well checked. But it was surfacing this time, and he might give himself away.

"I even thought *you* might have killed Margot," I said— "until Clay told me Julian found her. Now I know it must have been someone inside the house who pushed her chair. Because Julian wouldn't have hurt her. Julian still loves her."

He stared at me for a long moment, struggling to contain his anger.

"Julian loved her all right—but what he loved was a woman who never existed. He made something up out of his imagination and he never saw her the way she was."

"Perhaps he knew her better than you did."

He snorted and limped back to the stove to take the steaming soup from the heat and pour it into an ironstone bowl. Then he brought it to me, with a carved wooden spoon to eat it with. I looked with wonder at the bowl, the hand-carved spoon. I wouldn't have expected such amenities from Emory Ault.

"Shan gave them to me one Christmas," he said, as though understanding my look. He used their first names easily, since he'd known them as children.

There was a greater complexity to this man than I'd thought. For the first time I wondered about him, wondered what his life had been like, why he was alone—whom he had loved. And what were the titles of those books he liked to read?

He carried his own soup to the table and sat down to eat, paying no further attention to me. The hot soup tasted wonderful, and so did the coffee he brought me when it was ready. I could feel strength flowing through me again, a strength that came partly from the fact that I was no longer afraid—not of the storm, nor the man. Emory would get me back to Graystones safely. He didn't like or trust me, but he would do as Julian wished.

He nodded his head over his soup bowl and spoke as if to himself. "Yes, of course it was one of those inside the house. And we know which one, don't we?" He raised his spoon and waved it at me like a baton, declaiming: "The golden Lucifer! Son of the fiery snow—child of the fastest slopes!"

I gaped at him in astonishment. Some of these books must be classics.

"When I was twenty-two I was an actor," he said. "I trod the boards before the footlights and all my glory lay in an audience's applause. And then one year when I wasn't working I happened to go skiing. On this very mountain which towers above us now in the storm. I never recovered. The sickness of the snows took me. I became what they call a ski bum, until Julian McCabe's father stepped in to back me as a skier. The rest you know." He took a drink of hot coffee in the manner of a man who quaffed mead from a goblet, still leaving me astonished. "But we were talking about who pushed that chair, weren't we? And we both know it was your brother."

"No!" I cried. "That's not true. Stuart never touched Margot or her chair."

He growled like the bear he sometimes resembled; the brief glimpse of the actor was submerged, obliterated.

"Why did you lie?" I demanded. "Why did you say you found her when it was Julian who did?"

There was an intense silence within the room, while the storm roared outside the hut's walls. A log fell on the hearth, sending bright golden sparks up the chimney. When Emory spoke again it was with a deadly calm that frightened me more than if he had raged.

"I've warned you before. Go away from Graystones. Go away from Juniper Lodge. You can do your brother no good here, and you may destroy yourself."

"How destroy myself?" I challenged him.

"Perhaps there will be an accident," he said obscurely.

I finished my coffee and began to put on my parka. "I want to get to the house. I've rested long enough and I'm warm now."

He waved toward the door. "Go along then. There's nothing to keep you from going."

"Except that I don't know the way."

I had never seen him smile before and I did not like it when he did. There was a dark mirth in his look as though the thought of me lost in a blizzard and freezing to death gave him considerable pleasure.

"There's that, of course," he said. "Well then, come along and we'll get going."

He was ready before I was, and I left the warmth and

safety of the small hut regretfully. The storm had abated not at all and the sting of the icy blast seemed worse than before. I held to his belt once more, looking back now and then toward the hut, in order to keep some sense of direction alive. But the snow cut in, whirling it from view, and the forest was trackless, directionless. I had no idea which way Greystones lay.

When Emory acted, it was so suddenly that it took me by surprise. With a movement that wrenched my wrists and tumbled me to my knees, he twisted the belt from my grasp and was free of me. He didn't even look around, but stamped off among the trees, moving more swiftly than I'd have believed possible. I tried to follow him, calling out desperately, but he vanished as quickly as the hut and I was left totally alone in a darkness lit eerily by snow. Only the trees I bumped into were visible. I sank into drifts to my knees, struggling frantically.

But in the way of frantic struggle lay disaster—death. It was better to stand still for a moment and try to think. If I could find my way back to the lodge—if only there were traces of our coming left in the snow—! I turned back along the immediate tracks Emory and I had made on the path from the hut. If I could find his cabin, perhaps I could find my way to the lodge.

But I saw quickly that blowing snow had wiped out our tracks even more quickly than new snow could fill them. I stumbled into a drift and fell to my knees while the wind howled about my head and the coldness pierced my bones. It was all I could manage to stand again, but I knew I must keep moving to stay alive. If I let weariness and despair conquer me I was lost. All I could do was judge the distance between the trees and try to imagine where a path might lie.

How quickly the warmth and light of the cabin had been

lost! Now the cold was penetrating, the wind sliced at me mercilessly. I stumbled a few feet in that blank horror that means a loss of direction. My disorientation was like being blind. No way had meaning for me, and if I took the wrong turn I would die.

Snow fell away beneath my feet and I sank to my knees in the soft menace. My face was growing numb, dangerously losing the sense of cold. There was even the temptation to give up—to do what Emory expected me to. I struggled to my knees and went on.

When I first saw the light I could not believe in it. Something glowed softly through the blasting snow, moving, growing stronger. I cried out desperately, and the wind snatched away the sound of my voice. But the glow remained and grew brighter, and I stumbled wildly toward it, falling, picking myself up, stumbling on, until it resolved itself into the concentrated light from a storm lantern swinging from a man's hand.

"Help me!" I cried again. "Please help me!"

Julian emerged in the glow of light and caught me about the shoulders. He asked no question, offered no explanation for being there, and I clung to him with relief and joy.

"Hold onto my arm," he said. "We're not far from the house. I'll get you there."

The lantern made an oasis of safety that the wind and snow could not obliterate. Light cut a small path ahead of us, illuminating little except more snow and trees. But Julian knew every tree, he knew the way. The house was closer than Emory had claimed, and I wondered weakly if he had meant all along to lose me in the woods before we reached the house.

The candlelight and lamplight of Graystones gleamed in the windows and on the tower stairs, and were glorious to see. Shan flung open the door, and in my haste to grasp at safety and warmth I stumbled again before I reached the steps. Julian set down his lantern and picking me up in strong arms, carried me into the house. He bore me, snow and all, to the leather couch in the library and laid me down on it gently. There was a fire on the hearth, and an oil lamp burned on a table.

Shan followed us and stood looking at me, anything but pleased. Whatever her earlier hysteria had amounted to, she appeared to be over it now, and I wondered vaguely if she'd developed it to keep Julian from coming after me, so that he'd had to send Emory.

Her brother spoke to her curtly. "Go ring the outside bell, Shan, to let Emory know Linda's been found. Then fix her some hot tea. Sweet. With cream and sugar."

Shan went off and moments later I heard the pealing of the great farm bell that hung near the back door. It clanged furiously as though some disturbing emotion drove the force of Shan's ringing. Even with heavy snow blanketing sound, the voice of the bell would reach through the woods and call Emory—tell him his plan had failed.

Julian pulled off my wet mittens, helped me out of the parka, and all the while he muttered over me with a sort of angry tenderness.

"Little fool. As soon as I knew you were lost, I came out to look for you. Emory's looking too. But in this storm it might have been hopeless. The woods go on for miles. Why did you run away from him? Whatever possessed you to run away when Emory was trying to get you back to the house?"

I felt dreadfully weak—too weak to be indignant over Emory's lie. Let Julian believe what he pleased. All I wanted was to rest. When my wet ski pants had been pulled off, Julian took a silk dressing gown from a closet and wrapped it around me. Only then did he get out of his own heavy clothes, and carried all the snow-encrusted things out to the vestibule.

I closed my eyes and let warmth and a sense of safety—a strange illusion of being loved and protected—flow through me. Shan came with strong, hot tea and sat down near my couch to hold the cup for me.

"Can you sit up, Linda? Drink this—it will do you good."

Once more I drank hot, reviving fluid, and life seemed to flow back into my veins. Shan was muttering too, crossly, though her pique did not seem directed entirely at me.

"Men can be ridiculous. Those two! Because snow is nothing to them, and they know every inch of these grounds, Julian sent Emory off with the utmost confidence to bring you here. And look what happened."

I found my voice. "He left me. Emory left me out there in the snow. I didn't run away from him. He ran away from me. He was angry with me, and—and he abandoned me."

Julian, returning to the room, heard my words. His blue eyes, which so often seemed intense with extremes of emotion, turned cold, all tenderness gone from them as he spoke to me sharply.

"Emory never lies to me. I don't know why you should, Linda. Nor do I know why you should dash off into a blizzard, running away from someone who wanted to get you to safety. Why should Emory be angry with you—or you with him?"

Shan said nothing, looking a little sly.

Hopelessness swept over me again. I could not tell him why without revealing who I was. And if Emory had not yet done that, then I mustn't. Not yet. There were no reasons I could offer, other than the truth—that Emory hated me because I was Stuart's sister and he felt I somehow threatened

Graystones, perhaps threatened Julian, and he would stop at nothing to thwart me. Yet he had not told Julian my identity.

"You're making this all up, of course," Julian said. "You behave foolishly for some unfathomable reason, and then you make excuses to blame someone else. Typically female."

He strode angrily about the room, not looking at me now, as though he could barely contain his dislike for me. I drank hot tea and let weak tears trickle down my cheeks. His words overwhelmed me, smothered me, bore down upon me like weights of lead. I was too weak to be angry, to deny. A strange, unfamiliar longing filled me—a longing to be comforted tenderly, as a child might be. To be held in Julian's arms and protected—as he had seemed to protect me for a little while. Always in my life I had been the protector—and even in my weak state I knew the foolishness of such a wish, and I wept because it was foolish.

Shan nodded and smiled at me, almost as though she approved of my weeping. "Julian always manages to have emotional women around him. Women who make things up out of their imaginations, and then weep when they're caught in their own stories. Like Margot. Like me. He gets very disgusted with us."

Her words brought me to life. I handed her the teacup and sat up, beginning to feel a strengthening anger myself. "I haven't lied to anyone! And I shan't cry." I dashed the trickle of tears away and stood up, wobbling a little. "If nobody minds, I'm very tired, and I'm going up to bed. I'll look in on Adria on the way. I promised her I would."

"She's asleep," Shan said. "She doesn't need you. You really needn't have been such a heroine, coming here in a storm like this. It's ridiculous."

I wanted to drop Julian's dressing gown on the floor as if the very touch of it was repugnant, but I'd have lacked dignity striding off in my long johns, so I kept it about me as I went out of the room. The unfamiliar darkness of the hall halted me at once, and Shan came running after me with a candle set under a storm chimney.

"Do you want me to help you upstairs?"

"No, thank you," I said and took the candle from her.

The tower was freezing cold and reminded me of the terror of the blizzard. Drafts swept around me, and if it hadn't been for the glass chimney my candle would have blown out. Picturesque these stairs might be—but practical, no. Shadows climbed with me as I went up the wedged, curving steps, and I was aware of snow flung wildly against dark panes.

At the second-floor level another candle, glass shielded, had been set on a small table, so the landing was not entirely dark. I stepped through the door into the upper hall, my shadow running ahead of me as I'd crossed the glow of lamplight.

Adria's door was ajar and I opened it further to look in. As Shan had said, she lay sleeping quietly. Not even that clanging bell had wakened her. I could just see her by candlelight, one hand under her cheek, her lips parted with soft breathing. How charming she looked in her sleep, and how exquisite the longing in me to take a sleeping child in my arms.

As soon as I reached my room, I took off Julian's wine-colored gown that had about it a scent reminding me of pine needles and wood smoke, and put on my own belted robe. I carried the gown to the door of Julian's bedroom and hung it over the knob.

It was then I remembered Clay's manuscript in the pocket of my parka. I hoped it had survived the snow soaking. I had better rescue it before anything happened to it. I felt stronger now and I went swiftly downstairs in my slippers and into the hall where my wet things were hanging. The library door was still open, and I got the envelope quickly, hoping to escape before anyone looked out and saw me, and more words had to be exchanged. I was in no mood to read the story now, even if there had been any lights, but I would pick it up later. Before I turned away, however, the sound of Shan's voice reached me and froze me where I stood.

"She's got to go, Julian. I won't have her here. As you can see, she's a liar, and that's not good for Adria. She keys the child up, excites her too much. I could hardly get Adria to sleep tonight, because she was worrying about the fact that Linda would have to come back to the house through the snow."

Julian spoke more quietly. "I'm not sure but what it's a good thing for Adria to have someone new to worry about and concern herself with. If she comes to like Linda it's one step away from the past."

From my place near the clothes rack I could see Shan, but not Julian. She stood with her back to me, and her gauzy robe hung draped from her arms as she raised them, like a priestess invoking some spell.

"There can't be any stepping away from the past, Julian. It's here—all around us. Graystones is alive with it. Those who die violently never sleep."

"Stop that!" Julian cried, and I heard the anguish in his tone, overlaid by anger.

"We keep them alive in our minds," Shan went on, paying no attention. "We can't let them rest because we're haunted—haunted by our own guilt and our own fears. All of us."

Julian said nothing, but he must have taken a step toward his sister, for she ran suddenly out of the room, her draperies floating about her as she vanished through the door to the stairs. She had not seen me where I stood in the shadowy corner near the clothes rack, and for a moment longer I did not stir. Then I moved cautiously opposite the library door and looked in.

Julian sat with his head in his hands, not stirring. Everything about him spoke of despair and defeat. This was Julian McCabe, who was afraid of nothing. Julian McCabe, whom the slopes had never defeated in the days when he had challenged them. I wanted to go and kneel beside him, to put my arms around him, offer him comfort and support in his dreadful trouble—whatever it was. The longing seemed part of my arms, my very body.

I made no move. The impulse was treachery, of course—a betraying of everything that was important to me. On the wall behind Julian hung a framed photograph of two skiers. One was Julian. The other's bright gilt head shone in the sun, and his gay young face was lifted toward the picture-taker. It was my brother, Stuart, standing there beside Julian McCabe. He seemed to look directly into my eyes across the room—challenging *me*. But I didn't need to be challenged by Stuart.

I fled up the stairs through the wailing of wind and the rattling of panes, and hurried to the haven of my room. It was quieter there, though very cold, with the furnace off for several hours. To some extent the tall maimed beeches held away the storm. Its full fury crashed against the opposite side of the house. Quickly I undressed for bed, blew out my candle and got between cold sheets, to lie shivering until the natural warmth of my body took away the chill.

XI

I fell asleep more quickly than I would have expected. My experience in the blizzard had exhausted me enough to counteract emotions and thoughts that might have kept me tossing. Once I awakened and lay for a little while listening to the sounds of the unabated storm. We would be thoroughly snowed in by morning. I reached a hand into biting cold and pressed the switch of the bed lamp. Nothing happened. The wires might be down a long time, with crews unable to work in the fury of such a storm.

My flashlight was within reach and I turned it upon the dial of my travel clock. Two in the morning. At least the house was silent. Adria had been troubled by no nightmare. Everything was still, the rooms of the house encased in stone walls that held off the storm. Even the natural creakings of an old house could hardly be heard against the sound and fury outdoors. But my bed was warm now, sleep-inducing.

I dozed, slept, wakened—to an awareness that my door which I'd closed when I came to bed was standing open. How I could distinguish between the darkness of my room and the farther darkness of the hall I didn't know. But all my instincts told me that the door had opened and that someone stood there staring at me through the velvety dark.

I thought wildly of Emory, creeping back to the house, which he could surely enter at will, and coming to finish what he had tried to do to me tonight. Or it could be Shan, who harbored some threat of her own toward me. My heart thudded and my mouth was dry, but somehow I managed a whisper.

"Who is there?"

At once there was a rustle and something hurtled across the room to my bed. "Oh, Linda!" Adria spoke in a hushed tone. "I'm glad you're awake. Linda, can I get in bed with you? I'm so cold and so frightened!"

I flung back the covers with immense relief and let the small cold body slip between the sheets and snuggle close to me. I held my arms about her and let my own warmth encase her until the shivering stopped.

"You can sleep here for the rest of the night if you like," I told her softly.

"I was afraid you wouldn't come back from the lodge. I didn't want you to come out in the storm, really—but I needed you so."

It was consoling to be needed. There was hardly anyone to need me now. Only Stuart—in jail. And he wouldn't need me, once he was out again. Not as he'd needed me as a little boy. I had been busy and active, and I'd dwelt as little as possible on the loneliness of not being needed. But holding Adria close to me, I too found warmth and comfort.

"I'm here," I said reassuringly. "What frightened you, darling?"

"The dream. Oh, it didn't come, really. If it had I'd have behaved in that awful way and screamed so that I'd have wakened everyone. I never mean to do that. It just—happens. Only sometimes I can tell when I'm going into the dream, and sometimes I can wake up and stop it. It's like walking down a long corridor. Everything's bright in the beginning and there are windows on both sides. But the windows come to an end and as I walk along, the corridor turns into a dark tunnel. I know there's blackness and horrible things I can't see at the end. And when I get there, the dream will begin."

How well I knew what a dream of this sort was like.

She began to shiver again and I held her to the warmth of my own body, stroking the damp hair back from her small face, feeling in my arms the frailty of her bones, and the soft, child's breath on my cheek. She hadn't gone to Shan. She had come to me—and I was touched, filled with an enormous loving.

"I couldn't go to Shan," she whispered, reading my mind. "She'd fuss over me, even though she'd take me into her bed. She'd tell me not to talk about it. She'd tell me to forget."

"And your father?" I said. "What does he do?"

"He gets worried and upset. I think I frighten him some-times, and he shouts for Shan and doesn't know what to do. He didn't used to be like that. A long time ago he used to just pick me up and love me and make everything feel better. But he doesn't love me any more. He—he's afraid of me."

I pressed my fingers over her lips. "No—no, you must

never believe that. It's good to say such things to me if you feel like it. Saying them helps to get rid of them. But they aren't true and you don't have to believe in them. You can tell me about the dream though, if you want to. I'd like to know."

For a little while she lay still in my arms, breathing quickly, lightly. Then she began to speak in a low, soft voice—sometimes so softly that I could hardly hear her words.

"At the end of the tunnel is my mother's room—with the balcony outside. She's sitting there in her wheelchair in the doorway, just ready to push herself toward the ramp that goes down to the ground. I'm there with her. She's wearing the blue pants with the white daisies on them that she liked, and a frilly white blouse. And she's angry, angry, angry. I don't know about what. When I come into the room to ask her something, she's angry with me. She tells me not to bother her, not to come whining around trying to get my way. She says my father spoils me and she's sick of it. She's sick of everything."

The light whispering voice paused, and I put a question very gently so as not to destroy her mood.

"What did you ask your mother that day that made her angry?"

"I don't even remember. She was already angry. It wasn't anything important. If I'd known how she felt I wouldn't have gone near her. Sometimes we just had to leave her alone. But she was awfully angry, and she wasn't being fair—so I got angry too. I—I put my hands on the grips at the back of her chair."

I waited and she went on.

"I said, 'If I wanted to I could push your chair. I could push your chair and it would go right down that ramp and make you fall out.'

"So she said, 'Go ahead and push.' Then she said I was my father's child. And she said I couldn't push her chair because the brakes were on. 'Go away and leave me alone!' she said. 'I never did like children, really.'"

Again there was silence, and once more I tightened my arms about the small body. "She was probably cross and didn't mean what she was saying."

"I know. Later on I wouldn't have really minded her saying that because I know she loved me sometimes. And she wanted me to do lots of things for her that she couldn't do herself. But right then I was angry. I pushed her chair as hard as I could—and then I ran out of the room."

"But the brakes were on," I said.

"If they'd truly been on how could the chair have gone down the ramp?"

I let that go. "What happened next? Where did you go? Did you run right up the stairs and meet Shan coming down?"

"No. No, I don't think so. But I'm not sure. It's all terribly mixed up. I think I stayed in the drawing room. I remember looking out a window at the beech trees."

"And you heard your mother screaming?"

Adria hesitated, as if she tried to sort everything out in order, and there was a wondering note in her voice when she answered.

"No—I don't think so. Not right away. I could see something moving in the window, but I didn't know what it was."

"What sort of thing?"

"Like—maybe like a ghost. I told Shan about that, and she said it was Margot's spirit rushing through the air."

I swallowed the indignant objection I wanted to make. "How could it be—when she hadn't screamed yet? She hadn't gone down the ramp—and you were far away in the drawing room."

"I—don't know. I—I can't ever figure it all out. She did scream, you know. But I'm not sure when. Anyway, I heard her, and I ran away and went to the tower door. And Shan was there on the bottom step. She told me to go upstairs and stay there. And then she went to the drawing-room window that was nearest Margot's balcony and looked out."

"And what did she see?"

"She never told me. She doesn't want to talk about it. She says I must forget it all. Nobody will let me talk about it. When the police came I was upstairs in bed. Shan said I was sick and I must stay there. They never knew about my pushing the chair. I never got to talk to them at all. When I told her I wanted to talk about it, she said I was all mixed up and I wasn't making any sense or remembering things right. So after that I began to feel more mixed up than ever. I never could be sure of everything that happened. Sometimes it seems to me as though it was one way—sometimes another."

"When you went to see your mother, how did you go into her room? I mean, what door did you use?"

"From the library," Adria said readily. "First I was there talking to Clay and Stuart Parrish."

"The door wasn't locked."

"No—of course not. I went through it."

"Afterwards did you see Clay or Stuart?"

"I saw Stuart. He went out the front door while I was talking to Shan. She sent me upstairs and I went in my room and shut the door. I remember I was awfully afraid. I kept on hearing her scream—inside my head. And I knew it was because I'd pushed her chair."

"But it wasn't, Adria dear. You weren't anywhere near her chair when it was really pushed. *If* it was pushed."

She hardly seemed to hear me. "A long time afterwards, Shan came upstairs and told me my mother was dead. She was very upset and she was shaking a lot. So was I. We—we cried together. She said it was terrible for my father. And she asked me what had happened when I was with my mother, and what I saw afterwards. But when I tried to explain everything, she hushed me and said it was all over and I must forget all about it. She said they thought Stuart Parrish had pushed the chair. But afterward the sheriff let him go, and then I began to see that it was really me. My father got upset when I tried to tell him, and afterward he couldn't like me any more. But he took Shan and me away, and we went up to Maine to stay with some old friends. He never talked about what happened, and we skied a lot when the snow came. But everything was different. And then that thing came out in the paper about Stuart being arrested and my father said we had to go home. I guess my father hoped it was Stuart, so it wouldn't be me. But when I tried to tell him it wasn't Stuart, he wouldn't listen. And now the bad dreams have come again. I have them nearly every night."

"Yes," I said, "I can see how that would be. Now we must try to get rid of those dreams. They only come because you're afraid of something that isn't true. Tell me, dear—the other day when I first met you, you were sitting in your mother's wheelchair. Why? Why did you get into that chair?"

"I wanted to see if I could tell whether it really happened the way I was afraid. I thought if I sat in that chair—and then my father started shouting at me—and—and—"

Her words trailed off and I held her and crooned over her, trying to soothe and calm and reassure.

"Tomorrow you and I will prove that it couldn't have happened that way, Adria. Tomorrow you'll show me your mother's room and we'll try something out. But now you can forget everything and go to sleep. It's going to be all right. I promise you."

Slowly the tension went out of her. She relaxed with her head on my shoulder and went sound asleep. I lay awake, listening to her quiet breathing, thinking about what I must do. If I removed Adria from all suspicion, I left Stuart in a more dangerous position than ever. But this was what I had to do. Adria mustn't be sacrificed. Once she was safe and free of her dreams, I could give my attention to discovering which one of them had really pushed that chair. Emory? Clay? Shan? Even Julian? No—not Julian. And probably not Shan or Clay. But very possibly Emory. I already knew there were dark things moving in him, dark threats he would not hesitate to put into execution. And Julian was taking his word against mine. But there must be a way to find the truth. There had to be.

I fell asleep at last, only to be wakened by a soft yellow glow as the electric lights came on in my room, and I heard the low reassuring rumble of the furnace. I released Adria from arms that were growing numb, and she turned over sleepily and did not waken. I slipped out of bed in the sharp cold to switch off the lights. Then I put on my robe and went to the window that looked out over the kitchen roof below. The wind had died down and over the snow on my window sill I could see a calm white night. The storm had blown itself out. Drifts were piled high against the house and the familiar world had disappeared. Tomorrow we would have to dig ourselves out. At the moment we were snowed in and the house seemed all the more quiet for being encased in high-piled drifts.

I think Adria and I might both have slept late in the morning, but we were awakened by Shan's outcry. She had found Adria missing from her room and was running down the corridor calling her name. Adria stirred beside me and nuzzled her head into my pillow as she tried to shut out the sound.

I patted her shoulder. "Sleep if you can. I'll tell Shan where you are."

She grunted sleepily as I flung on my robe and went into the hall. Shan was white with alarm. She rushed up and down with her fair hair flying and her filmy nightgown floating around her as she went to one door after another, rapping and calling.

"It's all right," I told her. "Adria's with me. She had a bad dream in the night and I let her come into my bed."

Julian's sister turned from his door and came toward me swiftly, a faint pinkness staining her pale cheeks. "Let me see her! Let me see her!"

I stood in the frame of my doorway. "Can't we let her sleep? She's had a disturbed night."

But I couldn't bar her way, and she swept past me into the room and flung herself upon Adria. "Dearest! Dearest! Why didn't you come to my room? You know you'd have been safe from bad dreams with me."

A strange thing happened as I watched her. Suddenly I was back more than a dozen years to a time when Stuart had gone out of his room in the middle of the night, and when I'd found him on the moonlit lawn I'd smothered him with alarmed affection as Shan was doing now with Adria. Once I'd been as foolish as she. And then Margot McCabe had died, and somehow I was growing up.

Adria came awake and rolled over to look at Shan, bending above her, and at me, near the foot of the bed. Her black hair lay in tangles over the pillow, and her expression was ominous, wrathful.

"Go away!" she told Shan. "I don't like you very much and I want you to go away."

Shan began to tremble. She looked so shocked that I felt sorry for her and annoyed with Adria. But the fray lay between them and I couldn't interfere.

"You don't mean that, dearest," Shan cried. "You know how much we love each other, and—"

"I don't love you," Adria said stubbornly. "You think I pushed my mother's chair. But—*she* doesn't." She nodded her dark head toward me.

There was anguish in Shan's eyes. She had shut all other loves out of her life to give herself to this child, and the child was repudiating her. She turned away in desperate hurt and moved toward the door. But before she went out of the room she turned her head toward me and her look chilled. There was something frightening about it—not indignation, not a human despising of me, but a sort of malevolence that was terrifying. I had two enemies now—Shan and Emory.

But she went out of the room and I sat on the bed beside Adria. "There are things we don't do," I told her coolly. "We don't behave cruelly toward people who love us."

She glowered at me with her blue eyes intense with some dark emotion, the rest of her face hidden by the covers. "Maybe I don't like you, either."

So the battle was to be waged all over again, and the closeness of the night was gone.

"I'm sorry if you don't like me," I said. "But we've things to do today anyway, so you'd better get up and get dressed. Do you want the bathroom first, or shall I take it?"

She stared at me as though I baffled her. Unlike Shan I

didn't dissolve into a hurt mass of suffering which would encourage her to hurt me more.

"What things?" she demanded, finding that she could not stare me down.

"We'll talk about that when we've had breakfast. The storm's over and it looks as though it will be a good day. So do get started."

She lay quiet for a moment longer, perhaps still testing her strength against mine. I knew her tragic need of love and reassurance, and I longed to put my arms about her and hold her as I'd held her in the night. But this was the wrong time. She was her own person, and I had to respect that and give her a chance to choose her own course. So I stood quietly waiting for her to move or answer me.

Abruptly she flung off the covers and at the same moment flung a challenge at me. "I'll race you to the bathroom."

I let her go, laughing and relieved. Later, when we were both bathed and dressed, she let me comb the tangles from her long, fine hair and brush it to a dark sheen. By the time we went downstairs we had the house to ourselves, except for the maid who served us breakfast, and the cook out in the kitchen. Even Shan had left word that she was going out in the woods to look at the storm damage. I'd discovered that some hand shoveling had been done close around the house, and now both Julian and Emory were out in jeep and tractor, plowing snow from the driveway and about the house, as Clay was undoubtedly plowing it from around the lodge. There was a roar of machinery outdoors.

Adria seemed more subdued now and a little uncertain with me. I suspected that she had not forgotten what I'd told her last night about our plans for the day, and that this was troubling her. She picked at her breakfast, drank a little milk, and pushed back her chair, though she didn't rise immediately.

"I think I'll go outside now. Sometimes Daddy lets me ride with him on the jeep pickup when he's plowing."

That wasn't my plan. For once we had the house empty, and I didn't want to lose this opportunity. I had to try what I planned—I had to give it a chance, even though the thought of this trial frightened me.

"You haven't forgotten that you're going to show me your mother's room this morning, have you?"

The blue eyes were wide. "Her room is locked."

"But you told me you knew where the extra key was."

"I—I've forgotten."

"That isn't true," I said.

She wriggled in her chair. "My father says I'm never to go in that room without him. And Shan says I'm never to go there at all."

I knew all these things and they concerned me. Yet still I had to go ahead.

"This time I'll answer to your father and Shan. It's my responsibility. You don't want to spend the rest of your life having nightmares, do you? This may be a way to end them. Let's go and find out."

She sensed that I wouldn't give in, and she slid from her chair and ran out of the room. I followed her, not knowing whether I had won or lost. But she waited for me in the entry hall. I took two outdoor jackets from the clothes rack and handed the smaller one to Adria.

"Let's put these on. It may be cold in Margot's room."

She obeyed me as if hypnotized, and I put on the other jacket myself.

"Now you can get the key," I said.

For a moment her face twisted, and I thought she might

burst into tears. My heart misgave me and for an instant I was ready to retreat. I couldn't force her in the face of tears. Then she shook off the spasm and ran into the library, to fumble in a drawer of her father's desk. When she turned toward me, she held up a key. I took it without comment and slipped it into the lock of the door between the library and Margot's room. I was not feeling as calmly self-possessed as I pretended. Yet I had to take the risk.

The key turned easily in the lock and I pushed open the door. Adria stood close beside me. I felt her trembling, and put an arm about her shoulders.

"There's nothing here to frighten you," I said gently, though I could feel a tightening at the back of my neck.

The room had scarcely been touched since Margot herself had occupied it on her last day alive. The door to the drawing room was closed and I knew it was now kept locked. The bolt was thrown shut on the balcony door. Margot's wheelchair stood in the center of the room, and Cinnabar lay asleep on its cushion.

Adria gave a small scream and clung to me. For a moment I was ready to flee from the room with her. Then I spoke to her calmly.

"I wonder why Shan keeps letting the cat in here," I said. "Will you put him out, Adria? We'll need to use that chair."

My matter-of-fact tone seemed to reassure her sufficiently so that she stood her ground, but she would not touch the cat.

"No—I won't put her out. She has a right to be here. She has a right to see whatever you're going to do."

It was a point I didn't care to argue, but I wanted the cat to go. I had never touched Cinnabar before, but I went to the wheelchair and reached for him. He sprang up, spitting at me, and jumped to the floor. But he did not retreat from the room, though the library door was open. He simply settled himself on the carpet and watched us with a fixed yellow gaze.

I stood for a moment looking about the room, trying to quiet my nerves. It was strikingly decorated, with walls of pale silver gray, a darker gray carpet, and accents of flame color in patterned curtains, in the bedspread and even in paintings on the walls. Nowhere were there any skiing scenes or anything which suggested snow and winter. Except at the windows, where real snow had piled itself halfway up, contrasting with flamboyant scenes of tropical flowers and brilliant birds. It was a beautiful and dramatic room, yet it was somehow empty. Not merely empty because the woman who had lived here was gone, but empty of the things that matter in a room. It might have been a lovely picture out of a magazine. There were no books, no evidence of the everyday matters with which a woman tied to a wheelchair might have occupied herself. It was as though she must have sat here with no interest in life. No interest except for the brooding in her own mind, except for the planning of the harm she meant to do. Eerily, a presence seemed to enter me—a consciousness of that vengeful resentment which had turned solely toward one man—Julian McCabe. It was as if the very air of this room had once pulsed with angry emotion, so that traces of it were still here to disturb the atmosphere. For the first time I sensed along my own nerves and with my own awareness what torment Julian must have suffered. There were forces abroad I might not be able to combat.

With an effort I flung off these imaginings and gave myself to the single purpose of our being here.

I went first to the balcony door and shot back the bolt. The door opened inward, so that snow fell across the sill and cold air swept in. I was glad I wore a jacket. Outside, the balcony was deep in drifts that flashed rainbow lights in the sun, and the ramp was fully buried. I wheeled the chair to the balcony door and called to Adria.

"Will you show me how to set the brakes?"

She came reluctantly and showed me the rubber-handled brake levers above each wheel. When she had set them both, I tried the chair to make sure it would not move, and then seated myself in it as calmly as I could. Adria stared with wide-eyed fascination in which there was a hint of terror. A terror that had to be quenched.

"You'll need to remember everything about that day," I told her, keeping my tone matter-of-fact. "We're doing this to stop those dreams. How do you know the brakes are on?"

She was intently serious now and less frightened. "I just put them on!"

"And how do you know they were on that day?"

She considered this for a moment before her face brightened. "I put them both on that day too. I remember doing it. One of them was stuck and worked hard."

"Why didn't your mother put them on herself?"

"She liked me to do things for her," she answered with confidence, and then went on wisely, "And it made my father feel worse if there were lots of things she couldn't do."

"But when the chair was found later, the brakes weren't on. So how can you be sure you put them on?"

Her stubbornness grew from assurance. "I'm positive. We talked about the sticking brake, and she tried the chair to make sure. They were both on."

"All right. We know both brakes are on now, and I'm sitting in the same wheelchair. So go ahead and push me. Push the chair as hard as you can, Adria."

She shrank back. "No—no, I can't!"

Cinnabar yowled at her tone, not helping me at all.

"Of course you can. Nothing will happen because the brakes are on. Push the chair and see."

She put her hands on the two grips at the back and then winced away. "No—you'll go down the ramp, and you'll be thrown into the ravine! You'll be killed like Margot was killed!"

"Adria dear, I won't," I said. "You can see all the snow out there. I couldn't possibly go down the ramp. Look!"

I released both brakes and wheeled myself at what speed I could manage across the sill into banked snow. The wheels came to an immediate halt.

"You see? Even if you pushed me a lot harder so that I was really rolling and tipped out into the snow, I couldn't hurt myself. So now I'm putting the brakes back on. You're watching, aren't you? Push the chair, Adria, push it as hard as you can."

This time she obeyed and put all her will and strength into trying to shove the wheelchair. It skidded an inch or two on the carpet, never going over the sill. Adria came around to the front of the chair where she could look into my face, and I saw hope rising in her eyes.

"So even if I did push her she couldn't have been hurt?"

"Of course she couldn't."

"What if I took off the brakes and then pushed her? What if that's what I did?"

"In that case, why would you remember putting them on, but not remember taking them off?"

The cry of shock that reached us from the library door was shrill with near hysteria. Shan came rushing into the room, still wearing her outdoor clothes. She snatched Adria away from the chair, but all her fury was turned upon me.

"Oh, how wicked you are, how dreadfully wicked!" She

let Adria go and rushed past me, plowing through the balcony snow. "Julian! Julian!" she called.

I could hear the sound of Julian's snowplow but he couldn't hear Shan over the noise, so she went floundering wildly down the ramp, hip deep in snow, stumbling out into the yard, waving her arms frantically at Julian. He must have seen her, for the sound of the motor was shut off, and a moment later he came stamping up the ramp and into the room.

I sat in Margot's chair, and Adria came again to stand beside me, though now tears were streaming down her face and she was trembling within the circle of my arm. Julian had turned quite pale.

"What do you think you're doing?" he demanded of me. "Haven't I given orders to keep Adria out of this room?"

Shan had floundered up the ramp after him and they were both shedding snow all over the gray carpet. I had to shout to make myself heard over Julian's voice and Shan's fluttering cries.

"Be still!" I cried. "Do keep quiet for a moment—both of you!"

For once I took Julian by such surprise that he stopped his own shouting and stared. Shan gave a last small squeal and fell into a chair. At once Cinnabar leaped into her lap, his ears back and his tail twitching. I was shaking by this time, but I held onto Adria. And when I spoke it was to Adria alone.

"We're going to show them, darling. Show them how you put the brakes on for your mother that day. Go ahead, Adria—show your father."

She cast a single terrified look at Julian, and then reached for the brake levers on the chair.

"That's fine," I said. I tried the wheels and the chair

would not roll. "Now you're going to push the chair just the way you did that day when you and your mother were angry with each other. Of course the only reason you pushed the chair was because you knew the brakes were on and you couldn't really hurt her. You just wanted to show her you were angry. Isn't that right? Now go ahead and push."

She went behind my chair and I could feel the thrust of her hands, feel the chair quiver and slide a tiny bit. That was all. Julian stood very still. Shan was whimpering.

"Did you see the chair move when you pushed it that day?" I asked Adria.

"I didn't stay to see. I ran through that other door to the drawing room. I went and stood at the far end of the bay window and looked out at the beech trees. I—I guess I was waiting for her to call me back. Only—she couldn't."

"Could you see the balcony and the ramp from that side of the window?"

"No. You can't see them from there. Only from the other side of the bay."

"So you didn't see the wheelchair go down the ramp. You didn't see your mother thrown, or who came to pick her up?"

Adria shook her head. "I only saw part of the beech trees and reflections in the glass—something moving past like a ghost."

"When did your mother scream? Right away when you pushed the chair?"

"No. She knew I couldn't hurt her—because the brakes were on. It wasn't until I was standing at the window that she began to scream."

"Come around here, darling," I said.

Adria came to the front of the chair where I sat, and I held her arms with my two hands, looking into her face.

"Do you see what all this means?"

There was a growing wonder in her eyes, a desperate hope. "Yes. Yes, I do see! Linda, I don't need to have bad dreams any more. What I was afraid of didn't really happen. Is that what you mean? Is that it, truly?"

"It couldn't have happened," I said.

She turned and ran to her father. "Daddy, I couldn't have hurt Margot! So you don't need to hate me any more. You can love me again, Daddy."

Julian looked utterly shaken, broken. He drew Adria into his arms with a great tenderness and held her to him, pressing his face against her hair. I left the wheelchair and went to Shan, who had watched everything stunned.

"Come out of here," I said. "Let them be alone. And I think perhaps you'd better not put that cat in here any more."

She rose and Cinnabar sprang from her lap. She came with me like a sleepwalker. I couldn't tell whether she was still angry with me, or whether Adria's innocence had relieved her from a burden too. She seemed to have retired inwardly to her own private world. In the hall she left me and ran out the front door. I went upstairs and collapsed on the bed in my room. I'd gone through with it—I'd done it!—but I felt more drained than triumphant.

I could still hear the astonishing sound of my voice telling those two who belonged here to be quiet. I could see myself standing up to Julian in his anger, and a reaction of fright and weakness swept through me. I hoped I'd succeeded, for Adria's sake. But I didn't know what would happen to me now. I didn't even understand my own extreme reaction to what I had done. The threat of having Julian ask me to leave was nothing new. So why was I so upset?

I tried to empty my mind of all thought, all emotion, as though it were a slate which could be erased. But such a slate never stayed empty for long. The endless writing always returned, and I could almost see the word being scribbled there repeatedly. The one word: "Brakes."

The wheelchair brakes! Why did the thought of them frighten me? They had been off when the empty chair was found tipped over against the broken guardrail. The chair had gone down that ramp brakeless. Why? When Margot felt herself going down the ramp, why hadn't she tried to stop the chair with the brakes at least? Perhaps because she had released both brakes when she was alone, and had started herself down the ramp? Perhaps she had never been sharply pushed from above at all, and whatever had happened had occurred after the chair was down the ramp. That meant that whoever had come upon her at the foot of the ramp had flung the chair against the guardrail with such force that it cracked and threw Margot into the ravine, the broken rail only stopping the chair, leaving her body smashed upon the rocks in the ravine for Emory—or Julian?—to find.

There was much in this picture that frightened me, and I tried again to thrust the thought of all of it from my mind. But one other image remained—a glimpse of the woman I was becoming. Someone always ready to fight for others, but never for herself. Why did I so fear to take hold with my own life? Why was I afraid of responsibility to myself—and thus quite dreadfully afraid of Julian?

After a time the sound of voices drifted up to me from the rear of the house. The murmur came from outdoors, and I roused myself to leave the bed and look down over snowy roofs to where the kitchen garden lay buried under drifts.

Emory was there beside his tractor, one foot resting on the snowplow's blade. Near to him stood Shan, her hands in her pockets as she faced him. They were talking together earnestly, and though I couldn't see Shan's face, I could see Emory's. His great head was bent toward her in a listening attitude, and the expression he wore was one I'd never seen before on that remote and reticent face. He looked almost benign—affectionate. Apparently there was someone else to whom Emory gave his loyalty besides Julian.

I couldn't hear their words, but I had the feeling that they were talking about me and about what had just happened in the library. The fact was not reassuring.

XII

I was still at the window watching those two in the yard when Adria tapped at my door. I called to her to come in, and she ran to fling her arms about me with a touching appeal she had never shown before. I held her to me, warmed and delighted. Perhaps in this house I'd done something worth-while, after all.

In a moment she stepped back so she could look at me. "My father wants to see you in the library, please. Will you go down to him right away, Linda?"

I played for time, immediately apprehensive, and she watched as I sat at the dressing table to brush my hair and repair my lipstick.

"Do you know what he wants?" I asked her.

"I—I think he's upset. But I won't let him send you away, Linda. I promise I won't."

That was hardly encouraging, but I managed a bright smile before I went out of the room.

He waited for me sitting in his big armchair before the library fire. When I came into the room he looked up at me somberly and gestured to the opposite chair, his gaze returning to the flames in the grate. I studied that carved profile, the touch of silver at his temple, the straight, unyielding mouth, and I was further disturbed. Beyond, I could see the closed door to Margot's room.

When he spoke, his voice was low and a little harsh—as though there was an echo of Emory in it. "I'm not sure how to put the things I must say to you."

"You brought me here to this house to help Adria," I reminded him. "But you don't seem pleased with what has happened."

"You have helped her. Perhaps you've helped her in a major way by releasing her from this feeling of guilt that has ridden her ever since her mother's death."

"I hope it's true that I've succeeded. Whether it is or not, remains to be seen."

There was silence again, and I felt a growing gentleness toward him, a new willingness to do whatever he wanted me to. A log fell into the fire, sending sparks aloft, and I was reminded of that other fire I'd watched in Emory's cabin.

"You didn't believe me last night when you accused me of running away from Emory," I said. "Will you believe me now? Will you believe that it was he who ran away from me, and left me lost in the storm?

He raised his head to look directly at me. "How can I possibly believe anything so fantastic as that? I've known Emory all my life. He's part of our family. Why should he try to harm someone I've invited to stay in this house? You might have died in that storm. Are you telling me Emory is capable of murder?"

For an instant I considered blurting out the truth—that Stuart Parrish was my brother. But there was still everything to be learned by staying in this house. Some of its occupants were beginning to crack and I mustn't be sent away now. Besides, I didn't want to leave Julian. I was almost ready to ask for some few crumbs for myself.

"I suppose only Emory can answer that," I said. "But you didn't call me here to talk about him."

"No. I want to apologize to you for the times I've been angry and rude. Perhaps you can understand that I've been under an unbearable strain. You've done a great deal for Adria. You've given her an affection that she seems to return." He still sounded somber, not altogether pleased.

"I understand," I said, though I did not, really. He was a man with scarcely suppressed fires that sometimes threatened and alarmed me. Sometimes he seemed carved of ice, but there was always fire too, just beneath—and I didn't know which I feared the most—the fire or the ice. Yet somehow, unreasonably, I wanted to ease his terrible self-reproach which I couldn't begin to understand.

"I'm afraid you can't possibly know all the ramifications," he went on stiffly. "But thank you for trying. Will you accept my apology?"

The words were flung down, almost like a bitter challenge between us.

"Are you sorry to see your daughter proved innocent?" I asked, my moment of softness toward him vanishing.

Ice was predominant in those cold blue eyes as he looked directly at me. "I don't think you believe that."

"It's hard to know what to believe."

"What you did may have succeeded. It might have proved disastrous."

"No more disastrous than what was already happening to Adria! Perhaps you thought you were trying to help her, but you were only making her think that because you had loved Margot, you could no longer love your daughter."

"That's not true!" The edge of fire bit into his voice.

I went on heedlessly. "You showed it whenever you looked at the child! I've seen it myself in your face. And Adria has been aware of it. Probably from the first, when it came out that she thought she'd sent her mother to her death."

"I was reacting to my own guilt." He regarded me with stony remoteness. "How could I behave naturally with her when I felt that the main fault was mine? Mine because Margot died."

I watched him in sudden dismay, remembering the things Emory had said and Clay too. Things even Julian himself had told me. That it was he who had reached Margot first, that he had every reason to believe that she'd been unfaithful to him, that she'd been making a play for Stuart.

He went on almost as if to himself—as if he searched aloud for answers. "For years she had filled me with nothing but disgust. Long before the accident everything was over between us. I knew she had lovers, that she was insatiable, ruthless. But she was also wary and cunning. She gave me nothing I could use against her. And she held Adria."

I heard him in dread. There was a depth of passionate anger in his voice that frightened me. A man like that might very well—

He broke in on my thoughts. "After the accident everything became worse. She wasn't merely tired of me then—she hated me, blamed me beyond reason for everything that had happened. Yet now I couldn't act against her. I couldn't try to free myself. Because she was helpless. Because I owed her care, if not love. But I'm not blameless. I showed my disgust, my discontent. I could hardly endure living in the same house with her."

His voice died away on the note of self-reproach and I sat listening to him in dread. I didn't want to hear the terrible thing that he might tell me. Not even if it saved my brother.

"I might have given her more during these last years," he said. "My open distaste must have damaged her further. Yet she sought more love affairs, almost under my eyes. She used Adria when she could. She was a constant source of—evil."

And so he had killed her—was that what he meant?

"I can see now that much of the fault was mine. After the accident, I mean. My loathing for her showed when I should have stifled it. So the fault was in me. If Adria had pushed that chair, then that fault would have been mine too. I could see that every time I looked at my daughter."

I relaxed almost imperceptibly. He had not meant that it had been his hand on the chair. Here was a torment such as I'd never imagined. There was a yearning in me to touch him, to offer comfort and belief. I spoke out of my own shock at his words.

"You can't go on feeling like that! You're punishing the wrong person. I don't know anything about you and Margot, but you can't torture yourself like this. Margot must have been more to blame than you. But the real question, the one clear answer you need to search out now is who caused Margot's death. Adria didn't. So who do you think did? Stuart Parrish?"

He moved his head despairingly. "I'm not sure. How can I be? Stuart was like a younger brother to me. I loved him. But I don't know whether he could be trusted."

"I should think he could be trusted not to injure you," I said.

I couldn't bear to watch him any longer, and I jumped up and went to a window where I could look out at the clean, snow-covered world. Behind me Julian was silent. I knew I must not press him further. Yet I spoke without turning around.

"Who took the brakes off Margot's chair? Someone who came into her room from the house? Or did she take them off herself before she went down the ramp and met whoever waited for her below in the yard?"

He stared at me, his face dark, ominous. "Is this your business?"

"I'm part of it now! Because of Emory and what he tried to do last night. Why can't you see that? Why can't you see that he's hiding something? Perhaps he's afraid that I've come upon the true answer. Perhaps that's why he wanted to lose me in the storm last night. Shan's outside now, telling him what happened here in the library with Adria. He's fond of Shan, isn't he?"

He answered only my last question. "He's fond of us all. He's been here all our lives. We were children when we first knew him."

"He had the chance. He was there in the yard. And he was careful not to reach her first down in the ravine."

I had his full attention now, though he did not answer that.

"Clay told me that Emory lied about finding her," I went on. "That it was you who reached her first. But now it's Emory who's concocted some sort of story that's supposed to convict Stuart Parrish. Are you going to stand by and let it happen?"

He seemed too lost in his own torment to notice my

partisanship. He turned his head from side to side as if to escape some intolerable pain.

"Stuart was like the young brother I never had. Yet all the time—with Margot—"

"Do you really believe that? A wild claim by Emory?"

"Emory would give his life for me. If I can't trust him I can trust no one."

"So you let him lie for you? About finding her!" The moment the words were out I was shocked by them. This time I had gone too far—too recklessly far. I had not meant to hurt him.

He had no interest in the flames now. He was staring straight at me, and for an instant I expected a violent outburst. Then, strangely, astonishingly, he began to laugh. The sound was not altogether happy, but it seemed to offer some release. There was unexpected relief for me too. Whoever was to blame for Margot's death, I knew it couldn't be Julian. That he found my accusation so outrageous that he laughed at me was reassuring.

After a moment he rose from his chair. The hand he put on my arm was scarcely gentle, yet he did not hurt me, as Clay had done. He simply marched me to the nearest window where we stood together staring out at snow-laden trees. Not far from the house was a grove of birches, their slender trunks weighted into an arch, with their heads frozen to the ground.

"Ever since the storm stopped during the night," Julian said, "the grooming crews have been out in the ski area. But there may still be some powder left. Not deep powder. Not the eighteen inches you can find in the West after a storm, where your tips disappear as you go down and all you have is your own skill and knowledge. It's a little like flying then, and the snow seems bottomless. Here there won't be more than three or four inches—but it's something. Clean, fresh powder."

His mood had changed completely. He seemed to have put aside his torment, and I wondered where all this was leading.

He tightened his hand on my arm. "Go put on your ski things, Linda. We've had enough of Graystones and insoluble problems. You're coming with me. Leave Adria behind this time."

I suppose I gaped at him, for he gave me a small, impatient shove. "Hurry up!"

This time I responded. He could be wildly mercurial, but his very changes were infectious. I found myself running up those whirling stairs, hurrying as I dressed. Excitement was rising in me, and an eagerness to thrust ugly questions behind me. Perhaps the mountain slopes would clear my mind.

When I went downstairs I found Julian in the hall, working on my skis with wax and a cork.

"You haven't been taking care of these," he said severely. "The edges need sharpening, and there are a few nicks that need attention."

"I haven't really got into skiing this winter," I said apologetically. Usually it had been Stuart who looked after my skis. I didn't care enough to bother myself. In this house, apparently, I would have to reform.

Julian left word with one of the maids that we were going out, but we managed to leave without either Adria or Shan seeing us. The driveway had been plowed, but we did not turn down it. Instead, Julian drove off along another newly cleared road that led away from the back of the property, which I'd never followed before.

We drove between banks of white left by a snow blower

and wound our way between snow-crested evergreens to a place where a long rustic building was the center of the tree farm. Other work buildings and sheds for tractors and jeeps spread out from the main building.

"I wanted to show you this," Julian said.

Trees in every stage of growth stretched away in acres along the valley. In a few places they even edged up the side of the mountain. There were evergreens and deciduous trees and ornamental shrubbery.

We got out of the car and Julian led the way, stamping through deep snow among rows of small evergreens, pointing out the various varieties. As he talked, he came to life as I had never seen him do before, and at first I was more interested in the change in the man who walked beside me than I was in the trees. I had been wrong to think that Julian McCabe had lost touch with life. Here was a Julian fully alive and absorbed in what he talked about. The growth of trees, the reclaiming of forests meant as much to him now as had his skiing in the past.

My own interest began to quicken as I listened and he told me about how wild forests grew, and about the controlled growth practiced on a tree farm. The nursery was more than a commercial venture, since Julian ran a consulting center that drew inquiries from around the country.

I followed between the snowy branches of waist-high blue spruce, and he talked to me over his shoulder.

"Perhaps our most valuable function is our experimental lab, where we're working on the treatment of tree diseases caused by insects and fungus. We're trying to find new methods of treatment, and when we find something sound that gets away from insecticides, we publish our findings around the country."

"I didn't know," I said, "—I never dreamed."

His laugh had a cheerful ring. "The ski slopes aren't all of my life, by any means."

We stamped through snow and grew cold, and Julian seemed not to feel it. In reclaiming trees he had quite evidently reclaimed himself and I felt a surge of happiness and pride in him that surprised me.

When we had walked long enough, he took me into the low wooden building with its gracefully overhanging roof. We stepped into a pine-paneled room, furnished in beige and brown, with a log fire burning at one end, and a half moon of upholstered green bench curved before it. There was no waste of good trees in keeping a fire going, he told me as we walked toward the blaze, since the mountain was cluttered with deadwood, the better for being removed and burned.

Corridors that led to offices and laboratory opened off the main room, and there was a receptionist behind an enclosed desk. She smiled at Julian and picked up a phone as we came in. When we were out of our coats and warming ourselves on the bench before the fire, a girl came from one of the farther rooms, bringing us a tray with a pot of coffee, sugar and cream.

Something had changed between Julian and me. Some current of antagonism that had flowed stubbornly at times had been reversed. We sipped our coffee companionably and pushed away Graystones and all its haunting. But there were other hauntings for me, and Julian was still curious.

"What happened to you, Linda?" he asked as I set down my cup. "What happened to mark your life? It's evident that it's been marked, you know. You give yourself away."

I looked at him uneasily. Part of the marking was because of Stuart's present trouble, and he must not find that out.

"I don't know what you mean," I said vaguely.

"I think you do. You're willing enough to live other people's lives, but you are afraid to have one of your own."

"That isn't true! It's just that—"

He put out a hand and covered mine where it rested on the bench beside me. "You don't have to tell me. I don't want to upset you."

Suddenly I wanted to tell him. I wanted to talk about something I had never dared face. I looked into the flaring of the fire and saw other flames from long ago. Haltingly, I tried to make him see that other fire that roared so fiercely in the night when I had been a young girl of fourteen. I told him of my young brother—though I called him by no name. There had been a pathway down the hall, there had been time to get through to our parents' room—and I had not taken it. I had been afraid. I had brought my brother downstairs and out of the house safely and easily—and had been praised later for my heroism. When there had been none.

"So our parents died," I told Julian starkly. "And it was my fault."

He leaned toward the fire's warmth, still holding my hand. "So all these years you've tormented yourself and been afraid to take anything for you. Because you felt you deserved nothing."

I shivered in the warmth. "I don't know. I tried to put it all away from me, forget it. Not think about it. I did everything I could to make my brother's life happy—to make it up to him."

"Where is he now?"

"He's grown away from me," I answered obliquely. "I shouldn't have told you all this. It's senseless to dump one's troubles on someone else."

"You'll feel better for it," he said. "You can put it in perspective now. If you had gone through the flames to that room where your parents slept, you might not have come out, and your brother might have died too. How you felt afterward was natural, but unreasonable. It's time you stopped holding life away."

I clung to his hand tightly for a moment, and then let it go.

"Thank you," I said. It was as though a weight was slipping away from me, ceasing to press me down. And I had Julian McCabe to thank.

He smiled at me and drew me up from the bench. The ski slopes waited and we went back to the car. We drove along the road we'd followed until it opened into the Graystones' drive, and we turned toward the lodge.

Clay was out in his own rig, clearing the drive. I waved to him as we drove past and he stared in surprise. I wondered if he knew what had happened to me after I left the lodge last night. Emory, at least, was nowhere around, probably still working on the far side of Graystones. Or talking to Shan. Briefly a concern for that conferring flashed through my mind, but I thrust it aside.

Snowplows had already been through on the roads, and traffic was stirring. Everywhere there was evidence of people digging out after the storm, and the world was glorious with its covering of clean white.

When we reached the base lodge, there were few cars around, and we parked not far from the main door. I went with Julian while he got me a chair lift ticket.

We had said very little on the drive, but our mood remained close, companionable, and I felt happier than I had for a long time.

Several of the runs were closed, while the cats worked on them, packing the snow and making it usable for the average skier who didn't care for loose powder. But there was still powder on the steepest slope and that was where Julian was taking me. Strangely, I couldn't have cared less. I had been pulled so taut earlier that the continuing release of tension was all I cared about. If I broke my neck in the process of unwinding it no longer seemed to matter very much. I had a sense of trusting Julian as an expert skier. He would look out for me. He would ask nothing of me that I couldn't manage.

We rode the chair to the top, above a transformed world. Even the scraggly pines at the top of the mountain were frosted and beautiful, and the day was marvelously clear, the sky swept clean of clouds, and colored a beautiful winter blue. I followed Julian down the ramp at the top platform without worrying about getting off, and he smiled at me.

"You were a bit scared when you came up here last time, but you're not today," he said.

"Euphoria," I admitted. "I suppose I had my wits about me last time. Today I'm merely reacting. Not thinking, not feeling. Perhaps I've nothing left to think and feel with. For now, that's all I want—freedom."

He looked as though he understood. Under the brilliant light his dark hair had a shine to it, the lines of his face seemed to have lifted, and his eyes were a deeper blue than ever. He was Julian McCabe now. I sensed his full appeal, sensed danger—and didn't care.

We skated along the top and stopped near the beginning of Devil's Drop. We had the mountain to ourselves. No one else had come up the lift ahead of us.

We could see all the world up here and we stood for a few moments responding to the great view. We could see the break in the long level range of the Blue Mountain that was the Delaware Water Gap, with the river snaking between precipitous cliffs. The countryside stretched out below us with its hills and dark masses of forest growth, its lakes and villages and highways. We could even glimpse a stretch of Route 80 with cars whipping past before the hills swallowed them.

Immediately below lay that fresh powder—and the way down. No one had taken this slope today and the course lay unmarked, awaiting our skis. It was an intoxicating feeling to be the first ones down. I looked at the steep white trail winding broadly between hummocks of pine as if it were perfectly in my power to go skiing down it with the best of them. My euphoria had lasted.

"It's easier to ski a steep slope than a gentle one," Julian told me. "You'll go faster and it will be easier to turn your skis. You won't need to edge as much in powder. Don't look all the way down, and don't lean into the mountain or your feet will go off without you. Though you can lean back a little more with powder. I'll go first and all you need to do is follow me and do what I do. I've seen you ski and you're perfectly competent. All you need is to develop some confidence."

At the moment I seemed to have all the confidence in the world, and I could even relax my muscles—which is the skier's answer to everything. When you're relaxed the knees and ankles absorb the bumps and stress. Julian pushed off ahead of me, and I followed without hesitation. I'd never gone so fast, but I was in control. Blown snow packs unevenly and the trail had a different feel—but I could sense it as I went down. The moguls were my friends and they helped me to turn. Julian's tall green figure flew ahead, his skis smoking, taking the course with utter grace, and I imitated him, giddily confident. It was easy. It was lovely. I'd never skied like this with Stuart. Everything clicked, just as they told me it would back in school. In moments we were schussing out upon the level near the base lodge and I was laughing in triumph.

"I did it! I did it! It was wonderful! Oh, do let's go up again."

He smiled at me and I knew we had both relaxed and thrust everything except the ski trails out of our minds.

"So now you're hooked," he said. "You'll never recover, you know. You've been a skeptic, but now the slopes have got you for good."

I didn't care. Someday I'd ski with Stuart like this. I'd show my brother what I could do. Of course Stuart would be freed. There would never been any trial. Ugliness couldn't exist in this beautiful clear world.

So we went up again and up again. And when I'd tired a little, we went inside to warm up and sat at our same table next to the window, where the red carpet glowed under our feet, and we could watch the slopes and drink glühwein. I was a little fearful at first that all the haunting would return the moment we were off the slopes, but it did not. There was a comradeship between us, born of the snow and the slopes— and of that earlier time before the fire—and we were warm friends. I liked him a great deal, and I had the feeling that he liked me, and that we enjoyed being together away from Graystones. There was something more than liking. I knew that as well—but it must be given time. I was glad I'd left Margot's Ullr safely hidden away beneath lingerie in a drawer. There must be a time of reckoning, a time when I would tell him the truth, but I wanted nothing to distract Julian now from this new, lovely feeling that grew between us.

The morning had to come to an end, however. We were expected at Graystones for lunch, and there was nothing to do but go back. Back to where tensions awaited us and could not be escaped. Nevertheless, I continued to feel happy all the way home, and luncheon in the apple-green dining room was not as gloom-invaded as I'd feared. Adria was cheerful, and so was I—a little of my euphoria lasting.

It grew partly from my introduction to the trees that were the other side of Julian's life, and the exhilarating experience on the slopes. Partly from the time I'd spent afterward with Julian, when there'd been a new liking and respect between us. Perhaps even a tenuous something more. Once during lunch I caught his gaze upon me almost tenderly, and I warmed in response. All the warnings I'd heard about Julian McCabe's appeal for women were lost on me—most happily lost. There was a fragile beginning between us, and I wanted nothing to break the spell.

Julian too seemed relaxed, and much less hag-ridden, and we carried off the meal with cheerful conversation. Only Shan was scarcely there. She seemed to have retreated into her other world where she was hardly conscious of what went on in the real world around her. Whatever her conference with Emory had been about, she had retreated from that too, never mentioning it. Only once did she emerge from her distant place and speak directly to me.

"There's going to be a beautiful sunset tonight, Linda. You must be sure and watch it from the top of the tower."

Julian looked skeptical. "How can you tell this early? Unless some clouds blow up there'll be nothing to catch the colors at sunset."

"There will be clouds," said Shan serenely. "Go up to the tower at sunset, Linda."

Julian refrained from snorting, but I knew he disliked these conceits of Shan's. While we were eating our dessert, he threw his own bombshell into our quiet.

"I'm going out for a while this afternoon," he said. "I'm going to drive into town and arrange to see Stuart Parrish."

Even Shan heard him, and I must have gasped, for she glanced at me before she spoke to her brother.

"Are you finally going to do something about Stuart?"

"I'm going to talk to him. I'm going to give him a chance to tell me what happened as he sees it."

I felt relieved and wonderfully hopeful. It was I who had managed this for Stuart. All my sniping at Julian had finally taken effect. But I did not dare betray my sense of relief. I concentrated on caramel custard and made no comment. But that was wrong too.

"I thought you'd be pleased," Julian said to me. "You've been accusing me of unfairness."

"I'm glad you're giving Stuart Parrish a chance," I told him. "After all, you were his sponsor and it seems rather strange that you've never interested yourself in him. Perhaps he deserves more consideration."

Shan looked as though she were about to say something, then changed her mind. An odd restraint lay suddenly upon us, and I knew that Julian felt it. After lunch he went off alone without speaking to any of us, and I heard him start his car and drive away. I think I said a small prayer then for Stuart and for Julian.

When he'd gone, I asked Adria to bring her schoolbooks to the drawing room, where we'd spend some time on lessons. She was slightly rebellious, since by now she knew I'd gone skiing with her father, leaving her behind. But it was not an open rebellion, and I went upstairs to my room for my own notebook and pen.

While I was there, something prompted me to lift the pile of lingerie in the dresser drawer and look beneath it. The silver Ullr was gone. I searched rapidly and in some dismay. Whatever happened, I didn't want it to fall into other hands. But it was clearly not in the drawer. I picked up my things and went downstairs to join Adria in the drawing room.

XIII

The first part of the afternoon went by uneventfully. Adria applied herself more willingly to lessons than I'd expected, and I knew she felt a growing affection toward me, and an over-all relief that was having its effect. For the first time, she wanted to please me.

It was I who had difficulty concentrating, because my thoughts were forever wandering toward the scene that was being enacted between Julian and Stuart. If only something good would come of their meeting. If only something of their old rapport could be re-established between Julian and my brother.

More than once I thought fearfully of the chance that Stuart might tell Julian who I was. I didn't want that to happen yet. Not when this tenuous feeling was beginning between Julian and me. Not when this new sensitivity I felt toward him, and suspected that he felt toward me, was in its early, wary stage, where the slightest alarm might dissipate it like mist. It needed time to grow, to put down roots, to develop into something strong and sure. Something strong enough to stand the truth which I must eventually tell him. I couldn't quite believe in it, even now, and it frightened me a little because I was sure that if Julian learned my identity too soon, it would be over before it had begun. Perhaps I was farther into it than he—dangerously far.

"You're not paying attention, Linda," Adria said plaintively.

I brought my thoughts back to her and apologized. I asked her then if she knew what had happened to the silver Ullr on a chain that I had put away in a drawer.

She shook her head. "I don't know. Is it gone? I told Shan about it before—before we tried Margot's chair. Perhaps she took it."

The thought was disquieting, but I let it go for now, and this time I paid attention to Adria's reciting—even though part of me was alert and listening—for Julian's return. When I heard his car on the drive, I set Adria some sums to do, told her I'd return soon, and went out to the front hall. I was there, waiting, when Julian came in the door.

Strain showed in his face, but I couldn't tell what it meant. He saw me waiting and smiled a bit ruefully.

"Nothing's simple," he said. "I think I believe everything that Stuart's told me. It was painful to see him in that place. When he gets out on bail I'm going to bring him here for a time and give him my support, if he'll accept it. He's been hurt by my neglect and he put up barriers against me at first."

I tried to keep my elation from showing—and my worry. It was wonderful that they were at least partly reconciled, and that Stuart was coming here. But this also meant that the truth about me must be told before he came. Obviously, Stuart had said nothing to Julian as yet.

"The difficulty now will be to pull Emory off the course he's chosen," Julian said.

"And to find out why he chose it," I said softly.

Julian nodded reluctant agreement. "I'll go out and have a talk with him now. If Stuart is innocent, then the whole question must be thrown open again." He closed his eyes for a moment, looking a little sick, and I knew he was thinking of the possibilities which remained—perhaps rejecting them all.

"Think about Emory," I said. "Stop seeing him as the old family retainer, or whatever, and really look at what he's been doing, the lies he's told—all that fabrication. About Stuart. About me."

I could sense his stiffening against me. He went up the stairs, leaving me to realize how very tenuous those moments in the ski area had been. Perhaps the mist had already carried them away as far as Julian was concerned. I felt sore and unhappy when I went back to Adria in the drawing room.

For the rest of the afternoon I saw nothing more of Julian. Nor was Shan about. Adria and I worked beside the fire until it was nearly time for me to go to the lodge. This afternoon I would take my own car and have it there to drive back after dark. That way I would take no chances. I wanted to see Clay again and find out what he thought of what had happened to me in the storm. In fact, there was a sudden eagerness in me to talk to Clay. He had been more open with me than anyone else, though he made me angry at times.

But first there was something else I would do. There was still Shan's mysterious sunset to be looked into, and I didn't mean to let her down. For some reason she had wanted me to go to the tower gallery, and I wouldn't disappoint her.

I put on my after-ski clothes and shaggy boots, and went up the tower stairs. The house was very still. Julian had gone out again—to see Emory?—and he'd not yet returned, and Adria was still out behind the house, busy with the snowman she was building. Shan I had not seen since lunchtime. I felt a little amused as I climbed the stairs, already suspecting what I might find in the tower. But there were a few surprises.

For one thing, the door to the top room was bolted on the stair side, and I paused to puzzle over this. It was not a new bolt, for the brass was dull, and I wondered why anyone would have had a bolt set upon a cul-de-sac like the tower. What could anyone want to shut in up there? Unless, I thought whimsically, it was ghosts. With Shan, that was the likely answer.

However, I didn't hesitate to slide back the bolt and pull the door open. The sight that awaited me was partly what I expected. Cinnabar was there, of course, and he did not look pleased about having been shut into the tower. But there was a difference in him this time. Someone had taken the trouble to wind a silver chain several times about his neck, so that a medallion hung beneath his chin. It was Margot's Ullr, missing from my drawer.

What it meant I wasn't sure, but I knew this was not one of Adria's pranks. If Shan had taken the medallion, it might very well mean that my secret would now be exposed to Julian—after this small delay while she played a trick upon me with the great orange cat.

I was sharply aware of the cold air of the tower. Though all the windows were closed, it was like being outdoors. I had not worn my coat, but I wouldn't stay here long. First, though,

236

I must give my attention to Cinnabar and the retrieving of the Ullr.

The cat had edged away from me, across the circular floor of the gallery, and was watching me balefully from beneath one of the windows. I spoke to him quietly.

"It's about time we came to terms, Cinnabar—you and I. We've been glaring at each other ever since I came to Graystones. I wonder if we could make friends? For one thing, I'd like my medallion back."

His ears pricked up at the sound of my voice, and the tip of his tail twitched with displeasure. I took another step into the tower, drawing the door shut behind me so he could not escape. He moved like a flash of light, streaking toward the door, but he was too late, and he skidded to a stop against the closed panel.

"You see?" I said. "Unless you're willing to make friends, how are you going to get out of here? That is, unless you really can walk through closed doors."

He settled himself before the door and set up a pained yowling. Nothing happened. I turned my back on him and went to look out one of the windows to see if there really was any prospect of a sunset. The sky was clear, and though a beginning pinkness could be seen over the treetops, there were no streaks of cloud to spread the reflection of color. I was not surprised. I'd suspected Shan of some secret purpose, and I was not yet alarmed.

From this vantage point, I could look down upon the front driveway with its piled banks of snow, to the place where I'd left my car. Julian had dug it out for me earlier and I would have no trouble using it. But what I saw made me search hastily for the window latch. Emory Ault was down there beside my car, bending over a rear tire. I could not open the window. Apparently they had all been sealed shut, and I pounded on the glass and shouted at him. If he heard me he did not look up, and a few moments later he walked away around the end of the house, out of my sight.

I had no wish now to stay and play games with Cinnabar. I distrusted Emory utterly, and I wanted to get downstairs and see what damage he might have perpetrated. Like Cinnabar, I streaked toward the tower door, and like the cat I was too late. The sliding of the bolt made only a slight click, and the footsteps that stole down the stairs were soft. But the evidence was clear. I had been locked into the tower.

It couldn't be serious, of course. I only needed to shout, and someone would come to let me out. I began to pound indignantly on the door, and to call out as loudly as I could. The uproar alarmed Cinnabar, and he sprang away across the tower, his fur bristling, his claws unsheathed.

Again nothing happened. No one answered my outcry either from within the house or from outside. I remembered uneasily that Graystones was built of stone, and that the tower with its enclosed stairs was really outside the main stone wall. Solid wooden doors closed off every floor from the drafty stairs, and it was possible that the noise I was making could not penetrate. Up here I was on a level with the rooftop, and in the winter all the downstairs windows would be closed, so that sound could not carry through from outside.

Once more I searched the driveway, but there was no one to be seen. If Adria was still with her snowman, she would be far away on the other side of this thick house. I tried banging on the windows again, but that helped no more than pounding on the door. The situation was thoroughly ridiculous, and of course not permanent, but the tower was cold, and likely to grow colder with the setting of the sun in the early winter dark. My sweater and after-ski pants weren't adequate, though the reindeer boots helped warm my feet, at least.

"What do we do now?" I asked Cinnabar.

He regarded me with distaste, and as I marched about the tower flapping my arms to keep warm, he continued to retreat from me, not trusting me at all.

It occurred to me that my one best hope was for someone to start up or downstairs and thus step into the tower. If that happened, I could surely make myself heard. I took up my post beside the door, with my ear pressed against the wood, listening for the slightest sound. The house had never seemed more silent. Now and then I pounded on the door—with no more results than before.

Outdoors the faint winter pink in the sky was turning gray, and across the drive the hemlocks were thick and black with shadow. I was cold, cold, cold. I moved my arms and jogged around the tower, pausing now and then to listen at the door, continually making as much noise as I could. Clay would be wondering by now what had happened to me, but he wouldn't think it important enough to investigate.

Once, for want of anything else to do, I tried to retrieve the medallion from Cinnabar. But I had convinced him that I was quite wild and he wouldn't come near me. I had been able to make friends with ordinary cats easily enough in my life, but with this one I'd got off on a wrong foot from the very first. In the thickening dusk the medallion caught what light there was, so that Ullr's face glinted in the gloom grinning at me. He was the god of skiing and helped not at all with someone locked in a Norman tower.

When the end of imprisonment came, it happened suddenly. I heard steps on the stairs, the bolt was drawn back and the door flung open. Light from the lower tower flooded my prison, and I could see Julian and Shan and Adria on the stairs, looking at me curiously. All three wore outdoor clothes and had evidently just come in.

"What happened?" Julian asked. "Adria said our house ghost was pounding down the door in the tower. How did you happen to be locked in up here?"

"Ask Shan," I said, and went shivering down the stairs past them.

"There's Cinnabar!" Adria cried. "She was locked into the tower too."

Even I turned to look at Cinnabar, remembering the medallion. The big cat stepped delicately, cautiously across the tower floor, having lost his trust in all humans, and was about to streak past us, when Adria caught him up in her arms.

"Look!" she cried. "Look what Cinnabar is wearing!"

I crossed my arms about my shivering body and looked only at Julian. He reached out to unwind the chain from about the cat's neck. Then he held out the Ullr to me.

"This is yours, I believe?"

"Hers!" Shan was scornful. "Look at it carefully, Julian. You know who it belonged to. Look for the markings that diamond on the back has scratched out! Margot gave it to Stuart—and who would Stuart give it to but his sister?"

He didn't need to turn the medallion over. Perhaps he'd known the first time he saw the Ullr in my possession, but had refused to believe the truth. He was still holding it out to me, and I had to take it from him. I saw the dislike in his eyes—the disgust for my falsehoods, my masquerade. For the first time I could see it all through his viewpoint as I'd refused to do before. I would rather have him burst into anger and dismiss me furiously from the house than to look at me like that. Coldly, he went down the stairs and disappeared through the lower door.

Adria understood none of this, and she looked from Shan to me and back again, beginning to stammer her questions. Shan spoke to her sweetly.

"I'm sorry to tell you this, Adria dear, but Linda is Stuart Parrish's sister. The sister of the man who pushed Margot's chair down the ramp. She has only been pretending to be our friend. I'm afraid your father is very disappointed in her."

Adria cried out softly and ran down to the second floor, pushed open the door and let it bang shut behind her. Shan stood on the steps above me laughing gently—her dryad's laugh. But she had the full ability of the human to destroy and demolish, and she had used it with an almost fearsome pleasure.

There was nothing I could say to any of them. Not even to Shan, who had planned this exposure in her own dramatic way. I walked woodenly down the stairs to the second-floor door, and followed Adria through it. The door to her room was closed, and I knew there was nothing I could say to her now. Tomorrow, perhaps—if I could get her to listen.

In my room I put on my parka and gloves. Then I went downstairs. Like Adria's door, the door to the library was closed, and I knew Julian was in there. While I stood hesitating, he opened the door a crack and stared at me, his eyes chill, his dark brows drawn down. I could neither run nor stand there, and I took an unwilling step toward him. He pushed the door open, waving me into the room. I walked past him, still unwilling, wanting only to escape the look in his eyes, the condemnation which I so richly deserved.

In the room I did not sit down, and he did not ask me to. He came to stand beside me where I faced the fire.

"Perhaps you've some explanation for me?" he said grimly.

I could not look at him. "I should think the explanation is obvious. I wanted to help Stuart. I've never believed he was guilty, and that means someone else is. No one was really investigating. I thought I could find something out."

"And have you?"

"Very little. But I've thought you should be doing more and—"

"What about the injury to Adria? Haven't you thought of that?"

I looked at him blankly. "What do you mean?"

"You've come here and gained her confidence, her affection. And now she must know who you are and that you've been falsifying yourself with all of us. But especially with her."

"That's not true! I'd like to talk to her when she's willing to listen to me. I think I can—"

"Fool her all over again?"

Blood was flowing in my veins again. Angry blood. "I've never wanted to fool anyone! Especially not Adria. I was caught and couldn't help myself. But I haven't falsified my feeling for her. There are times when I've put her good ahead of Stuart's. Don't you think it would have been an easy out to believe that she had pushed that chair? But I didn't believe it, and I had to disprove it."

His gaze dropped from mine for the first time, and he took a quick, angry turn about the room. His face had a flushed look and his eyes were bright.

"I would have said you'd be trustworthy under any circumstances," he flung out at me. "I believed in you—I liked you."

By this time I was too angry myself to be cautious. "What difference does that make if you can't trust me now? You've liked a great many women. One more or less hardly makes any difference. I've heard the stories about you. Perhaps I've some right to be angry too. Perhaps I might have expected greater understanding from you, greater trust. Yes—trust. I've pretended, yes. Because I couldn't help myself, once I'd chosen this course. But I've never let you down, never injured anyone here in any way."

He paused beside a window and turned to stare at me. But I wouldn't wait to be torn apart again. I flung away from him and ran toward the door, and into the hall. When I stopped to pull on my boots, he made no move to come after me. I was still shaking as I let myself out the front door and crossed the drive to my car. There was only one place for me to go right now, and that was to the lodge. I needed Clay to listen to me. He might not always approve of me, but he would listen. And he already knew who I was.

I got into the car, started the engine, and began to back in order to turn around on the drive. The action of one rear wheel was unmistakable. I had forgotten that I'd seen Emory near the car. When I got out and went to the right rear tire, I found what I expected. It was flat. Not because someone had let out the air, but because it had been slashed with a knife. I could just make out the cuts in the dim light, and I could feel them under my fingers. So that was that.

Without really caring very much one way or another, I began to follow the drive the long way around toward the lodge, on foot. This evening there was a waxing moon and the way was not fully dark. The short-cut path would still be filled with snow, so I had to take the drive. As I rounded the first turn, I saw the light of Emory's cabin off through the trees. How close I had been to safety during the blizzard, without knowing it. But there was no storm tonight. I had no need to feel afraid. Especially, since I could see a figure cross before a window of the hut. Emory was there inside. He was not out looking for me.

Something drew me toward the cabin, and I stopped behind a tree to watch the square of light that was a window.

Someone else was in there with Emory. I saw the movement of a second shadow, and then Shan crossed the room toward him. I stole closer, wishing I could hear, but their voices did not reach me. When I was near enough to the window, I could see that Shan appeared to be pleading with him. Her back was toward me, but I could see Emory's angry face.

He was waving a folded sheet of paper at Shan. She tried to snatch at it, but he held it away and strode toward the wood-burning stove. But before he could take off the lid and drop the paper into the fire, she hurled herself upon him and pushed him away from the stove. Slight as she was, he fell back before her attack, the paper still in his hand. Again Shan seemed to plead with him, and this time he shrugged and dropped the folded sheet into a steel strongbox that stood on the table. Then he got into his parka, took his skis from their wall rack and came toward the door.

I ducked around the corner of the house, hoping he wouldn't see my tracks when he came outside. Fortunately by now the snow had been chopped up with footprints, and he seemed not to notice mine. Peering around the corner, I saw him go stalking toward his car, with his ski poles and his skis over his shoulder, leaving Shan behind. The door banged, and I knew she was in the hut alone. Once more I had to see what was happening and I moved to a window.

If ever I had seen a woman who looked terrified, she was one. Her face was pale in lamplight and drawn as if in pain. After a moment in which she stared fixedly at the door through which Emory had gone, she seemed to fling herself into action. She reached into the strongbox and drew out the folded sheet of paper they had quarreled about. She thrust it into her jacket pocket and ran out of the house. I stood well back in shadow and watched her.

I heard the sound of Emory's car, and so did Shan. We

both watched through the trees as he drove off toward the road. Shan stood for a moment staring after the car. Then she moved and there was nothing drifting and unfocused about her now. Every line of her body showed purpose as she ran toward Graystones. I knew I had to follow her. I had to find out what was going on.

Such urgency winged her feet, however, that she was out of sight by the time I reached the house. I stood uncertainly in hemlock shadow and watched for a moment. I wasn't sure whether she had gone for her own car, or if she'd entered the house. Lights showed me the library on one hand, and the dining room across the hall. But I couldn't see all of the library, and there was only a maid in the dining room, setting the table for dinner.

Then my eye caught movement on the lighted tower stairs and I saw Shan running up to the second floor. She vanished through the hall door, but her room was at the back of the house and I didn't know whether that was where she had gone. I waited for a few moments longer, and as I was about to give up, a reflection of light fell upon the trees at one end of the house. I went to where I could view one of the attic windows that was set into the end gable. I could see Shan's dim figure moving about in those high recesses, and I wondered what on earth she could be doing up there.

Whatever it was didn't take her long. In a moment the light went out and she reappeared in the tower, running down the stairs. This time she hurried out the front door and went toward the garages at the back. In moments she had backed her car out, turned around and was off at high speed down the curving drive. Like Emory, she carried her skis in the rack on top of the car.

Julian must have heard the sound of squealing wheels, for he came to the library window and looked out. Well hidden in my clump of hemlock, I looked at him as if he were miles away—looked at him and knew how lost he was to me. What stabbed through me in that moment was no longer tenuous and uncertain. I was no longer angry. Where there had always seemed time to draw back before, that time was now past. I was committed—and lost. Perhaps Stuart was lost too, when it came to receiving any help from Julian. Perhaps Julian would be so angry with me that he would refuse to do anything for my brother—and that would be my fault. So that somehow I had failed them both.

I knew how much I needed counseling, and there was only one person to turn to. I stole through the trees until I could reach the drive at a point out of sight of the house. Then I hurried desperately toward the lodge.

Dinner was already in progress, but Clay had eaten earlier, and he was alone in his office. I flung myself into the chair across from his desk without taking off my things, out of breath and thoroughly distraught. He looked at me for a moment without surprise and then knelt to pull off my boots, and helped me out of my parka. When I started to talk, he listened to me, gave me all his attention while I told him everything that had happened since I'd left the lodge last night.

Once when I came to a break, he asked if I'd had anything to eat for dinner, and when I said I couldn't eat, he went to the kitchen and brought me back a bowl of hot oyster stew and crackers. This I could manage, and I ate the stew while I finished my story, including in it the things that had happened most recently—my being locked in the tower, Julian learning who I was, and the strange scene in which Emory had rushed off in his car taking his skis, and Shan had gone up to the attic, and then had sped off in her own car, also carrying skis.

"Why?" I demanded of Clay. "Why should those two go dashing off with skis at this time of the evening—as though something desperate was happening?"

He could only shake his head. "It will work out," he assured me. "When they come home, we'll know. Julian saw Shan leaving—he'll ask her."

"I feel awfully queer," I said. "As if something was going to happen. Something terrible."

He came around the desk and took my cold hands into his. "I don't doubt that you're terrified after all that's occurred. You don't need to play hostess tonight. If you like you can have your room upstairs and stay there. Why not go to bed now and relax? I can give you a sleeping pill, if you like. Tomorrow you can begin to work things out. Or perhaps they'll work themselves out."

I studied his bearded face with the wide cheekbones and mouth, the gray eyes that watched me with kindness and sympathy. I had the feeling that Clay was good. He might make his own rules in some ways—he might even be trying to protect someone, and he might have been angry with me at times for this very reason, but he was solid, he was good. He would never hurt me.

"Sometimes I think you know a lot more than you're telling," I said.

He gave my hands a little squeeze and dropped them, his look grave, perhaps a little remote, and I knew there were matters I could not push with him. He would befriend me, help me, lend a listening ear. But there was a barrier I must not pass. Nevertheless, I had to ask another question.

"What is Shan up to? I know she feels possessive toward Adria and jealous of me, but I think it's more than that. I have a feeling that I'm almost onto something."

"That may be. Shan has something on her mind. I'd like to know what it is myself."

His concern for her was real, but I had no time for it now.

"Why has she set herself against me? Why should she try to torment me in so many petty ways?"

"Be glad they're petty," he told me. "Be glad she's not like Margot. When Margot crashed she wanted to take the world with her. Now then—suppose you go up to your room and get some rest."

I shook my head. "I'm all right now. I feel better. And there's nothing to frighten me here. It will be good for me to move around and talk to your guests. But I'll need to go back to the house afterwards. There's too much hanging fire there. I'm worried because Julian may decide against Stuart —thanks to me."

"Julian's not like that. He may throw you out"—Clay smiled wryly—"but I don't think he'll take his anger with you out on Stuart. He'll probably guess that your coming here was your doing, not Stuart's."

Through the office door I could hear guests coming in from the dining room, and I stood up. "I'll go out there now. And thank you, Clay. Thank you for listening—and for everything."

"I'm afraid I haven't done much good."

"You've done a great deal of good. I don't feel so frantic now. Clay, I haven't read your story yet. Too much has been happening. But I will soon."

He shrugged. "Take your time. A writer learns not to wait around breathlessly for an opinion. Don't worry about getting back to the house tonight. If you must go I'll take you. And, Linda—I'm glad you've come here. Perhaps you're the catalyst we've needed. Perhaps you're dangerous to have about, but I think you're causing something to happen—to come out in the open. We've needed that."

I turned away from the warmth in his eyes. He still belonged to Shan, while I—I belonged to a Julian who certainly didn't want me.

I went out without answering him, to move among the guests. This, I realized suddenly, was the weekend Friday night. Events had moved so quickly since I'd come to Juniper Lodge that I'd lost all track of time. There could be days in a life when events were so closely packed that you lived a lifetime in their few hours.

Surely next week Stuart would be out on bail, and he'd come to Graystones. Then he would be able to help me—if Julian allowed me to stay. All the answers might very well lie with Emory, as Stuart had claimed all along. With Stuart here, perhaps Julian could be drawn into a real search for the truth. Except that I had the strange and growing feeling that no one at Graystones truly wanted to know the truth. Because they were afraid of it? Afraid of what might happen to someone they loved and wanted to protect?

I was more than a little absent-minded that evening. I found myself catching words and phrases when people talked to me, without really concentrating on their meaning. At least the weekend crowd was large enough so that they mostly amused themselves. The editor from Connecticut had come with his combo and they were keeping everything on the same attractive informal plane—singing their own songs, getting the group to join in.

I don't know when it was that I realized Clay was no longer in evidence. I needed to relay a question which had been asked me by a guest, but he was nowhere in the lounge. I tried his empty office, and then went out to the kitchen where the help was finishing up. No one knew where he'd gone, no one had seen him, and he'd left no word.

I looked in the rear vestibule where outdoor things were hung, and saw that his jacket and boots were gone. I flung on my parka and dashed outside along the snow walk that led to where he kept his car. It too was gone. Whether he'd carried his skis with him or not, I didn't know, but I had the feeling that Clay too had driven off to the slopes to see what was happening with Emory and Shan. In a way, I was glad of that. When he came back he would surely have a few answers.

The combo was playing, and the guests were doing fine on their own. I went out to the kitchen and made myself a sandwich, suddenly hungry, and while I ate I talked with the boy who was taking dishes out of the big washer and stacking them for tomorrow's use.

"Have you ever gone skiing at night over in the area?" I asked.

He grinned at me, ready any time to talk about skiing. "Sure. Who hasn't?"

"I haven't," I said. "What's it like?"

He shrugged, clattering dishes. "There're lights on all the trails. And it's colder—and maybe quieter. You feel—sort of alone when you go down the slopes at night."

"Is it more dangerous?"

"Not if you take care. The light's not as bright, of course, as by day. But sometimes there's a moon. Like tonight."

I finished the sandwich and went back to my duties. I didn't know why uneasiness had begun to grow in me, but I felt increasingly jittery, and when the phone rang in Clay's office, I ran toward it. It rang three times before I got through the lounge and had the door closed behind me. When I picked up the receiver my hand was shaking.

"Hello, Linda?" That was Clay's voice, and I felt an immediate and unjustified relief.

"Yes!" I cried. "Why didn't you let me know you were going out?"

"Don't waste time on questions," he said curtly. "There's been an accident on the slopes. A bad one. Emory Ault. He's been killed in a fall. Ski Patrol is going down for him now. I've phoned Julian and he's coming out right away. But he wants you at the house—to stay with Adria. Otherwise Adria will be alone. Shan's at the base lodge. Will you hurry? I'm sorry I can't get you back to the house, but you'll be all right—now. I've got to go, Linda. Good-by."

He hung up and I stood staring at the phone for a moment before I put the receiver back. Emory—dead? Did that mean the end of all our troubles? Did that mean they'd now let Stuart go—because the prosecution's main witness could no longer testify? There was no telling. It would depend on the evidence they'd collected. But I knew what Clay had meant—that I'd be all right *now*—because Emory was gone. It was hard to believe that he could have fallen to his death. Though the fact had just been given me, I found it hard to accept. In his sixties Emory had been more alive than many who were younger.

I returned to the lounge and spoke to a man who was a long-time guest and knew how things ran better than I did. He agreed to take charge if there was any need—keep the fire going and the guests unalarmed. I had to tell him there'd been an accident and that Clay had to stay away, but he asked no difficult questions, and I hurried into my things and started back to the house.

This time I took the short cut, in spite of deep snow. I couldn't endure the delay of the drive. Sometimes I went into snow over my boot tops, but I didn't care, and I managed to plow through in better time than I could ordinarily have managed. Lights were on in the library and in Adria's room upstairs. I went in to Julian at once.

He was waiting for me, ready to leave, and he looked a little gray. His eyes told me that I meant nothing personal to him at all—I was simply someone who worked for him, and he gave me directions curtly. Adria was still awake. He'd told her he must go out and that I would be here to stay with her. He hadn't told her Emory was dead. Let that wait until morning.

Then he was gone, and I stood at the window watching his car out of sight down the drive, before running upstairs to Adria.

She was sitting up in bed, reading a book, and when I came through her open door I saw that she had been crying. She regarded me coolly, distantly. I had lost Adria too, now that she knew who I was. Any earlier sympathy she might have felt for Stuart was gone, and I knew Shan had been getting her insidious work in again.

"Why did everybody rush off?" Adria asked.

I sat down in a chair beside her bed, feeling breathless and upset. "I think something's happened over at the area. I expect we'll find out tomorrow."

"An accident, probably," she said darkly. "They happen every once in a while. Mostly it's skiers who get reckless and think they're better than they are. My father says it's terribly important to be in control and not take silly chances."

I nodded without speaking. Emory! Emory, who was an expert, had fallen to his death. Enough of an expert to have taught Julian McCabe and Stuart Parrish. I felt cold and increasingly frightened.

Adria seemed to dismiss my presence and returned to the

pages of her book. Once I asked her what she was reading, and she mumbled at me, clearly annoyed by the interruption. After a while I got up and looked out the window, but moonlight showed nothing stirring, and from here I could not see the lights that must still burn in Emory's hut, waiting for someone who would never return.

I needed something to read myself, and I told Adria I'd be right back.

"You don't have to stay with me," she said, sounding as curt as her father.

I paid no attention, but went to my room and took the envelope containing Clay's story out of my dresser drawer. Perhaps his words could distract me in these dreadful moments of marking time. Because no matter what I told myself, I did not think anything had ended. Something terrible had happened out on the slopes tonight. Though I didn't understand what it was, I had the strong conviction that when I knew what had occurred everything would be worse than ever.

I settled down in a chair not far from Adria's bed and opened Clay's manuscript to the first page. This was a carbon copy, and I couldn't tell whether it had ever appeared in print or not.

He wrote well—as I already knew from the article he had done about Graystones—and the mystery story caught my interest at once. Even if I hadn't known Clay, it would have held me, but now it held me doubly because I felt I knew some of the characters. The victim was a woman skier, based, I could guess, on Margot. The house in which she lived was a disguised Graystones, and she was found dead in the attic of the house. She had gone there with the intent to hide something, and had apparently accomplished her purpose before she was felled with a blow from a mysterious attacker. The murderer was a young man who had been seeking her favors and been repulsed by her. Based on Stuart?

Suddenly I could read no more, and I felt an unexpected anger against Clay. He had given me this story deliberately, for a purpose. Yet in the past he had always seemed sympathetic toward Stuart, and he had treated me with kindness and consideration. So why—this? I knew now that it had never been published. He wouldn't have dared because of Julian's wrath if he ever saw it in print. The next time I saw Clay I would give back his story and demand to know what he meant.

"What are you so mad about?" Adria asked, and I saw that she was watching me over the top of her book.

"I'm just—worried," I told her.

"Because your brother killed my mother?"

"He didn't do anything of the sort," I told her sharply.

"Shan says if he did we shouldn't blame him too much."

I had no answer for that, and my hands were shaking as I folded the manuscript pages and replaced them in the envelope.

"It's time for you to go to sleep now. Put your book away and I'll turn out the light."

"Aren't you going to stay with me while I sleep?"

"Of course not. You don't have dreams any more. And I'll be right down the hall in my room if you want me."

With more obedience than I expected, she put her book aside and settled down on her pillow. I pulled the covers over her, but I dared not bend and kiss her cheek as I wanted to do. When she was settled, I turned out the light and went to the hall door.

"I'll leave it ajar just a little," I said. Then I had to soften toward her, no matter how she rejected me. "Sleep well,

Adria dear. And don't worry. Your father will take care of everything."

"He couldn't before." Her voice was only a whisper across the darkened room. "When my mother died."

"Go to sleep, dear," I said again.

Her voice grew a little stronger. "Why didn't you tell me you were Stuart's sister?"

I heard the break in my voice when I tried to answer. "Oh, Adria, I couldn't! I couldn't tell anyone. I wanted to try to help my brother—because he isn't the one who pushed that chair."

"So you had to sneak around and *pretend* to be my friend, and—"

"No!" I cried. "You mustn't ever believe that. I wanted you for my friend first of all."

"I don't believe you," she said. "So just go away and leave me alone. I don't want to talk to you any more."

I heard tears in her voice, but there was nothing more I could say or do. I slipped away into the hall and started toward my own room. On the way, I began to wonder where the attic stairs might be, and when I reached my room I paused only to put Clay's story away, and then wandered down the hall to the very end of the house. There was a bathroom here, and a door I took to be a closet, but when I opened it I saw a narrow flight of stairs running upward into gloom. For an instant I was intensely aware of the great house enclosing me, deserted except for Adria and me. A sense of echoing loneliness pervaded the very halls. But I was not to be stopped.

A search near the door showed me a switch and when I flicked it a dim light came on high overhead. There was no rail, and I climbed carefully, touching the walls for balance. The top step ushered me into a vast, echoing area where the discarded hoardings of generations had been stored. Two dim bulbs hung from the steeply peaked rafters, one near the stairs, and another toward the far end of the house. It was cold and drafty, and I cast a glance behind me toward the stairs now and then, remembering that I'd been locked into the tower earlier. But no one bothered me here, and no orange cat appeared.

On every hand were trunks and boxes, pieces of old furniture, discarded pictures, chipped dishes. Had the family never thrown anything away? Cobwebs hung from low portions of the rafters, and there was dust everywhere. Shan must have done no housekeeping up here in her lifetime. But where Shan might have brought that piece of paper from Emory's hut in order to hide it—if that was what she'd done—I couldn't tell. There were too many possible hiding places, and tracks in the dusty floor led this way and that, as though members of the family must have come up here now and then, leaving footprints behind like marks on bare snow.

I was shivering with cold and uneasiness, and I stayed no more than five minutes before I gave up and went downstairs to my room. I wondered if there might be some customary hiding place in the attic, where generations of children had hidden their treasures, and which Shan might still use. I would have to ask Adria, coax her to tell me. One thing I knew—the attic would draw me back again to its dusky reaches.

The thought of Adria depressed me all over again. Shan had used to good effect the weapons I'd placed in her hands. How I was to counteract them, I didn't know.

At least I was warm again by the time I heard cars on the drive, and heard Shan and Julian come into the house. I was still dressed, and I ran downstairs and followed them into the library.

XIV

Julian was pouring himself a drink when I walked into the room. Shan had flung herself into a chair and she was weeping openly, with tears running down her pale cheeks, her long fair hair over her shoulders, her Norwegian sweater inappropriately cheerful in its colorful design. They both saw me come in, but only Shan burst into words.

"It's your fault!" she wailed. "If you hadn't come here so treacherously, none of this would have happened. Why didn't you go away? We tried hard enough to get you to leave. Then there'd have been no accident. Emory would never have been out on the slopes tonight."

Julian's voice cut coldly through her words. "There was no accident. Emory has skied that slope most of his life. He could do it in his sleep."

"Of course it was an accident!" Shan's voice had gone shrill. "I saw it happen. And so did Clay. Emory was careless. He was angry about—about"—she flung out an accusing arm, pointing at me—"about *her*. He wasn't careful as he should be."

Julian took a long draught from the glass in his hand. "Emory was too good a skier not to be careful. But we'll say nothing about that for the moment. Let it seem an accident."

More secrets? I thought. Because Graystones must not be connected with another—murder? I glanced at Shan, weeping uncontrollably and felt my flesh creep. What lay between her and Emory? What was the meaning of that scene I'd witnessed tonight at his cabin?

"Before he went out this evening, Emory slashed the right rear tire on my car. I saw him do it."

Shan wept the harder, and Julian stared at me. But when he spoke he addressed himself to Shan.

"Go to bed. You're nearly out on your feet. And nothing more's required of you until tomorrow. I want to talk to Linda for a moment."

She flung me a look of loathing and ran out of the room. Julian did not ask me to sit down.

"Is Adria all right?" he asked.

"Shan has turned her against me," I said.

"What else can you expect? The McCabes have never cared for deception. It's something we never forgive."

I laughed my derision. "The McCabes are up to their necks in deception. Isn't it time you had a look at that?"

He stared into the depths of his glass. "I had a phone call tonight. There was no time to tell you earlier. Stuart is to be let out on bail tomorrow. Do you want to drive into town and bring him here?"

For a moment I could hardly speak, my relief was so great. "Perhaps—perhaps he'll never be tried now—now that Emory is dead."

"I wouldn't be too sure of that." Julian's voice was dry.

"But at least you'll let him come here? You'll talk to him, try to find out the truth?"

His look was skeptical. "I'll hear him out, at least. He's asked me to do that."

"Would you like me to leave?"

He spoke curtly, remotely. "You'll stay. For the moment. I'm not through with you yet. Go to bed now. And bring Stuart here in the morning."

I went out of the room feeling wounded and a little sick. Yet if I had not come to Graystones, if I hadn't played out my masquerade, Julian would not be bringing Stuart home to his house. He would never have listened to him. As Clay had said, I'd been a catalyst. So I'd done some good in helping Stuart, after all. And nothing else mattered.

I kept repeating that to myself as I climbed the drafty tower stairs and went down the hall to my room. Shan's door was closed, Adria's was still ajar. When I stopped to listen, I heard her soft breathing, and knew she was asleep. Fortunately she had not heard her father and her aunt come home.

The night seemed endless. When I dropped off to sleep, it was I who dreamed. Ghostly faces moved through the mists of my restless sleep. Shan, Clay. The dead Emory. Adria. Stuart. But never Julian. It was as if I could not even summon him to me in my dreams.

I was up early that Saturday morning and down for breakfast before anyone else. I didn't know when the jail door would be opened, but I wanted to be there waiting— however long. When I went out to the car I found that the spare had been substituted for the slashed tire. Julian's doing, undoubtedly, and I was grateful.

The day was gray, but there was no snow, and the highways were clear, with no great amount of traffic.

In town I found a parking place near the jail and went up the steps to ring the inconspicuous bell that would admit me. One of the guards let me in, and I found Stuart's lawyer, Henry Bainbridge, already waiting. He rose from the hard bench in the hallway and shook hands with me—a small, balding man, with a fringe of sandy red hair. I was glad to see him alone, and I sat beside him on the bench.

"You've heard about Emory Ault's death?" I asked.

"Yes. The news was on a local radio station."

"Will it mean that Stuart will be let off?"

He blinked sandy lashes and looked away from me. "We don't know yet. I've just had a copy of the letter that's part of their evidence put into my hand. It's—pretty bad, Miss Earle."

"You'd better tell me," I said.

He opened a briefcase and took out a sheet that had been xeroxed and handed it to me. The letter was handwritten on Margot's personal stationery. It was dated one week before her death. I read it to myself.

> *Dear Emory:*
>
> *Thanks for staying around last night. Stuart has been threatening again to kill me. He is jealous of my every move, and he watches me constantly. I'll have nothing to do with him, and he can't bear it. If anything happens, Emory, the police should be told where to look.*
>
> *Yours,*
> *Margot*

I read the letter through and then handed it hastily back to Mr. Bainbridge, as though the feeling of it burned my fingers. I did not need to read it twice. The words would be with me forever.

"Has Stuart seen this?" I asked.

"Not yet. I want to show it to him this morning."

I was sorry Stuart had to see it. Somehow even in the copy it carried the taint of Margot's twisted character. Whatever her purpose in writing that note, she had meant to make trouble for Stuart. Probably to revenge herself on him. Because he had rejected her.

"There's something wrong with it," I said. "Something phony."

Mr. Bainbridge regarded me warily. "What do you mean?"

I stiffened on the hard bench beside him. "You don't believe Stuart actually pushed that chair, do you? Or prepared that break in the guardrail ahead of time so the chair would go through? He's not capable of that."

"I'm here to defend your brother," he said quietly. "But I'd like to know what you mean by phony."

"The whole thing is phony, of course! It's made up out of whole cloth. If Margot had been afraid of anyone, she wouldn't have gone to Emory, she'd have told Julian."

"I gather they hadn't been too close lately. Perhaps—"

"No. No matter how she felt, she'd have known he'd protect her. That's why we have to find out why she wrote anything to Emory. And I think Shan McCabe knows."

"We've a lot to discuss. Can we go somewhere to talk before you take Stuart back to Graystones?"

Before I had time to answer, a door at the far end of the hall opened, and beyond it I could see another door of chill gray steel with windows set into it—a door I had not seen until now, since Stuart had always been brought directly to the visitors' room, where I had met him. Now the door to the cells opened and a guard brought him out to the office, where he went through the formality of checking out. In a few moments he had been released and joined us in the hallway.

I slipped my hand through the crook of his arm and squeezed comfortingly. He tried to smile at me, but something had happened to his bright confidence. There was pain in his eyes, and his healthy skier's tan had paled.

"Let's go somewhere for coffee," I said. "Mr. Bainbridge wants to talk to us, and he has something to show you."

We drove to a nearby diner, Stuart and I in my car, and Mr. Bainbridge in his. When I sat beside Stuart in a booth, with the lawyer across from us, and steaming hot cups of coffee on the table between, Stuart was shown the xeroxed letter.

He read it through twice and then looked from one to the other of us, plainly shocked. "But none of this is true! I never threatened her. I never tried to make love to her. It's true that she made a play for me, but Julian was my friend, and I'd never have touched her—even if I'd wanted to. I didn't. She was repulsive to me."

I knew every cadence of his voice, and I knew he was telling the truth.

"Anyway, this is only circumstantial evidence," I said. "They can't convict a man with a warning letter. Any angry woman could write what she pleased. It isn't real evidence."

"That's true enough," Mr. Bainbridge agreed, "and of course that's what we'll claim. But Emory Ault apparently had much more to say, and there are transcripts of all his evidence."

"With Emory dead—" I began, only to have Stuart echo my words.

"Emory—dead?"

Of course he couldn't have known. "He was killed by a fall on Devil's Drop last night."

Hope came into Stuart's eyes. "I won't pretend to be regretful. I never liked the old man, and he never liked me. As a skier, I was no substitute for Julian in his eyes and he resented the fact that I was good. Good enough so I didn't need him very much. Anyway—doesn't this change everything? If he was their main witness and he's gone, won't I be let off?"

"We can't tell yet." Mr. Bainbridge sipped coffee gravely and seemed to consider. "As I say, they have transcripts of all his evidence. Whether this will be strong enough to use, I don't know yet. There's a possibility of the whole thing being called off. But we'd better not be too hopeful. We can't count on it."

"Anyway, just calling it off isn't good enough!" I cried. "Stuart has to be vindicated, exonerated. He can't go through his life with a shadow like this hanging over him."

Neither man said anything, and I supposed they were both thinking that it was better to be let off than to risk life imprisonment. But that wasn't for me.

"There's a murderer loose at Graystones," I reminded them. "And you're going to help me expose him, Stuart. I'd begun to think it was Emory. But now we have to look for the one who killed Emory on the mountain, as well as for the one who pushed Margot's chair."

"Killed Emory!" Stuart cried. "What are you talking about?"

"Julian said last night that it wasn't an accident. Though that's not the story he means to give out to the papers."

Both men gaped at me, and after a moment Stuart touched my hand gently. "Take it easy, Linda. This is hard to believe. But if it's true, then you'd better get out of this area as fast as you can. I don't want anything to happen to you."

"Enough has," I said, and I filled them both in on some of the things that had been happening since I'd last seen Stuart.

Mr. Bainbridge listened somewhat skeptically, and I suspected that he thought I was being hysterical. But he too urged that I leave Graystones as soon as possible.

I shook my head stubbornly. "No. First we find out the truth. And perhaps Stuart can accomplish that better than I. My brother won't be safe until the truth is known, whatever it is."

We parted shortly afterward, and Stuart took the wheel to drive us back to Graystones. He seemed to need the feeling of freedom that driving gave him after his confinement, but he always drove too fast, and I was glad when we reached the mountain and turned in at the Graystones' drive.

Clay was outdoors, still shoveling snow from around the lodge, and when he saw us, he hopped down from the snowplow and ran across to where Stuart had braked my car. He shook Stuart warmly by the hand and smiled at me.

"I hope you're out for good, Stuart. Linda's been in a bad way worrying about you."

"I hope so too." Stuart sounded more cheerful, now that the county seat was well behind him. "It's good to see you, Clay."

He would have driven on, but I put my hand on his arm. "Wait a moment. Clay—you were on the slopes last night. What really happened? Shan said you were there and you both saw it."

He spoke to me across Stuart. "Yes. Emory was going down at a crazy speed. We were behind him, coming more slowly. About a third of the way down there's a ridge on the right which isn't very dangerous, because skiers always turn below it. But he didn't turn. He simple edged his skis a little uphill and went right out over the ridge. There's a sheer drop beyond, straight down the mountain. When we crawled up to the ridge, we could see his body caught on a ledge far below. Ski Patrol had a bad time getting him out."

"But Julian said it wasn't an accident—" I began. "He said—"

"Of course it wasn't an accident. Fast as he was going, I don't think Emory ever lost control. He went up and over that ridge on purpose."

"You—you can't mean—"

"I'm afraid I do," Clay said gently. "Emory Ault killed himself."

I heard the slow expelling of Stuart's breath. "Then that's it. I thought all along that with these lies he was manufacturing, Emory had something to hide. There's our man. He must have gotten desperate, knowing I was coming out. But how we're going to prove that he pushed that chair of Margot's, I wouldn't know."

"If there's anything to that, you'd need a motive," Clay said. "And I don't see one."

"We'll find it!" Stuart spoke with new confidence, as he started the car.

For the rest of the way to the house, I sat beside him in silence, trying to assimilate this new information about Emory. If it was true, it opened dozens of new questions, and I wasn't sure they would lead us to the answer I wanted.

But now, as Graystones' tower rose into view, Stuart came

to life. Something of the old brightness returned and his eyes were alive with eagerness.

"What a heap of stone!" he cried, and there was affection in his tone. "It's a monstrous old place, but I think I've been happier there than anywhere else." He threw me a quick apologetic look. "Don't mind, Linda. It's just that Julian and skiing and all that belong to Graystones, and there've been times lately when I wondered if I'd ever see it again."

When we'd parked the car and walked toward the front door, Julian was waiting for us. His greeting to Stuart was on the guarded side, but Stuart seemed not to notice. He had always trusted others readily, never believing that people might not like him, might hold him off, or distrust him. His exuberance over being "home," as he called it, reached through Julian's reserve, and in a few moments the two of them had settled before the library fire and were talking of old times. Tragedy was put aside for the moment—and so was I. With neither one paying any attention to me, I wandered out of the room and went upstairs to look for Adria.

I met Shan on the way, and if she still felt loathing toward me, she concealed it. She said she and her brother were driving into town soon to make the final arrangements for Emory. So would I look out for Adria? The old man had no family, and of course Julian was taking care of everything.

"Do you think he killed himself?" I asked directly.

Her face began to work as though she might burst into tears, but she controlled herself and put on her vague, unfocused look that seemed to see through and beyond me.

"I don't know what happened," she said, and drifted past me down the stairs. At the bottom step she paused and looked back. "If your brother wants to stay, he can have his old room, next to yours. Julian has had his things put in there.

Even his skis." She did not sound either pleased or displeased—all that lack of focus was back, as if she had drifted off into a world of her own that only she knew.

I went up to the second floor and looked for Adria. She was in her room, reading again.

"Where shall we have lessons today?" I asked. "Do you have a choice?"

She shrugged indifferently. "Shan says Emory is dead. She says he fell on the mountain."

"That's what happened. And do you know that my brother, Stuart, has come back to Graystones? I went to town and got him this morning."

"Why is my father letting him come back?"

"Perhaps because your father knows Stuart hasn't done anything he should be imprisoned for."

Adria thought about that for a moment. "Does he wear stripes, like on television?"

"Of course not. He hasn't even been tried, and perhaps he never will be. I don't think anyone will prove that he has done anything wrong."

"Does that mean that even though he may have pushed my mother's chair, he may still go free?"

"You've got it entirely wrong, Adria." I was beginning to lose my patience. "Perhaps you'd better ask your father to explain it to you. In the meantime, let's get your books together and take them downstairs."

Her mood was contrary. "I'd rather stay here."

"All right. It doesn't make any difference to me. Have you written the theme I asked you to write?"

"About skiing? I've started it."

"Then suppose you get on with it now. But first, Adria— I've been reading a story by Clay Davidson, and it made me wonder about something. Can you tell me if there has been any special place where children in the McCabe family have liked to hide things? I mean some place which you might use even after you grew up. A place Shan might use?"

She thought about that for a moment. "There's the attic."

"That's pretty big. Where in the attic?"

"If I tell you, it won't be a secret any more."

"Does it have to be a secret? What if there's a treasure I'd like to hide? Couldn't I use the same place?"

I was winning her over, in spite of her determination to hold me at arm's length. She smiled confidingly.

"All right, I'll tell you. When you go up the stairs, you walk right to the middle of the attic—halfway between those two bulbs that hang down. Then you turn right and walk to the wall. There's an old Halloween lantern hung on a peg. It's made out of cardboard like a jack-o'-lantern, with the eyes and everything cut through. My grandfather made it when he was a little boy. You can lift it down off the peg and hide something inside, if it's not too big."

"That sounds like fun," I said, and made no further comment.

We busied ourselves with lessons, and Adria was tractable enough—not showing any warmth toward me, but at least not rebelling from my rule.

While we were at work, Stuart came upstairs and looked in at us. "Hi, Adria. It's nice to see you again."

The look she gave him was guarded, though she answered politely enough. I went with him to see to his room and he began to take out his ski clothes at once.

"I've got to get out on the mountain," he said. "For me, that's a cure for everything. Is it all right if I take your car?"

He'd had an unhappy experience that he needed to work out on the slopes, and I understood. He'd sold his car some time ago when he needed money, and when he stayed at Graystones there was usually one available.

"Do you want me to go with you?" I asked.

"I don't want anybody with me. I'm not filled with patience today, and I need to be out on those trails by myself."

Again I understood, and he came to kiss my cheek, held me to him for a moment before I went back to Adria, my eyes swimming. I heard him go down the hall and out of the house, and I felt again that marvelous sense of relief—as though a terrible burden had been lifted from my shoulders. But I knew that was an illusion. I wasn't free of it yet.

I kept Adria at work all morning, and we didn't go downstairs until we were called for lunch. Julian and Shan were back. Stuart was still out on the slopes, and I knew he would stay there. Both Shan and Julian were subdued after their grim morning's errand, and there was little conversation at the luncheon table.

I had a strange sense of marking time—as though this particular period was suspended between zones of action. Now that Stuart was back and his presence might threaten, I sensed a tautness, as of a wire stretched to breaking point. If something severed that wire, it would zing away into a dangerous flailing, from which only some terrible injury could result.

During the meal I watched Julian for some sign that would mean he had relented toward me, but he was formal and cool whenever he spoke to me. He had accepted Stuart back with a semblance of old affection, but for me he had nothing but this chill disapproval.

Nevertheless, I had to talk to him—when I could find the chance. He went off after lunch, not catching my eye, and I returned to my room and lay down on my bed to collect my thoughts and decide exactly what I must say to him. Now that he'd taken Stuart into the house, I didn't mean to let important matters go.

After an hour or so I went downstairs looking for him. To my surprise I found him in Margot's room, with two maids and a number of cardboard boxes. He appeared to be directing them in the packing up of Margot's possessions. I wanted to give a small cheer because this was a step in a healthier direction, and I felt it would be better for Adria as well if this room was dismantled and redone, so that a presence would no longer seem to haunt it. This was a corner turned, but I dared not comment on the fact.

When I asked if I could speak to him for a moment, Julian regarded me distantly, but he came into the library with me, closing the door between the two rooms. He made no motion to sit down, and I was left standing on my feet.

"What do you want?" he asked me curtly.

I no longer felt sore and wounded. I had reached a place where I was numb. I couldn't feel anything. I put my question straight out.

"Have you seen the letter to Emory that Margot is supposed to have written? Stuart's lawyer showed me a copy this morning."

"Of course I've seen it," he said. "That letter was one reason why I've been keeping hands off where Stuart was concerned."

"But now you've changed your mind about it? Perhaps you've decided it wasn't written by Margot at all?"

"Of course it was written by Margot. I know her handwriting. The police have even checked it with other writing of hers."

I raised my shoulders helplessly and let them drop. "But now, in spite of that letter, you've brought Stuart to your home."

For an instant some flicker of emotion showed in his eyes, and he spoke to me more kindly. "If you want to know, I suspect that letter was written out of spite—as Stuart himself says. He's been open with me about it and about how Margot felt toward him. And he toward her. I should have given him a chance to tell me so himself before this. But I believed in the letter at first."

"And now you don't?"

"Margot was quite capable of spite. She may have been trying to stir up some sort of ill-feeling against Stuart with Emory. I don't think she had any real conviction that Stuart meant to injure her. If she had, she'd have been upset enough to tell me. She wouldn't have gone to Emory. But I didn't think this out clearly enough in the beginning, when the shock of what happened was on us all."

"That's what I think too—that she would have gone to you, not Emory. Emory didn't even like her. Julian, do you think it's possible that Emory—?"

"No," he said curtly.

I wasn't sure I accepted that. "What are you going to do next?"

"Next?"

I flung away from him suddenly and walked across the room, stopping before a window with my back to him. "Of course there's a next! If someone pushed Margot's chair, then that someone is still around. It's not enough if Stuart is released and there's no trial. I want his name cleared! You should want that too."

"I hope Stuart appreciates your loyalty. I hope he appreciates this wild scheme of yours in coming here and not letting us know who you were."

"I don't expect appreciation. That doesn't matter. He

didn't want me to come. He thought it was foolish and that I might stir up trouble."

"Which you've done. Thoroughly."

I couldn't turn and face him. I didn't want to be thrown off my course, and I went on talking over my shoulder.

"It had to be stirred up, didn't it? It had to be brought into the open. Perhaps this wasn't the best way—but what other way was there?"

He came up behind me and his touch was light on my shoulders as he turned me around. "You put yourself into what could be a dangerous position. Don't you see that?"

"I don't care!" I cried, and couldn't stop the tears that came into my eyes.

He kissed me gently and I found myself stiffening under his hands, not understanding his sudden gentleness—not trusting it. Julian McCabe had never seemed to me a particularly gentle man.

"I'd like to have had a loyalty like yours in my life," he said.

"Then—you will help him? You'll try to find the real answer?"

For just an instant his eyes seemed to blaze with the fire I had seen in them before, and then the heavy lids came down, smothering the flame, and he released me, stepping back.

"Do you think I want that any less than you?" he asked.

"I don't know! I don't know anything about you! I only know that I'll never stop searching for the truth. I'll never stop until Stuart is cleared completely!"

Heavy lids hid his eyes, so I couldn't tell what he was thinking, and I wanted to listen to no more. I ran out of the room toward the stairs, toward the privacy of my room.

It was true that I knew nothing about him, and probably

never would. Why the sudden gentleness, the kiss that was tender, the light touch of his hands on my shoulders—and then always the fire, the sense of a volcano about to erupt and hidden just in time. One moment he was angry with me, the next he seemed to have forgiven me. He was volatile as Stuart never was. Stuart always knew exactly what he wanted—to be a skier. Julian sometimes seemed to whirl, driven by a multitude of desires. Sometimes I felt I preferred Clay's quieter ways. Clay could be a little deadly too if something displeased him, but he never frightened me as Julian could.

I sat on my bed and twisted my fingers together. What about me? What did I feel? Where did I stand? Yesterday I'd been filled with a wistful sense of belonging to him, even though he was lost to me. Today I was less sure of anything so tender and wistful. At the moment when he held me, kissed me, there had been fire in me too. A response that shook me. Yet a moment later I was flinging challenges at him, turning him from me.

Time, which had seemed to rush, now extended endlessly. What could I do? How could I bring everything to a head so that the truth would explode upon us and there would be no more groping, no more searching and uncertainty and fear? But would that explosion bring more danger, more death?

At least there was the attic. The attic and a Halloween lantern. That was the next step, in any case.

I opened my door cautiously and looked into the hall. There was no one there. Shan's door was closed and so was Julian's. Adria's stood ajar. Moving as quietly as I could, I went to the door that hid the attic stairs and opened it softly. A moment later I stood at the foot of the stairs, looking upward. Dim lights burned overhead, though I had not touched the switch, and I wondered why. Was someone up there—or had I left the lights on when I was last there?

I climbed the stairs, treading lightly and looked about those echoing reaches that covered the top of the house, shadowy with piled boxes and trunks and ghostly furniture. There was no sound, no movement anywhere.

"Is anyone here?" I called.

The silence was intense. Then something creaked beneath the high slanting roof. But then, old houses were always creaking. I didn't think anyone was here, and I followed Adria's instructions, walking to the center of the attic and stopping at the point that was equidistant between the two hanging bulbs. Where the roofs slanted down on either side, the attic was dark with shadows, and there was the smell of ancient dust, of mice and airlessness.

XV

I walked toward the place on the right where the roof slanted to meet the wall, and I had to duck my head to keep from striking it. I could see the jack-o'-lantern now. It sat upon a discarded bureau, leering at me from the shadows with its orange face and black cut-out triangles of eyes. Adria had said it was usually hung on a peg, but that didn't matter. I took it from the bureau and found the cardboard flimsy and battered, as I thrust one hand through the opening at the top.

There was nothing there. I could feel the stub of a candle set in a metal holder—but nothing else. My hope that Shan might have hidden the paper she had taken from Emory's hut up here was dashed. Unless she had hidden it and taken it away again. Or unless someone else had found it—which did not seem likely.

Not far away there was a slight skittering sound, and I stiffened and held my breath. The stillness pulsed in my ears. If it had been mice, they were now being as still as I. But the sound had been too close for comfort, and I began to sidle away into the shadows, crouching under slanting rafters, trying to remove myself soundlessly from the place where I'd been.

But it wasn't possible to be quiet up here if one moved at all. Boards creaked under my feet, and once an old dress form that I bumped into went over with a terrible clatter. While the echoes still rang, I heard that stealthy skittering again. Was it coming toward me or running away?

The scene from Clay's story flashed through my mind. Was I to make that story come true? Would someone come to the attic at some future time and find me lying here, struck down by whoever it was that hid from me, and whose steps were surely coming close?

I had chosen the wrong direction in moving away, and the footsteps—sounding bolder now—had cut me off from the stairs. Was I to make a dash for it, or try to circle the attic and get back to the place of escape?

When the laughter began it was an eerie sound. Elusive, female laughter, tantalizing, tormenting. Whoever laughed hid herself from me and laughed to taunt me.

"Shan!" I cried. "Come out of there. Stop playing games."

The laughter rose eerily out of blackness, rising to a pitch, shattering like glass as it fell back down the scale. Then someone ran into the center of the attic, in full view, and I saw that it was not Shan but Adria. She held a folded sheet of paper in one hand, and she waved it at me in triumph.

"See! I found the treasure first! You can't catch me now—I've got it. It's mine!" She ran from me toward the stairs and I could hear her clattering down them. Then both lights went out and I was left in the dark. Far away at either end of the attic, a narrow gable window showed gray light. But for illumination the windows were useless. I must now fumble my way, bumping into things, knocking things over, feeling the creepiness of a dark attic as vast as this, as I made my way toward what I hoped were the stairs.

I could move with no speed, lest I miss my step and go plunging down those stairs. Once, when a pile of furniture hid the windows, I lost my sense of direction entirely. It was frightening not to know which way to turn, or where the stairs might lie. Then I came out into pale light again and saw the opening in the floor ahead of me.

Even now I couldn't hurry as I went down. I had to press my hands against the wall on either side, and feel for each step. The door at the foot of the stairs was closed, and I went down into pitch darkness. I was nearly at the bottom when the screaming began. It was shrill, wild, terrifying. I stumbled down the last few steps and burst through the door, running down the hall to Adria's room.

She was standing in the center of the floor with an open sheet of paper in one hand, wailing aloud.

"What is it, Adria?" I cried. "Give me that paper!"

She stopped her keening instantly and flung herself toward the fireplace. Before I could stop her, she thrust the paper down upon banked embers, and I saw it flare into flame, curl to black ashes at once.

Now others were coming upstairs, running toward Adria's room. I saw her face stretch to wild tension as the screaming began again, and I whirled to see Julian in the doorway and Shan just behind.

"What's happened?" Julian cried. "What's going on here?"

"I—I don't know," I faltered. "We—we were up in the

attic and—and—oh, never mind. We must do something for her."

I ran to Adria, but she waved me off as though I were some demon out of her dreams. And when Julian would have touched her, she screamed more shrilly.

Shan watched for a moment, white-faced. Then she said, "I'll phone the doctor," and ran out of the room.

Julian took stern measures. He slapped her, not too hard, across each cheek and shook her into silence. The rasping screams were cut off abruptly, and Adria tore herself away from him and flung her small body across her bed, sobbing more quietly now. When I moved toward her with a soothing hand outstretched, she rolled to the far side of the bed, staring at me in frightened agony.

Julian shook his head at me. "You'd better not stay. You can tell me later what you think has happened."

But when he would have stepped to the bedside, she rolled away from him in wild, senseless fright.

I went to my room and put on outdoor things. Then I ran downstairs, to meet Shan coming up. She passed me without a word, all her concern for Adria. I let myself out the front door and hurried along the short-cut path to the lodge.

Not even Clay could be counted on—not after giving me that story to read. But if he was available, he would listen to me, at least. I found him working in his office, checking through the guest list for the weekend. When I fell into the chair across from him, breathing hard because I'd hurried so, he began to talk to me quietly, soothingly.

"It will be a big night tonight, out on the slopes. This won't be the main festival of the year, but there'll be some exhibition skiing this afternoon, and more things doing tonight. Are you going out there?"

I shook my head. I wasn't going anywhere.

"I brought your story back," I said and handed him the envelope.

"What did you think of it?"

"It made my flesh creep—as you knew it would. Why did you give it to me to read? That's pretty thinly disguised stuff."

"I thought you'd be interested."

"Why? Because a young man like Stuart was your villain?"

"Not like Stuart. Not really. You're touchy, Linda. Reading meanings into my words."

"And I suppose the woman who dies wasn't Margot?"

"Let's say she was based on Margot. Perhaps I was writing out some of my own antagonism toward Margot McCabe."

"The attic was certainly real. I've been up there since I read the story."

I told him what had happened. Told him about the paper I'd seen in Shan's hands in Emory's cabin. A paper she had apparently hidden up in the attic. Adria had found it in the old jack-o'-lantern ahead of me, read it, burned it, and gone hysterically to pieces.

"I can guess what that letter might have been," Clay said gravely. "I believe Margot wrote something to Emory Ault—something which was supposed to incriminate."

"I know that. I've seen a copy of her letter. It's being held by the police as evidence against my brother. So Shan couldn't have got hold of that. The letter said that Stuart was threatening to kill Margot and that she was afraid."

"Stuart?" Clay sounded surprised.

"Of course. This is part of the evidence they're holding against him."

Clay opened a ledger on the desk before him and began

to look through the pages. I thought he meant to show me something, but instead he closed the book.

"I'll tell you something," he said. "Maybe my theory is wrong, but I have an idea that the letter Emory turned over to the police, and which you've seen a copy of, is a forgery."

Hope leaped in me. "What do you mean? How do you know?"

"I don't know. That's the trouble. I'm only guessing. If there was another letter—the real letter to Emory—and it's the one Shan hid and Adria found, I doubt that Stuart was mentioned in it at all."

"But why should you think that?"

"I've seen Emory copy handwriting, and do it so effectively that most people wouldn't recognize it as forgery. It was a sort of parlor game with him. I've seen him amuse Adria with mirror writing, for instance. If you copy handwriting upside down, or from a mirror, you can duplicate it quite well. Though not well enough to deceive an expert. I suggest that you call Stuart's lawyer and get him to have that handwriting checked by an authority. If it develops that it wasn't Margot's, then Stuart may be home free."

There was something missing here. I still didn't understand why Clay should have leaped to such a conclusion.

"But why—" I began, only to have him reach across the desk and cover my hand with his.

"Hush, Linda. Let me worry about this for a while. Don't mention it to anyone else. There's something I have to decide before I can tell you any more. Just give me a little time. If the prosecuting attorney should conclude that with Emory's death he hasn't a strong enough case against Stuart, maybe you won't need to go into this matter of the letter at all."

"But I will," I told him. "I've already tried to make you

understand that it's not good enough just to have Stuart go free. I want to see him cleared."

"Loyal big sister," he said, faintly mocking. "You're a nice child, Linda. Wrong-headed sometimes—but nice."

"I'm not a child!" I cried impatiently. "Talking like that doesn't change anything."

He was grave at once, though his eyes were kind. "No, it doesn't, does it? Why don't you go back to the house now and let me do a bit of thinking? If I come to any useful conclusions I'll let you know. Will that do?"

"I suppose it will have to," I said. "For now. Though I don't understand in the least. Clay, if there was what you call a *real* letter, and Adria found it today, she's already destroyed it. So where can you go from there?"

"Have you thought about why she destroyed it?"

"I don't know what to think."

He stared at me remotely for a moment. "What if Margot wrote, not only to Emory but also to me?"

"Clay—" I began, but he tightened his grasp on my hand, as he'd done once before, hurting me.

"That's enough," he told me. "Go back to the house and let me think. But don't count on me to save your brother. I can't promise that."

I drew my arm away from his touch. "If there is another letter then Julian needs to know. Perhaps I'd better tell him about this talk of ours. Perhaps—"

He broke in on me harshly. "If you do I'll deny everything and make a fool of you. You've got to leave this to me, Linda. Stay at the house tonight. Don't go out of it. Not for any reason."

"What about my job here?"

"Forget it. I've realized that your getting here has become difficult, and I've called up a girl who used to work for me.

She's married now, but she'll fill in for a few days. You needn't worry."

I stood up and moved toward the door. "So I've been fired," I said lightly.

He came around his desk at once and put an arm about my shoulders. "Let's talk about that another time, Linda. Just stay indoors and take care of yourself while I wrestle with this and figure out what to do."

There was nothing more to be said. I left him, feeling distressed and dissatisfied, and hurried back to Graystones.

When I came through the front door Julian called to me from the library, and I went in to find out how Adria was.

"The doctor has given her a sedative. She'll sleep through the night, and I've brought in a nurse to stay with her. She seems to have developed some strange antagonism toward all of us. I can't understand it. Can you clear it up, Linda?"

I could do no clarifying, but I told him what had happened—about the letter Shan took from Emory's cabin, and about the scene in the attic, and Adria's burning something in her bedroom grate. I heeded Clay's warning and said nothing about his suspicion that the letter held by the police might be a forgery, or that Clay himself might have still another letter. Julian seemed to make little of any of this. He was as puzzled and troubled by Adria's hysteria as I.

He had, however, a suggestion to make. "Let's put all this aside for now. It will be a good thing for all of us to get out of this house tonight. The evening is supposed to be clear, and there's to be a moonlight spectacle over at the ski area. You ought to see it. Adria won't need us at present, so you and Shan and I can go over together. Stuart too, if he wants to come. Suppose we leave right after dinner."

I remembered Clay's words about not leaving the house tonight, but of course he hadn't known about this. He'd probably thought of me wandering about the grounds alone. As long as I was with Julian, I was safe.

"I don't know that I feel cheerful enough for watching spectacles," I said. "But I'll go, if you wish."

There was that unexpected tenderness in his eyes again, and I turned away from it. Not because I wanted to, but because too much was nagging at me, disturbing me. If ever I answered that look I wanted to be free of worry about Stuart. I still could not be sure Julian would help as I wanted him to.

The rest of the afternoon was uneventful. Stuart came back from the slopes early, a bit tired after his lack of exercise —but quite ready to go out again that night. Adria slept soundly, with the nurse beside her bed, and Shan stayed in her own room, though she'd told Julian she'd join us tonight. We had an early dinner, then hurried to dress for the slopes. The four of us got into Julian's big car to drive off, with our skies clattering on the car roof, and this time there was no Clay to see us go. I wondered if he would be looking for me at the house tonight. I'd told Julian that I was free at the lodge because Clay had another girl coming in.

On the drive to the ski area Shan was subdued. She had put on a cheerful green and yellow skiing outfit, but she was anything but cheerful. Adria's behavior had left her brooding, and not even Julian could get her to snap out of it. Stuart was himself again, with his special gay exuberance, and it warmed my heart to see the characteristic shine about him. All his optimism had returned and he was sure there would be no trial, no further trouble. Julian lacked any real exhilaration tonight, but Stuart made up for any lack in the rest of us.

When we'd parked near the base lodge, Julian and Stuart got our skis down from the rack and we went around to the other side of the lodge where there were low benches and put them on. The evening had cleared of clouds and a nearly full moon was rising over the countryside. The ski area was alive with lights and music and the voices of people, the sounds of skis. Snow bunnies were out for the fun, and more than once some incautious skier ran across my skis as we made our way to the chair lift. That was definitely a no-no. Skiers must be constantly aware of others on the slopes. All the lifts were busy, but there was no long line, and we took our turn at the chair without too much of a wait. Shan and Stuart went up together and Julian and I followed.

There were lights everywhere, making the snow trails sparkle, and the black patches of trees seemed darker than ever. Our chairs swayed over the dusky lake, and climbed toward the sky, our shadows following us below. The music and voices grew fainter as we mounted, and the bite of cold air from the mountain struck us. Now there was exhilaration for us too. I could sense it in Julian, feel it in myself.

At the top of the lift was another world—a bright moon-lit world with intensely black shadows. Daytime shadows might be gray, but at night they were jet. We lost Shan and Stuart, and Julian led me in a herringbone up to the very top of the mountain, where the moonlit countryside lay spread out on every hand. The lights of villages and highways were scattered across the land, and overhead glittering winter stars seemed myriad and very far away. It was breathlessly quiet, with hardly any wind, the scrubby pines around us standing very still in their own deep shadow.

We snowplowed along the top of the mountain where the state park began, and Julian found a great snow-covered rock, where we could stand with our skis edged into the snow for stability, the tips pointing out over the abyss. I could feel Julian's hand at the back of my jacket, and for an instant—

with that plunge down the cliff before us, I felt the imminence of danger. There was just the slightest pressure to his hand, and if it increased I would go plummeting down upon snowy rocks that looked deceptively soft far below, and would shatter anything that fell upon them. Then his hand tightened, grasping a fold of my parka, pulling me back to safety, so that I fell against him and we tumbled in the snow, laughing together, our skis in a tangle. How could I ever have feared the pressure of his hand at my back? His eyes were bright with starlight when he leaned over and kissed me. And this time his kiss was not gentle. There was a demand behind it, a dominating of my will. And I didn't care. Our faces were cold until they touched and then they burned like fire.

Julian managed to get to his feet first, and he pulled me up. We untangled our skis and started back toward the slopes. That moment when I'd felt his hand pressing was already in the past, forgotten. Later on I would remember it, but not now.

It was a night of snow and fire.

When we reached the top of the trails we saw that skiers were going down the slopes carrying lighted flares that flamed in the night. They did christie turns, traversing back and forth across the fall line, while the flares marked their movements in streaks of light against the mountain.

We stood together and watched, and Julian's arm was about me. There was snow all around us, and there was that newly lighted fire within. I couldn't be cold now. I knew my cheeks were glowing in the wind, and when Julian started down Devil's Drop, and I followed him, I felt warm under the cold moonlight. I took the turns around moguls in Julian's wake, feeling strong and sure and utterly exhilarated. When we schussed out upon the level, we found Shan waiting for us.

"Have you seen Stuart?" I asked.

She answered me shortly. "Where do you suppose he'd be? Up there somewhere. Among the stars, probably. Once he's near the slopes, he doesn't touch ground. And he's not exactly gregarious when he's on skis. Julian, I've a frightful headache. Will you take me inside, please?"

"Would you like to go home?" he asked, quickly concerned for his sister.

"No. Just get me a table inside, and order me some coffee. When I've taken some aspirin I'll be all right. I don't want to spoil your fun."

"Would you like to come inside?" Julian asked me as he bent to take off his skis.

I shook my head. I wanted to stay outside and watch the slopes, mingle with the crowd, feel the ski excitement enter my blood. And sense this other, new excitement that almost made me forget about Stuart. When they'd gone, I began to move about, thrusting myself along with ski poles—tasting the night. I'd never been able to do this until I'd met Julian. Now I belonged to this world too. I wanted to be a better skier than I was. I could savor the feeling of being a little better each time out, the satisfaction of learning, growing, until all this became second nature and part of my developing control.

When Clay pounced on me, I was startled. He grasped my arm to keep me from passing him.

"I want to talk to you," he said.

I looked at him doubtfully. "Shan has a headache. Perhaps Julian will stay with her for a little while, but he'll be back soon, looking for me."

"Maybe not so soon. I asked Shan to get him away so I could talk to you. Get out of your skis. I know a place where we can go."

I loosened the bindings and stepped out of my skis. Clay

picked them up and I followed him, carrying my ski poles. He led me to a small redwood building with a peaked roof and when he opened the door for me I realized that this was the chapel. On Sundays it would be used interdenominationally by whatever group wanted to hold a service. The rest of the time it was open for meditation and rest—for whoever wished to come here.

The redwood sides peaked into a roof overhead, with racks along the slanted walls for skis. Bales of straw were set in rows to serve as benches on each side of an aisle. The floor was covered with bluestone pebbles, and there was a cast-iron heating unit at the far end, forming a small open fireplace where wood could be burned. It was cold at the moment, and there was no one here.

When Clay closed the door behind us, I clumped over stones in my ski boots and sat down on a straw bench to stare at an overhead candelabra made of skis, with peaked roof timbers rising above. Clay had touched a switch at the door so that the lights came on, and I sat for a moment savoring the peace of this place. No sense of alarm had filled me as yet.

When Clay had rested my skis and poles against the wall, he dropped onto a straw bale beside me.

"I warned you not to go out tonight," he said. "I told you to stay in the house—go nowhere."

I shrugged lightly. Exhilaration had not faded, and there was only peace between these walls.

"Don't be silly. I'm with Julian and my brother and Shan. What can happen to me?"

He didn't answer that, but reached into his jacket pocket and took out an envelope. "I've decided to show you the letter that Margot wrote to me three days before she died."

He held out the paper toward me, and I stared at it blindly.

XVI

I had no desire to take the envelope from him, and he had to urge it on me.

"You'd better read it, Linda. This one's genuine. I haven't shown it to anyone else because I don't know what it means, or what it might open up."

The envelope was unsealed, and as I slipped the single folded sheet from it, I recognized Margot's buff stationery. I had seen pieces of it about the house in Adria's possession. I had only to open the single sheet and read what was written there. Strangely, I did not want to.

"Read it," Clay said.

"I wonder if I should. Perhaps if I read it something will be terribly changed and there'll be a road I can never go down again."

Clay leaned forward, his eyes searching mine. "Are you sure you want that road, Linda?"

He leaped too quickly to a conclusion I was growing afraid to admit to myself. I sat in silence, with the buff sheet between my fingers, and all exhilaration seeped away.

"You want to save your brother," he reminded me. "So read."

The mention of Stuart settled the matter. I opened the folded sheet and held it up to the light. Black handwriting slanted boldly across the page. The wording was almost the same as it had been in that other letter. As though she had composed this carefully, and chose not to change very much. Emory's and Stuart's names were missing from this version.

> *Dear Clay:*
>
> *Thanks for your help. Julian has been threatening again to kill me. He's jealous of my every move, and he watches me constantly. I'll have nothing to do with him, and he can't bear it. If anything happens, Clay, the police should be told where to look.*
>
> *Yours,*
> *Margot*

I read it twice and then raised my eyes to Clay's in question, not wanting to believe—refusing to believe.

"This was why she didn't go to Julian for help," Clay said. "It was Julian she was afraid of all along."

I shook my head as if to refute the evidence of the letter. "But then why did she use Stuart's name in her note to Emory?"

"I've already told you that. She didn't. I think she wrote 'Julian' just as she did in mine. Only Emory saw his chance to protect Julian and blame Stuart, whom he'd convicted in his own mind anyway, and he made a copy, a forgery, using your brother's name. Probably he was ready to perjure himself with lies in order to save Julian and convict your brother. Why do you think Emory killed himself, Linda?"

"But did he, really?"

"Of course. A skier like Emory wouldn't have had such an accident. Ask Shan—she knows. We both saw him go over. It was deliberate. Because the time would come when his tangle of lies would be exposed and he would have to condemn Julian. He couldn't bear that. What he planned for Stuart just wasn't going to come off. In good part thanks to you. Of course one reason he kept still about your identity was because he didn't want all this coming out. But he'd have liked to get rid of you when you began to seem dangerous."

"But why should he hate Stuart like that?"

"Because he believed he was having an affair with Margot, betraying Julian. There was a time when he felt the same about me."

"But I know Stuart wasn't having an affair with her!" I cried. "I know he wasn't! Perhaps I can't always tell when Stuart lies to me. But when he tells the truth with conviction, I know it. And he was speaking the truth then. He told Julian the same thing—that she had made a play for him, and he was trying to avoid her. But I don't believe this version either."

Clay nodded. "That's one reason why I've held it all this time and have shown it to no one. Because Margot was capable of vicious spite, and might simply have been trying to stir up trouble. She tried to stir it up with me once. She taunted me, mocked me, because I wouldn't take up our affair again. Just a day or so before she wrote me that letter, she threw all sorts of things in my face, raging at me. If she did that to Julian he could well have exploded in anger and killed her. Which is another reason why I've held back this letter. It could be full of falsehood. You notice she thanks me for helping her. What help? I gave her none. If she was telling the truth and Julian stood in the yard and pushed her chair through that guardrail—then I didn't want to see him punished for it. I know what a demon Margot could be. However she ended, she deserved what happened. I'm on Emory's side there."

That was a harsh judgment, and I winced away from his words. There was something called justice that couldn't be taken into private hands.

"And now? Why have you shown it to me?"

"Because I've come to believe in its possible truth. I don't want to see what's happening to you. I've seen other women fall in love with Julian McCabe, and I'd rather see him exposed, see this letter turned over to the police, than to see you hurt. Don't you know how I feel about you, Linda?"

I could not look at him because I was remembering the look in Julian's eyes, and I didn't want to erase that memory with another. I felt utterly torn and devastated. Because I could not stand by and let Stuart go to trial in order to save Julian. Even if I loved Julian—and how was I to tell what love was, when all these emotions were so new and untried?—I would still have to sacrifice him for the truth and for Stuart's sake.

Clay bent toward me, his hands on my arms. "Don't look like that, Linda. You're tearing me up."

I was tearing myself up. I stood up, absently brushing a wisp of straw from my ski pants. "Where are you going now?" I asked.

"I'm going to take you back to the lodge, of course. And

keep you there until you have time to get your things and get away."

I shook my head dully. "No. I don't want to leave now. I must talk to Julian first."

"Talk to him! You can't do that. I think he's already afraid of you because all you talk about is clearing Stuart. And if you clear Stuart, you have to bring out the truth—about Julian. Has he made love to you, Linda? Because that's what he'd do. To make sure you were on his side."

I walked away from him and picked up my skis and poles where they leaned against the wall. "I have to do it my way. Are you going home now?"

"Not right away. If you won't come with me I'll go inside and look for Shan. Take care, Linda."

Outside, I bent to put my skis on and fasten the bindings. I waved to Clay, who stood by, watching me unhappily. Then I pushed off toward the chair line.

Since most people were watching the trail where the exhibition skiers were coming down, I had no trouble this time and got a chair to myself right away. Strong lights on the lift towers helped to light the area, and as my chair creaked upward, the long shadows of my skis moved along the ground below, across snow that looked yellow white beneath the lights. Beyond my chair a few skiers were coming down the slope. On the bright trail I could see them clearly, and there, well away from the others, was my brother, Stuart.

How beautifully he came down the mountain—all youthful grace and strength, his turns skillfully balanced, his carving perfection to give him the greatest speed and maneuverability. He did not see me, intent upon his contest with the mountain, and I felt a lump in my throat as I watched. How could I have forgotten for a moment that he must come first in my life? That his safety, that justice for my brother must weigh above everything else.

The rest of the way up in the chair I made myself think about Julian in a new light, forcing myself to remember and remember. The way he had not come to Stuart's aid, but had stood back from the first. Clay's evident belief that what Margot had written him was true. Margot's fear of Julian, her fear for her life. Shan lying to protect her brother, conniving with Emory because they both wanted to protect him, at whatever cost to anyone else. No wonder they had hated my coming, done everything possible to disturb me and frighten me away, lest I come too near the truth that was so dangerous. Then Emory's suicide—flinging himself down the mountain because he knew his fabrications wouldn't stand up in the final test and that the whole dreadful truth was going to come out. Rather than bring himself to testify against Julian, he preferred to die.

My chair had passed the halfway station, but I hardly noticed where I was. I felt a little ill. Yet still reason piled upon reason. Even Stuart had tried to protect him. I'd felt all along that Stuart was trying to shield someone—now I knew it was Julian. And there was Adria's unexplained hysteria upon reading the letter she had found in the attic, and her burning of it in the grate. Because her mother had written that her father was trying to kill her. Written it in the real letter to Emory. Under such an accusation, Adria's slim emotional balance had cracked. There was no telling what would happen to her now.

Yet still something in me could not entirely accept the clear evidence. I had to see Julian first. I had to talk to him. I had to give him the chance to condemn himself before I lowered my final judgment and went to the police.

The chair almost spilled me out at the top station because I was not alert to leaving it. I schussed down the ramp and snowplowed out a little way from the lift. I could not bring myself to ski down right away. Soon, soon, I must go and look for Julian, find a way to talk to him alone—yet in the midst of others, where I would be safe enough.

The top of the mountain seemed lonely now, and the cold was growing intense. Most people were off watching the exhibition skiing on another slope. Only a few diehards were still skiing on their own. One of them was my brother. I saw Stuart coming up the lift alone in a chair, and this time he saw me. He waved his ski poles at me and shouted, "Wait for me!"

I stayed where I was, near a red snow fence, where slopes split off in different directions, plunging down the mountain between stunted pines. Nearby someone had left a snowmaker, looking like a machine gun on a tripod, its blue hose snaking away across the snow. I waited for Stuart to reach me.

He lost no time, skating toward me the moment he left the ramp, sliding to a stop, his skis inches from mine. "Clay sent me up here after you," he said. "I don't know what he's worried about, but he's got something on his mind."

I answered him directly. "I know who killed Margot, Stuart."

"Take it easy, Linda." He patted my shoulder with one mittened hand from which dangled a ski pole. "Clay said I should get you home right away. Since we don't have a car, let's go down the back way. We can talk when we get to Graystones. You're shivering and it's getting colder up here."

I shook my head. "No—I'm not a good enough skier to take that back trail to the house."

He wasn't taking me seriously, or Clay either. "Sure you are. I've been watching you and you're plenty good. All you need is a bit more confidence. The trail will do that for you."

"No," I repeated. "I'm going to wait and talk to Julian. You go ahead, if you want to. Perhaps I'll try it later."

"He should be up soon. I saw him outside down below, putting on his skis."

My heart thudded. I didn't want to talk to him alone up here. "Wait for me, Stuart. After I talk to Julian, I'll go down with you."

He had never been particularly sensitive to the fears and trepidations of others. Perhaps I had never taught him to be. Perhaps I had always put his feelings first in my life, and that hadn't been wholly good for him. Now, when I needed him most, he failed me.

"No point in my waiting. You can come when you're ready —or let Julian take you home in the car. I've been out here most of the day and I'm not in the best possible shape, so I'm tired. We'll talk down at the house later. Besides—I think I know what you're going to tell me. It was Emory, wasn't it? And he's killed himself because he couldn't face up to having the facts come out and me go free."

"I think you know better," I said. "But go ahead. Perhaps I'll follow you in a little while. If I'm brave enough to try the trail."

He skated off toward the end of the mountain where the trees would open upon that winding trail that led back to Graystones far below. I watched him go, wondering if I had the courage to face Julian alone up here.

When Stuart was out of sight, I searched the chair lift as it climbed steeply up the mountain—and I could see Julian. He was only a few chairs away from the top—and he saw me too. He raised his hand to me, the ski poles dangling. And suddenly I knew I could not stay and face him. Not up here. What accusations had to be made, or whatever questions asked, had to be carried out where there would be others near at hand. I could no longer trust myself with Julian alone. Once he guessed what I knew, I might be in as great a danger as Margot had been.

I did not return his wave, but skated off along the rough mountain top in Stuart's wake, hoping that I might catch up to him. Perhaps Julian would think I had not seen him and make nothing of it.

I was not used to skiing an ungroomed surface, and I quickly gave up skating and pushed myself along more gingerly in a snowplow. There were banks where the snow was thin, half-ridden rocks, roots across the way. I wasn't going to like this at all, but I had no choice. Only the moon lighted my way—there was no electricity up here—and where the trees gathered tightly together, shadows deepened, and the white ribbon of the trail twisted away through black trees on either hand.

Once I reached the trail it became worse, because now there was a downward tilt to the earth, and a winding path to be traversed. I didn't know how to do it. After a few moments of slow snowplowing, of catching my ski tip in a bank and nearly falling, I cupped my hands about my mouth and shouted for Stuart. But he had gone on well ahead of me, and he would travel faster, so there was no answer. I could see his ski tracks ahead of me in the snow, clean and competent, sometimes neatly jumping an obstacle—not stumbling about as I was doing. I could see by his tracks that he was alternating between a schuss and wedeln.

The trees were taller now, and while I was better hidden from the top of the mountain, the light was dimmer down here. In the distance I heard Julian shouting my name, and wondered if he had heard me calling Stuart, had already guessed that I would be coming down this way. Now I was afraid of him. For the first time I was afraid of him and he would sense that fear in my unanswering flight. He would be after me at once—coming a lot faster than I could manage on the same trail. Coming after me, driven by all that fire and ice.

I pushed on down, trying to wedel, falling, tangling my skis, giving Julian more time before I was up on my feet again. Now I had to speed whether I could or not. I let myself schuss straight ahead, trying to avoid the rocks, the roots, trying to maneuver the turns without falling. But now I had too much speed. In another moment I would go cracking into a tree to wreck myself. If I tried to snowplow that would throw me. There was only one way I knew to slow a schuss that was getting out of control. I sat down and let my skis go out from under me, sliding a little way on the seat of my pants, leaving sitzmarks behind me. It was not a proper fall and my skis didn't release. While I was scrambling up I could hear him coming behind me—the swish and rattle of his skis—the unmistakable sound of a skier coming fast.

Terror was a spur. I was off again, schussing, taking the turns with more skill than I knew I had, faster and faster— until I had to sit down again and slow myself. All around me the trees were tall now. I was well down from the top— but how much farther I had to go I had no idea. There was no sign of Stuart, except for the trail he had left in the snow. I tried to follow it, knowing he would choose the best way. I concentrated on one obstacle at a time—and never mind the far course. That was what Stuart had taught me.

On again, schussing. There! I'd barely missed a hidden rock that would have sent me head over heels. If I had a real fall Julian would be on me in moments. And I was alone on the mountain, where I could so easily go into a tree, or over the edge—by "accident"—and no one any the wiser.

That there was an edge to the trail now, I became all too aware. On my left the trees had opened to show a moonlit glimpse of countryside, far below. The trail was skirting the steep side of the mountain now, and off to my left was a plunging drop-off. My terror increased, yet I could do nothing except pray and try to carve my edges into the snow so that I wouldn't go careening off into space. But you carved in turns, not in schussing, and all thoughts of skiing technique forsook me. I skied by instinct, sometimes by the seat of my pants—and I was going fast, faster. Wind whistled in my ears and my hair flew out behind me beneath its restraining band. I was no longer cold, but the fingers that grasped my ski poles were growing a little numb. I was holding the poles too tightly. I must relax. Relax, relax—that was the only command I could give myself. It was the prime rule of all successful skiing. And nothing about me was relaxed.

As I got up from my last sitzmark, I could hear him coming. My speed had been nothing compared to his, and he'd not had to waste all that time sitting down, as I had done. I turned my head to look up the long stretch I'd just come along, and I saw him, bearing down upon me. He didn't trouble to shout, but his face was drawn in anger and tension. There was no use in my trying to schuss now. He would simply run me down. We were close to the edge of the mountain and anything could happen. I stood with my back against a tree, my skis pointed uphill across the fall line to brace me—and waited for whatever was about to happen.

He saw me and his eyes burned with anger—perhaps as wildly as they had done that day when he'd come upon Margot's chair coming down the ramp and had pushed it through the guardrail he had earlier prepared so it would break. But there was no guardrail here—only the sheer cliff beyond the trail. And my brother was far away from my reach, where he could no longer help me.

I braced myself as the grim man on skis bore down upon me. It was because he was watching me instead of the trail, that the thing happened. He did what any expert has done at times—his skis struck a hidden rock and he went catapulting into the air in a terrible fall. Both his skis released and he lay stunned in the snow. Granting me time—unexpected time.

I was off again, with hope renewed. The mountain couldn't go on forever. And once Graystones was reached, Stuart would be there. And Adria and her nurse. I would no longer be alone and helpless. I managed the next steep curve with precision—and found Stuart ahead of me, leaning against a tree, smiling at me brightly.

I practically tumbled into his arms, nearly falling out of my skis, and he set me upright, smiling. "I could hear you coming—what a clatter! But you were doing fine. I told you you could come down this trail if you tried."

I was too much out of breath to do more than blurt out words. "Quick! Julian. Back there. He's fallen."

I don't know whether he understood what I meant—that Julian was pursuing me. But he sensed the need for action. And he seemed to understand that I wasn't asking him to rescue Julian.

"Come along," he said. "I'll go ahead and you can follow me."

He could wedel and do quick stem turns, but I had to schuss again, and I almost bore down upon him before I slowed myself by sitting. He turned to look back at me, laughing a little, and as I got to my feet I listened. There was no sound on the trail behind us. Julian must have knocked himself out. I waved to Stuart to start ahead. But this time he waited for me.

I saw that we were two thirds of the way down. I recognized this place. We were just above the lookout point where Julian and Adria and I had come that day. And now that I was with Stuart I needn't be afraid any longer, even if Julian recovered and came after us. Yet something in me ached willfully, unreasonably for the man who had fallen back there—and who was about to fall further because of all he had brought upon himself.

"Quick!" Stuart called. "Come here quickly, Linda. I can hear him coming again."

Yes—he was up. I could hear the swish and the clatter. I didn't know what Stuart intended, but I gave him my hand and let him pull me, sidestepping up the back of the lookout rock.

He put his arms about me and held me tight. "You couldn't let anything be, could you?" he whispered. "You couldn't let well enough alone so that I could get out of this by myself. You had to keep stirring around until you found out the truth. And I know you all too well, my darling sister. You'd protect me up to a point. But now that you know, you'll throw me over because you can't wrestle with your conscience."

His words tumbled out while I stared at him in horror, unbelieving, not accepting what I'd heard. Unable to accept.

"We've got to get back to the house," I said. "Don't let Julian catch us."

His arms about me tightened and I felt myself being thrust toward the plunge down the mountainside. His face was one I knew very well. All the brightness of Lucifer was there, and the high elation that was part of Stuart—and a will that was without mercy. My body was lifted, my skis raised in the air, and I dared not struggle. Far below lay the world—but it was an empty world for me—all space and nothingness. I hoped I would be unconscious before I struck the first rock.

"Put her down!" cried the grim voice from behind us.

I could feel Stuart turn as he looked toward the trail. I could feel my skis touch the rock beneath as he lowered me, and for an instant his lips grazed my cheek.

"I wouldn't have let you drop, Linda. I only wanted to frighten you, punish you a little."

I bent my knees, clutching at reassuring rock as he released me. Then he leaped out into the air, and dropped into a perfect landing on the trail, with knees bent, sitting back a little, his skis carrying him like the wind. His speed was tremendous—desperate. He meant to make the turn. I saw him edging, but one ski tip caught on a branch lying across the way, and he went headlong into the woods. I heard the dreadful crack as he struck a tree, crashing to the ground. The moonlit night was filled with echoes—and then silence.

I released the bindings on my skis so I could step out of them. Then I huddled against the lookout rock, moaning a little. The earth was spinning too fast for me. I couldn't catch up. I was too dizzy to stand, though I knew I must go to where Stuart lay.

Julian did not stop for me. Once he was sure I was safe, he got out of his own skis and followed to where Stuart lay flung upon moonlit snow, where something dark and shining spread around him.

In a moment Julian was back. "He's still breathing. I've got to get down to the house fast and phone Ski Patrol. If he lives that long. Can you stay with him, Linda? He can't hurt you now."

"Of course," I said, and let him pull me to my feet.

For just a second he held me against him, his face in my

hair. "I was so furious with you. Because you wouldn't stop. Because you had to go headlong into danger. Clay told me about the letters—and I guessed. But now I'm only thankful you're alive. Wait with him, Linda."

He put on his skis swiftly and went down the last third of the trail to the house and telephones. I left my skis lying in the snow and plodded to where Stuart lay. I knelt in the snow beside him and bent above him, my tears flowing unrestrained. Dark wetness seeped across the snow, and I took off my parka, peeled my sweater over my head and then wadded it to stanch the flow of blood from his scalp.

While I put on my jacket again, I talked to him. "Julian's gone for help. It will only be a little while. Oh, Stuart, Stuart!"

Moonlight fell upon his upturned face, and I could see the flicker of his eyelids. He opened his eyes and looked up at me, and something in his look beseeched me.

"I know," I whispered to him. "I know you'd never have dropped me."

But he wasn't thinking of me. His gaze shifted from my face, looking off into the distance.

"She never put her brakes on," he said so softly that I could barely catch the words. "When I pushed the chair, she never tried to fight me. She let it go—straight to her death."

"It doesn't matter now," I told him. "Don't try to talk."

He paid no attention to me. "She would have told Julian we were having . . . affair. Not true. She'd have made him drop me. All the skiing ended. . . . I . . . couldn't let her. She wanted . . . to die. She . . ."

His head fell sideways and there were no more words. I felt his pulse under the mitten and found a faint beat. He was only my little brother whom I'd loved for so long. I bent and let my lips graze his cheek as he had done mine. Then I got up and began to stamp about in the snow because I was shaking so, because I was terribly cold and frightened.

Though it must have been quite soon, it seemed forever before the Ski Patrol men, wearing their parkas with the big yellow crosses on the back, came down the trail by snowmobile, dragging a sled behind them. They were quick and efficient, and they had strapped Stuart down under blankets by the time Julian came back up the trail, climbing in walking boots, without his skis.

The ambulance was already on its way, and the snowmobile went ahead of us toward the house. Julian put his arm about me as we walked, and I used my ski poles for a cane. Back at Graystones, doctor and ambulance had already gone by the time we got there. Shan had brought Julian's car home, and he drove me to the hospital in East Stroudsburg. Stuart was unconscious and all that could be done was being done. There was a good possibility that he would pull through. The sheriff was there, but we told him as little as possible. We still knew too little ourselves.

The doctor gave me pills to help me sleep, and Julian drove me back to the house. I couldn't talk to him. My brother had caused Margot's death—the only person he had been protecting was himself—and there was nothing I could say. He left me to my silence, and I could not tell what he was feeling.

All I remember of that night was that Shan looked in once or twice, and Julian sat beside my bed until I went to sleep. All the words that must be spoken were left until tomorrow.

XVII

First of all in the morning there was Adria, to whom the truth must be told, to whom reassurance and comfort must be given. Julian was alone with her for a long time, and when they had talked enough, he brought her to my room, where I was dressed and waiting for whatever the day might call for.

Julian said the doctor had phoned, and Stuart had a broken shoulder and a scalp wound, concussion. But I could see him later in the day if I liked. He was not mortally hurt and he would live.

Adria came straight to me. "I'm sorry about Stuart's getting hurt. But I'm not sorry it was Stuart who—who—"

I caught her to me. "I know, darling. But it could never have been your father. We know that, don't we?"

But had we known? Didn't we both feel guilty over our lack of trust? There was much we owed Julian now.

When Adria went away, he spoke to me a bit grimly. "Clay and Shan and I sat up and talked late last night. We compared notes and reconstructed as we haven't done properly till now. Would you like me to tell you our conclusions while you have breakfast?"

"Of course," I said, as grave as he.

Until now we had all had only bits and pieces. It had taken Stuart's wild actions to pull everything together. The answers were simple and quite terrible.

Margot had told Julian more than once that she could no longer endure life, and that was his fault—but if she went she would find a way to take him with her in one way or another. As she considered that he had destroyed her life, she would destroy his. Unfortunately, he didn't pay enough attention to her threats. So she began to write her letters, drop her hints that Julian meant to harm her. A letter went to Emory and one to Clay, each blaming Julian if anything should happen to Margot. She got a boy from town, who was going away to school in another day, and brought him in to saw through the guardrail for her. She had him take out a piece, telling him that she wanted to put ornamental iron in its place. She had him nail it back loosely in the meantime. She could be persuasive enough, plausible enough when she chose, and the boy asked no questions, and was gone before the "accident" happened. Not until a few days ago had he come to Shan and told her about the curious job he'd done for Margot.

Next, Margot planned her course of action so that someone would push that chair. She tried hard to infuriate Julian, so that he would be the one, but he only stamped away from her, angry, but not one to strike out at her violently. She tried to torment Clay, to get him to act, but he laughed at her. There was only Stuart left. When she attempted to promote an affair with him, he would have nothing to do with her. And he took no action until she told him she meant to go to Julian with a story that Stuart had been trying to make love to her, that he was undercutting his benefactor in every way. Here she had fertile ground. Stuart could not bear to lose Julian's patronage, but even then he acted without planning when he pushed the chair, goaded by Margot.

On that last morning he must have gone from the library, where he'd been talking to Clay, through the drawing-room door to Margot's room. He was the "ghost" Adria had seen reflected in the windowpane, moving behind her. He went to make one last plea with Margot, and when she wouldn't listen he lost his temper. Her chair was poised at the head of the ramp—purposely—and he pushed it as hard as he could, perhaps more in angry reaction than with any dire intent. Then he ran out to leave the house by the front door. Margot's chair, unchecked by brakes because she didn't want to check it, flew down the ramp and across the few feet of yard at that narrow place, to break through the weakened guardrail and fling Margot into the ravine.

Julian and Emory were working in different parts of the yard. Julian saw the chair strike the rail, and he ran down to the ravine and was the first to find her. Emory believed that Julian had killed her, and when the police arrived he got in his word first—that he was the one who had found the body. Julian could see endless questionings arising if he contradicted Emory, so he let it go. At the time, it didn't seem to matter.

But Emory had already found what he thought was a scapegoat. He had no belief that Stuart had really killed Margot by pushing her chair, but he decided to pin the thing upon him, save Julian, and punish Stuart for the affair he had supposedly been trying to promote with Margot. Emory never really cared whether the wrong man was charged or not, so long as he saved Julian. He didn't care who was hurt—and that included me, whom he regarded as dangerous to Julian's safety.

He talked a bit to Shan, who was upset, but went along with his deception in order to protect her brother. Shan hoped it was Stuart, wasn't entirely sure it was Julian, feared that it was Adria, and much of the time retreated into her own world and shut the whole thing out. Until my arrival on the scene.

Clay, too, was undecided. He rather thought it was Julian because of the letter. But he meant to keep still and see what happened when it came to Stuart.

But as he had pointed out—I was the catalyst. I had begun to make things happen, and I stirred up forces against me without realizing why. It was fortunate that I had stirred up better things too—the change in Adria. And perhaps even in Julian.

I ate my breakfast and listened in silence. When I had heard all I could bear, I excused myself and went up to my room and began to pack. I'd had nothing more to offer him by way of information, and I could stay here no longer. My own world had collapsed about me at that moment when Stuart had held me over the abyss. I still did not know whether or not he would have dropped me, and perhaps I would never know. But I knew now that it was his hands which had sent Margot to her death. Perhaps if it had not been for what she herself intended, Stuart might have hurt her, punished her spitefully, but it was unlikely he would have caused her death. But how the law would look on all this no one knew as yet. There would be grim days ahead—and a trial to get through I could not stay at Graystones.

Julian had been kind to me, solicitous. He had kissed me and put his arms about me. And that was that. I knew how I felt about him, but there was nothing to be done except put distance between us and start recovering. To be near Stuart, whether he was in hospital or jail, I would stay in town.

In my packing I came upon the Ullr medallion, and I set it ruefully upon my dressing table. It belonged to Julian, not to me—and I couldn't bear the sight of it. But the thing that really destroyed me was the small carving of a skier that Stuart had made for me so long ago. I drew it from the pocket of my suitcase and felt the smoothness of the wood in my fingers, knew by heart the poise of the small carved body as it came down some imaginary slope. I dropped to my knees beside the open suitcase on my bed and wept bitterly, the small carving clasped in my fingers.

Julian found me there. He came tapping on my door, and when I didn't answer he opened it and looked in—saw me beside the suitcase, with my head on my arm, the little skier in my hand.

He came in and closed the door gently behind him, bent to take the carving from me. "It's like the one he did for Adria, isn't it?"

"I failed him!" I wept. "I did all the wrong things while he was growing up. If *I* had been different—"

"Poor little mother," Julian said. "Though of course that's what every parent thinks at times like this. And through no fault of yours you had to be more parent than sister. But who's to weigh the import of genes against anything else? I doubt that Stuart was like others in his family. His mold was his own. Except to learn from the past, it's never profitable to go back to distant reasons for causes, and it's not the way the law looks at things. It is the hand that pulls the trigger which kills, and Stuart was apt to be trigger-happy."

"Don't talk about him like that!" I cried, the old sore anger against Julian rising in me.

"We'll have to talk about him a lot. And about Margot. And Emory—and all of us. It's silence that has let us down. Silence for too long. If it's any comfort to you, the law, while not shifting blame, will take into account that there was no planning on Stuart's part, and that Margot, who wanted to die, goaded him to what he did. And now perhaps you'll tell me where you're going, why you're packing?"

I dashed at my tears with wet fingers. "I don't know. To town for a while until I know about Stuart. I'll be out of here as quickly as possible. Perhaps you would drive me in?"

He carried the carved skier across the room and placed it beside the medallion. "Stuart will be back eventually. He'll be on skis again. Stay here and wait for him."

I raised my head and stared at Julian as he went on casually enough:

"After all, you have a job here. It will last until Adria goes back to school. I think she should be able to return next term, don't you?"

"I don't want to stay here," I said, and got resolutely to my feet. "There are too many—too many—"

"Memories of a bad time? But don't they need to be erased with better memories?"

I shook my head. "Every time you look at me you'll remember Stuart. And how can I be of any use with Adria, when I did so badly with my brother?"

"You'll do all the better now for having learned. So stop reproaching yourself." His words were curt. "I don't know of anyone I'd rather trust Adria with—permanently."

He looked quite furious with me—prickly and angry, as if he resented having to argue with me. Quite suddenly I smiled at him.

He caught me by the shoulder, whirled me to him, engulfed me in his arms. His kiss was hard on my mouth.

"Does that make it any more clear? Adria needs a mother. And I need a wife. A proper wife. But quite aside from practical matters of that sort, I don't want to live without you. You're a stormy petrel, and quite wrong-headed at times. You make me angry. You annoy me. But will you please say that you love me, Linda?"

His second kiss was more tender as I raised my face to his. "You already know that I do."

Something struck a window and splattered. Outside, Adria was throwing snowballs. We went to the window and looked out. Her face was radiant as she laughed up at us.

"Come down and play with me!" she cried. "Both of you!"

Both of us. Julian waved to her and we went to put on our outdoor things and join Adria in the yard. Now was the time to begin making new memories to overlay the old.

Appearing from nowhere, Cinnabar walked amiably down the hall with us, permitting our company. Old ghosts had been laid, and he was only a big orange cat.